The mattress sagged. Sarah rolled over, a smile on her face.

Daniel started in surprise, his heart pounding. He clutched the bedlinens and stared back at her. His first thought was, *She looks angelic.* Which was daft. Then, *What the hell is she doing here?* He didn't remember having gotten in bed with her last night, but that didn't mean... Could he have sunk so low as to seduce Sarah?

What was the matter with him? Of a certain, he was a scoundrel. But to have taken advantage of an innocent like Sarah? His friend?

Hoping to figure things out, he risked a wary second glance at her. Yep. She gazed back at him as steadily and as trustfully as ever. Just as she had yesterday, when they'd... exchanged vows.

All at once Daniel's wedding rushed back to him, complete with Sarah's prettiness and that disturbing thing she'd said after he'd carried her inside the house.

Now I believe we're married.

THE SCOUNDREL

BY

LISA PLUMLEY

First published in Great Britain 2008
by Mills & Boon, an imprint of Harlequin (UK) Limited,
Large Print edition 2011
Eton House, 18-24 Paradise Road, Richmond, Surrey TW9 1SR

© Lisa G. Plumley 2006

ISBN: 978 0 263 22388 0

Harlequin (UK) policy is to use papers that are natural, renewable and recyclable products and made from wood grown in sustainable forests. The logging and manufacturing process conform to the legal environmental regulations of the country of origin.

Printed and bound in Great Britain
by CPI Antony Rowe, Chippenham, Wiltshire

When she found herself living in modern-day Arizona Territory, **Lisa Plumley** decided to take advantage of it—by immersing herself in the state's fascinating history, visiting ghost towns and historical sites, and finding inspiration in the desert and mountains surrounding her. It didn't take long before she got busy creating light-hearted romances like this one, featuring strong-willed women, ruggedly intelligent men, and the unexpected situations that bring them together.

When she's not writing, Lisa loves to spend time with her husband and two children, travelling, hiking, watching classic movies, reading, and defending her trivia-game championship. She enjoys hearing from readers, and invites you to contact her via e-mail at lisa@lisaplumley.com, or visit her website at www.lisaplumley.com

In loving memory of Verna Plumley

Chapter One

August 1882
Morrow Creek, northern Arizona Territory

There was only one thing Daniel McCabe didn't understand about women—how a man could be expected to choose from among them. Beginning with the raven-haired ones and ending with the feisty ones, there was an endless variety of females for a man to sample. Settling down with just one seemed nigh unthinkable.

Curling his fist 'round the pint of Levin's ale on his table at Jack Murphy's saloon, Daniel smiled at the rouged-and-powdered beauty before him. Her costume shimmered of fiery satin; her bosoms pushed at its neckline in a way that made him wonder about the architecture of corsets. To make so much of so... *much*, the garments had to be fashioned of something sturdier than mere muslin and whalebones. Something more akin to tiny versions of the sleigh runners he'd been shaping at his blacksmith's shop before coming here today.

The matter might require closer investigation, he reckoned. Much closer. How else to further his grasp of architecture and design? A man never knew when an intimate knowledge of such things might prove handy.

With a wider grin, Daniel propped both booted feet on the nearest ladder-back chair. Who was he fooling? If there was one thing he understood, it was ladies' undergarments. The corset or garter had yet to be designed that could defeat him. 'Twas a point of pride, much like his knack for forging steel and wielding a twenty-pound hammer.

The snap of Jack Murphy's bar towel pulled Daniel from his reverie. He glanced up to see the man scowling at him.

"Yes, Rose's charms are a sight to behold," the barkeep said in his drawling brogue. "But I brought you here to get your opinion on building a stage in that corner, McCabe. Not to watch you beguile my dancing troupe."

"It's unavoidable, Murphy. I can't help it."

"Try harder."

"All right." Reluctantly, Daniel spread his arms. "You heard him, ladies. I am not in the least charming, nor as irresistible as you might think. I am a serious man, with serious work to be done."

The women on either side of Daniel giggled, plainly disbelieving. They did not budge.

Both were costumed as extravagantly as Rose. Both flirted just as boldly as she did. One laid her arm enticingly across his shoulders and pressed herself against him, her feathered headpiece tickling his nose. The other cooed over the fineness of his arms, honed by years of blacksmith's labor. Each lady had promised him admission to her boardinghouse room later that evening, if he desired to receive "private dance instruction."

To be sure, a man could hardly help but develop an interest. In waltzing, of course.

The lady to his right snuggled closer, not the least bit daunted by Daniel's claims of seriousness. Their traveling ensemble had arrived in Morrow Creek two days past. They were set to perform at Jack Murphy's saloon before moving west to San Francisco, if Murphy could construct a stage for them.

The barkeep's exasperated gaze signaled his interest in doing exactly that. The Irishman was new to the territory, and Daniel liked him. He decided to try a bit harder.

"I warn you," he told the troupe next. "I'm not a man for settling down. Neither am I a sweet talker, a fine dancer or even the least bit a dandy." He nodded at his flannel shirt and rough-hewn canvas trousers. Although both were clean, they had seen hard use.

"Stay away. You'd do well to cozy up to Murphy, instead. He's a man of industry. Purpose. And coin."

"Coin?" Murphy scoffed. "I was, before your aces turned up last night."

"I never said I wasn't lucky."

The barkeep rolled his eyes.

"Only that you were a fine prospect for these ladies. Far finer than me."

The women turned contemplative gazes upon the Irishman. One fluttered her fan. Another fluttered her eyelashes. As a group, they returned their attention to Daniel, undeterred.

Murphy snorted. He strode to the corner of the nearly empty saloon, his boots ringing across the scarred floorboards. With hands on hips, he surveyed the area where the makeshift stage was meant to be built.

Daniel shrugged, his grin wide. "See?" he called out to his friend. "There's nothing I can do."

"Hmm." Rose sashayed a little closer. "I'd wager there are a *few* things you can do. Quite well, at that."

Her ribald gaze swept over him, taking in his oversize frame and nonchalant pose. Daniel gave her a wink. He liked a woman who wasn't afraid to go after what she wanted—just so long as what she wanted wasn't *him* in a marriage noose.

Contemplating what diversions the night might hold, he pulled out a Mexican cigarillo. Eagerly, the lady to his left held out the table lamp to light it with. With an arch of his eyebrow, he murmured his thanks. These women *were* uncommonly bold. But at least they weren't like most of the women in town—many of whom were inconveniently marriage-minded. Dallying with one of Murphy's dancers would prove pleasurable...and pleasure, above all, was what Daniel lived for. Life was too short to be spent among missed opportunities.

It was also too short to shirk a promise to a friend.

Regretfully, he stood. His cigarillo's plume of rich tobacco smoke trailed his progress across the room to join Murphy. In his wake, the dancers sighed.

Daniel offered them an apologetic over-the-shoulder glance—coupled with a smile to promise he'd make up for their disappointment later. Maybe he'd finish his ale, order a bath and invite one of the ladies to join him. Cleanliness was a virtue, after all. Or maybe that was patience. Either way, he reckoned he had things square.

He squinted at the space Murphy indicated. "You already talked to Copeland about getting the lumber from his mill?"

The barkeep nodded. "It'll cost me plenty. But even

after paying Rose and her girls, a dance show ought to make a profit."

"Even after you factor in paying off Grace Crabtree?"

Murphy tilted his head in confusion.

"She's bound to cause a ruckus once she hears you've got dance-hall ladies here," Daniel said. "I've known them Crabtree girls all my life. Grace is the most trouble of the lot. She's all het up over women's suffrage. Other things, too."

"That's got nothing to do with me."

"You'll see. Grace is a meddler. If she decides to make this place one of her damnable 'causes'—"

"My saloon isn't a—"

"That's what Ned Nickerson thought," Daniel interrupted. "Until Grace and some of her friends chained themselves to the awning of his Book Depot and News Emporium, protesting because he didn't have some lady author's highfalutin book or other. In the end, Deputy Winston had to haul 'em away."

Murphy frowned. Most likely, Daniel figured, he was imagining a passel of troublemaking females all picketing his saloon. With reason. Grace was a handful, and she knew most everyone in town. The Crabtrees in general were a bunch of original thinkers, prone to all sorts of oddball behavior. With one exception, of course.

"I could put in a good word for you with Grace's

sister," Daniel offered. Murphy was out of his depth—whether he realized it or not. "Sarah's the only sensible one of the lot. She'll see that Grace ought to leave well enough alone."

With a skeptical shake of his head, the barkeep strode the width of the corner, measuring the space available for his stage. For a moment, he was silent.

Then, "I can cope with Grace Crabtree."

The man was deluded. "Have you never tangled with a woman before? Most of them are beyond reason."

"I can cope with Grace Crabtree."

Clearly, Murphy hadn't spent much time with the fairer sex.

Daniel shrugged. "It's your funeral."

"No, it's my saloon. I'll see no one interfering with it."

"Oh, yes, you will. Mark my words."

One ale and two flirtatious encounters with the pouting dancers later, Daniel finished his measurements for Murphy's stage. Although he wasn't a carpenter by trade, he'd done his share of building, all the same. By the time he was old enough to reach for a straight razor for his peach fuzz, he'd grown a head taller than most men. Because of that, he'd learned to erect barns, raise roofs and rebuild storm-damaged houses...all while apprenticing as a blacksmith.

Now that he'd finished his plans for the stage, it had grown late. Murphy's saloon was packed to the rafters with miners and merchants, ranchers and lumbermen. Tinny music accompanied Rose's impromptu dance beside the piano—as did raucous cheers from the men watching. She fluttered her fan and swiveled her hips, belting out a rowdy rendition of a sentimental tune.

Comfortable at his table with dancers again on either side, Daniel smoked his second cigarillo. He tilted his head and aimed smoke rings at the fancy lanterns overhead, feeling satisfied. He had a whiskey at his elbow, a bellyful of Murphy's tinned beans and bread, a friendly obligation fulfilled and the promise of a delectable evening's entertainment ahead. A man's life didn't get much better than that.

"Daniel McCabe!" someone yelled. "McCabe?"

He glanced sideways. Several men stepped aside for a boy in a baggy suit and low hat. Daniel recognized him as the clerk from the railroad depot. He made his way through the crowd, an expression of urgency on his young face.

"Is Daniel McCabe here?"

"Over here, boy." Lazily, Daniel indicated the one remaining chair at his table. "Why don't you sit a spell?"

The dancers murmured their agreement. The clerk gawked at them, at their impressive bosoms, then at the empty chair. A blush rose clear from his starched collar to his eyebrows.

"No, thank you, sir. I couldn't."

"Sure, you could. I have one lady more than I can handle, anyway."

The dancers tittered. They leaned his way with joint protests. Another minute and he'd forget the boy was there at all. Resolutely, Daniel focused on the clerk.

"Well?"

"Well, uh… I came to bring you a message. You've got a delivery down at the railroad depot."

"A delivery? I'm not expecting anything. Are you sure it's for me? McCabe?"

"I'm sure. We haven't been able to determine much else about it, but we know one thing for sure. It's for you."

"I'll get it tomorrow." Daniel raised his whiskey in the clerk's direction. "You man enough for one of these? I'll buy you a boost for your trouble in coming down here to find me."

"Oh, no. You've got to come with me. Tonight."

A portion of Daniel's good cheer evaporated. "I've got plans for tonight. Believe me, they don't include hightailing it to the train depot."

Inconveniently, the boy held fast. He didn't so much as glance at the proffered glass of Old Orchard.

Daniel held out a coin instead. "Here. If you're

not a drinking man, take this to the apothecary. Get yourself one of those medicinal soda waters they sell. Maybe it'll grow some hair on your chest."

The clerk's blush deepened, but he straightened his spine doggedly. "I'm afraid I'll have to insist you come with me."

Daniel raised his eyebrows. "You *insist?*"

The boy's Adam's apple bobbed. "Uhhh...yes, sir."

Squinting against his cigarillo smoke, Daniel eyeballed the clerk. He was plain ruining his night—*and* his plans for Beatrice, the dancer to his right, too. There was something downright intriguing about that feather in her hair....

But if the boy had to "insist" one more time, he looked as if he might piss his britches. Daniel had that effect on men sometimes. He didn't mean for it to happen. There was just something about his size, his strength...his reputation for bending steel.

He heaved a sigh, drained his whiskey, then stood. "All right. Stay here, ladies. I'll be back before you can say 'lickety-split.'"

He would *not* be back before "lickety-split."

In fact, he'd be lucky to get back before his dancing girls pulled foot for San Francisco, Daniel realized. That much became clear the moment he stepped on the platform at the train depot and spotted the commotion there.

He surveyed the gathering crowd. At this time of night—when lanterns illuminated the platform and a dark breeze made the nearby ponderosa pines swish and creak—most people should have been abed, not at the depot. But there was a sizable crowd there, all the same. Ambling nearer in the clerk's wake, Daniel cocked his head toward the mysterious thumps and muffled swear words he heard. Some kind of scuffling reached him next.

"C'mere, you little hooligan!" the stationmaster said, grabbing for something Daniel couldn't see.

Whatever it was, it managed to duck away. Several women squealed. The whole group surged backward in a clatter of boot heels and ladies' button-ups.

"All aboard!"

To Daniel's right at the waiting train, the conductor issued his standard boarding call for the westbound 8:47 passage. Then, hardly waiting for any response, he jumped on the train and signaled the engineer. Smoke bellowed from the engines as the cars pulled out. The train looked, Daniel would have sworn, to be in a marked hurry.

Curious.

The clerk nudged him. "Looks like your delivery's still here," he observed, nodding to the crowd.

From within it came more scuffling. More swearing. More squealing. Apparently, Daniel's "delivery" was a part of that mess.

At the realization, a sense of prickly unease rushed over him. Something was akilter here. Worse, he'd just been called into the thick of it.

Regretfully, Daniel let pass a moment's mourning for the waltz lessons he'd doubtless be missing. Then he strode forward. He wasn't a man to back down from a challenge, no matter how much cussing and fighting was involved. Or how much mystery.

At Daniel's approach, the murmuring crowd parted. In its midst, he glimpsed the beleaguered-looking stationmaster, then someone about waist height. A child. Before he could do more than take note of the boy's dirt-smudged face, big dark eyes and wild demeanor, the child glanced up. Recognition sparked in his expression.

"You're here!"

An instant later, the boy hurled himself at Daniel's midsection. The tinned beans, bread and ale he'd consumed for dinner were jostled mightily by the impact. Wincing, Daniel took the child by the shoulders and set him apart.

Or at least he tried to. The boy was uncommonly wiry and determined, to boot. When Daniel gently pulled, the child merely...*stretched* a little, his grimy fingers clenched fast on Daniel's leather belt.

Confused, Daniel looked up. Although the crowd

had not dispersed in the least, the stationmaster had already begun retreating to his usual post. The man brushed his palms together and waddled across the platform, shoulders sagging with relief. The clerk, too, scurried to the depot's entrance.

They both moved, it occurred to Daniel, with the same haste the train conductor and engineer had employed.

"Hold, there!" Daniel bellowed.

At his shout, the boy started. His scrawny shoulders jerked. A mighty snuffle issued from the vicinity of Daniel's shirtfront. Awkwardly, he lowered his voice.

"What about my delivery?" he demanded.

"You're holdin' it," the stationmaster said.

The clerk nodded.

Daniel frowned.

The crowd watched avidly. Their expressions put him in mind of the sight that probably greeted a lion tamer when he looked out from inside the circus ring. What the hell was going on here? Had everyone gone daft?

"I was not expecting…a *child*."

"We've heard that afore!" someone shouted from the crowd.

Titters followed.

"Yeah. Long about April, after a long winter's *rest*."

More chortles. Daniel didn't find this situation funny

in the least. A child had attached itself to him—a child who appeared to know him. Experimentally, he took a step sideways. The boy trundled right in time with him. 'Twas like having a third boot. Or an extra arm. Or a squirmy, four-foot shadow. One that smelled like cabbages and surreptitiously wiped its nose on Daniel's shirtsleeve.

Again he tried to wrench the boy free. This time, he accomplished a full three-inch space between them before the child locked his bony arms around as much of Daniel's middle as he could reach and hurled himself forward once more.

Something inside Daniel lurched a little, as well. Most likely, it was the further settling of his dinner. But it felt a scant bit like some mush-hearted emotion...concern, maybe. Staunchly, he shoved it back. He placed both hands over the urchin's ears.

"You'll have to take him back," Daniel commanded in a low voice. "This is a mistake. I can't take delivery on a *child*."

"He's yours," the stationmaster said. "Good luck."

"He's not mine."

Several onlookers snickered. Exasperated, Daniel rolled his eyes. There'd be whispers now. By morning, rumor would have it that he'd fathered ten bastards between swallowing his morning coffee and arriving at the depot. That was the way of things in Morrow Creek.

Drawing in a deep breath, Daniel moved his hands away from the child's ears. As he did, he became aware of the boy's gritty, unkempt hair—and the striking disparity between his beefy hands and the child's small head. Clearly, the boy was too helpless to take care of himself. He needed someone to watch over him. At least for tonight.

But it could not be Daniel. The notion was preposterous.

Who would place a child—however stinky, scrawny and troublesome—in the care of a renowned bachelor like him?

The boy shifted. From someplace within his bedraggled coat, he produced a packet of twine-wrapped papers. He let loose of Daniel's belt just long enough to offer the bundle.

"I'm s'posed to give this to you." His gimlet gaze latched on the stationmaster, who'd lingered to watch. "*Only* you. I rec'nized you from the picture my mama showed me."

Daniel examined the boy's defiant face. Though dirt-smudged, his features looked familiar. They looked…a little like his own. God help him.

Scowling, he accepted the papers.

The crowd pushed nearer. A deeper scowl sent them back again, affording Daniel room—and lantern light—to read. The moment he glimpsed the handwriting on the fine stationery before him, he knew nothing would ever be the same again.

Briefly, he closed his eyes. He'd need strength to confront the revelation awaiting him. Strength, and a goodly measure of whiskey, too. But since the whiskey was back in his old life—the life that included dancing girls, carefree days and no one watching him with hopeful, little-boy eyes—Daniel knew he might as well get on with it.

A minute later, he put his hand on the child's shoulder. Ignoring the curious onlookers, he hunched low, so only the boy would hear him.

"Eli, you did a fine job of this. You should be proud, coming all this way on the train by yourself."

Solemnly, Eli met his gaze. "I know. I won this coat playing marbles."

After that, the truth was plain. Daniel could harbor no doubts at all.

Gently, he squeezed Eli's shoulder. Then he addressed the waiting crowd. "This boy is mine," he said gruffly.

New murmurs whisked across the platform. Daniel couldn't be bothered by them. In truth, he'd never cared for rumors. He couldn't be troubled even by those concerning him.

"Come with me, Eli. It's time we went home."

Chapter Two

Two months later

Sarah Crabtree's first proposal of marriage came between geography and literature during her inaugural year of teaching. She blamed it largely on student boredom and vowed to make her lessons more involving. The second came a year and a half later, coupled with a ten-year-old's favorite frog and a promise to "study 'rithmatic harder." She pinned her pretty pink gown for that one and vowed to dress more sensibly.

Neither of those proposals prepared her for the third one, though, which she received on a blustery afternoon in late October. For it, she could find no excuse at all...but she did promise herself to remember it. Because it came from the man she'd been sweet on for years, and it wasn't likely to be repeated.

It started out innocently enough, after lessons

had ended for the day. She'd just climbed on the schoolhouse ladder to shelve some books when her longtime friend Daniel McCabe strode in, filling the small timber-framed room with the scent of the outdoors, his loud footfalls and his undeniably masculine presence.

"That's it," he announced, stopping beside her ladder in clear exasperation. "I need a wife."

I volunteer, she almost blurted.

No, that would never do. She'd hidden her feelings for too long now. She couldn't go casting them about willy-nilly at the first opportunity. Clenching her hand on the next book, Sarah made herself affect an airy tone.

"My, my, Daniel. *Those* are four words I never thought to hear from you."

"Well, you just did. I mean it, too."

At the grumble he gave, Sarah chanced a downward glance. Yes, Daniel looked exactly as burly and wonderful as he always did. Also, fairly perturbed. The realization stifled the sigh she'd been about to unloose. Hoping to improve his mood, she tried teasing.

"You don't fool me." She moved down a few rungs, skirts swishing, for the next armload of books. "You'd as soon pluck out every hair on your head as settle down with one woman."

"Hmmph. I think I'm doing that anyway. Maybe it's time to get some help."

"Help pulling out your hair?" Sarah grinned. "Grace would volunteer. Her ladies' aid group is making handwoven hair switches for convalescents this week."

He stared, agape. Hiding her grin with a studious-looking scrutiny of the volumes in her arms, Sarah grabbed the ladder. She climbed higher. Sometimes she thought Daniel truly didn't understand her sister's altruistic nature. Many people did not.

"No. I want to keep what's left." Ruefully, he rubbed his scalp.

She caught the telltale motion and looked around for the one person who could always rile up Daniel McCabe. Little Eli was just visible through the schoolhouse window, hopping outdoors in the autumn-crisped grass.

Hmm. Perhaps Daniel had reached the end of his renowned patience. A child like Eli could do that to a person. The whole town had been predicting it since Daniel took the boy in.

He saw the direction of her gaze. Frowned. "Last month, Eli nicked penny candy from Luke's mercantile. Two days after that, he let loose all of old lady Harrison's chickens. It took her hours to find them all. A week ago, he got caught pulling the girls' hair on the way home from school."

"An eye for the ladies," Sarah murmured. "Like father, like son."

His sharp-eyed look stopped her. She didn't know what he was so irritated about. Although Eli was the very image of Daniel himself, Sarah didn't really believe all those rumors about Daniel having illegitimately fathered the boy. Daniel claimed Eli was his nephew, and she trusted him. He knew that. But whatever their relationship, the saying fit.

Daniel was a rogue. Eli was a rapscallion. They were a matched set, an ideal—if troublesome—twosome.

"Yesterday, he swapped my coffee beans for dirt clods," Daniel went on, obviously too beleaguered to take exception any further. He strode across the schoolroom, past the desks and the children's hastily pushed-in benches. "When I took a big slurp of the brew, he laughed his fool head off."

"You couldn't tell the difference?"

"Afterward, I could. And *now*." His glare could have pierced the windowpane, it was so severe. Beyond it, Eli frolicked, unconcerned. "Another tussle at school. This is the third time this month."

"You don't have to tell me," Sarah said gently. Eli's adjustment to life in Morrow Creek had not been easy—and it had not yet been fully accomplished, either. "I've been trying to help him. To help you both. You know I have."

Daniel inclined his head, silently acknowledging the visits she'd paid to their bachelor house, the books she'd read, the meals she'd delivered courtesy of the Crabtrees' cook. But he didn't stop pacing—and he didn't look much relieved, either.

"But," she continued, "I won't allow any child to disrupt my classroom or my other students. That's why I had to ask you to come collect Eli yourself today."

Daniel fisted his hand, frustration evident in every line of his hardened body. "I can't keep leaving my blacksmith's shop like this. I need to earn my living."

"You need to be a father to Eli."

He shook his head. "That's not enough." He wheeled around, his expression newly determined. "What I need is a wife. A good one."

That again. He couldn't be serious. Daniel McCabe was the most well-known scoundrel in the northern part of the territory. Although Sarah hadn't captured his heart for herself, she knew she didn't have to worry about another woman accomplishing that miracle, either. Daniel didn't *honestly* want a bride. The very idea was outlandish. He was simply overwrought right now because of Eli's shenanigans.

She shelved another book, then gave him a complacent wave. "A 'good' wife, hmmm? I may be wrong,

Daniel, but I don't think you're in any position to be dictatorial."

He snorted. His raised eyebrows made her smile. Clearly, the notion that he might not always be in command of things came as an astonishment to him.

"A wife will take care of Eli," he said, his enthusiasm for taking a bride undimmed. "A wife is what I've needed all along. I should have gotten myself one weeks ago."

"You can't order a wife from the Bloomingdale Brothers' catalog, like a new suit."

But Daniel wasn't listening. He was running his hand through his hair again, thinking. He pulled his palm away and frowned anew.

"I've pulled out more hair than I thought these past weeks. At this rate, I'll be bald before winter's out."

She glanced downward, bemused. Nothing had changed—Daniel still possessed enough thick, dark hair for a man and a half. Besides, he'd still be handsome to her, even with no hair at all. Sarah wanted to tell him so, to put his mind at ease. But experience had taught her better than that.

Instead, she settled on, "Bald, eh? All right, then. I guess you'd better hurry up with that wife business."

"Hmmph."

Pointedly, she peered at the crown of his head. "You wouldn't want to scare away any potential brides."

Amid another surreptitious examination of his locks, he stilled his hand. "They're that fussy?"

As a spinster herself, Sarah had no idea. But she knew Daniel didn't, either. So she nodded knowledgeably. "The savvy ones are. The ones who want a husband with a full head of hair."

He furrowed his brow, looking increasingly worried. She felt a little deceitful, carrying on this way. But she simply couldn't resist. It wasn't often Daniel was uncertain about anything—especially anything to do with women. Besides, this was all in fun. He'd forget the whole idea by tomorrow.

"But you don't want a potential bride who scares easily," she cautioned. "That wouldn't do."

He nodded, encouraging her. Perhaps foolishly.

"You need someone with fortitude," she opined.

Another nod.

"Someone who's organized," she offered. "Someone who's efficient and orderly."

He made a face. "I'm not opening a mercantile. I'm getting hitched."

Noncommittally, she shelved another book. Daniel was taking this far too seriously. Ordinarily, the two of them teased each other often. But this time…a prickle of unease nagged at her. Could Daniel really mean to find himself a wife?

Before Sarah could contemplate the matter further, a rustle at the schoolhouse doorway alerted her to another presence in the room. She didn't need to turn around to know who it was.

"Hello, Emily."

The nine-year-old girl murmured a quiet greeting.

"Your slate is there at your desk, right where you left it. I thought you might be back for it."

"Thank you, Miss Crabtree."

Emily snatched up her slate and ran out, pigtails flying. Satisfied, Sarah blew a dust mote from her shelf and resumed working.

Below her, Daniel glanced out the window. Emily—one hand protectively on her hair—was making her way cautiously around Eli. After she'd passed, the boy went back to hopping.

"How did you know who that was?" Daniel asked. "You didn't even turn around."

She shrugged. "This is my job. Just like your new mercantile will be your job. Yours and your organized new bride's."

He did not take the bait. He only went on discussing his impending marriage…as though it might actually take place.

"All I need is a woman who's amenable," Daniel

said, his usual certainty firmly in place. "And knowledgeable about children. That should be easy enough to find."

Sarah rammed in another volume. She'd had just about enough. A jest was a jest, but this... Daniel was beginning to sound downright resolute about finding a wife. Even worse, he'd already rejected *her* as a candidate! No matter that he didn't know it yet. Those wifely qualities she'd suggested to him— bravery, fortitude and keen skills in the areas of organization, efficiency and order? They happened to be some of *her* personal best. He'd dismissed them out of hand.

A woman who's amenable. And knowledgeable about children.

Hmmph. She possessed plenty of amenability. And who could be more knowledgeable about children than a schoolmarm?

It wasn't that she wanted to make herself a potential candidate. Not *exactly*. Not for an arrangement like this. Sarah wanted a love match. She wanted Daniel. She'd already made up her mind to wait until she could have both. This new scheme of his was trying her patience in the extreme, though.

Experimentally, she plastered an amenable simper on her face. She glanced down to gauge its effect.

Daniel looked oblivious. He'd crossed his arms

over his broad chest and was studying the pine plank floorboards.

"She should be passing fair to look at, too," he said decisively, adding another item to the list of his potential wife's qualifications. "That wouldn't hurt."

His anticipatory chuckle got her dander up. Sarah shoved in the next book. There were any number of women who were "passing fair to look at" in Morrow Creek. Not one of them was good enough for Daniel. Or Eli, for that matter.

She'd obviously have to do something about this. Scuttling her plans to give Daniel time to realize the obvious—that they were meant for each other— Sarah set her expression in a dubious frown. The amenable simper hadn't felt a natural fit, anyway.

"Having a wife *might* help," she agreed as she put away a book of poetry. "But on the other hand…"

At her hesitation, Daniel squinted upward impatiently. Just as she'd known he would.

"Out with it, Sarah. 'On the other hand,' what?"

"On the other hand, planning a wedding can require an awful lot of time. Time you don't have, as you pointed out yourself."

"Fine. I'll let my bride plan the wedding."

Oh, that would be lovely! Seduced by the very thought, Sarah let her imagination run unchecked. Visions of a fairy-tale wedding swirled in her head—a wedding between her and Daniel. Her imagination dressed her in her finest gown and Daniel in a fancy suit. Eli carried flowers. The whole of Morrow Creek gathered for a celebration fit to rival even her sister Molly's grandiose marriage to Marcus Copeland last month.

She would serve spice cake from her sister's bakery, Sarah determined, and memorize all her vows....

"Because I don't have time to waste," Daniel said, interrupting her reverie. "Eli needs a woman's influence. Now."

Her daydream popped like so many soapsuds. But perhaps there was still a way to salvage this situation.

"Are you sure there's not more to it than that?" Sarah glanced downward. Her heart squeezed painfully at the sight of him. "Maybe there's another reason you want a wife."

Like love. Longing. An overly delayed realization that your ideal partner has been here all along, alphabetizing dusty tomes about literature and history.

He scoffed. She wanted to kick herself for voicing the question at all. Aggravated, Sarah shelved the next book. She often forgot herself around Daniel. They'd been friends for so long.

Her family always said that her tendency to ignore the obvious—usually in favor of some dreamy notions of her own—would get her in trouble someday.

Dangling her lovelorn hopes in front of a confirmed bachelor like Daniel McCabe most definitely counted as trouble.

Well. She'd simply stop doing that, then. Easy as that.

"Steady my ladder, would you, please?" Sarah asked briskly, needing very much to move on. "I want to grab that next pile."

Instead of doing as she'd asked, Daniel slid the stack of books from her desk himself. Effortlessly, he offered up the heavy volumes one by one. Then he absently steadied her ladder with both big hands on a lower rung. She felt its wooden frame wobble with the impact, then turn as solid as the earth beneath Eli's kicking feet.

That was Daniel, Sarah reflected. He set her off balance without even knowing it…yet always remained nearby for her to rely upon.

Although she'd never have revealed as much to him, his presence was the aspect of her day she looked forward to most. Between planning lessons, grading schoolwork and traversing the path between her schoolhouse and the Crabtrees' lively household, Daniel was always in her thoughts. Without him, her days would feel half as sunny…and twice as lonely.

An unwelcome thought occurred to her. What if

he found a disagreeable wife? One who disapproved of their friendship?

Obviously, she could not leave such an important decision up to Daniel. Sarah decided to return to the reason for his newfound interest in matrimony— the wayward boy he'd found unexpectedly in his charge.

"About Eli," she began. "I know you've had your share of troubles with him, but I'm not so certain he needs a woman's influence. After all, you're a capable man who—"

"Does my smithing fire need its pit to contain it?"

Oh, dear.

"I've decided," Daniel said. "That's that."

No. That most definitely *wasn't* "that." It couldn't be. If Daniel got himself a wife, he'd be lost to her forever. Desperately, Sarah cast about for another tactic.

"And you?" she asked.

"What about me?"

"Do you also need a woman's influence?"

His hearty laughter rang out. She'd have sworn it rocked the very ladder she stood upon. Sarah clutched its top rung, then ladled some starch in her voice.

"I expect that's a no?"

"*I* influence women. Not the other way 'round."

"That's what you think," she grumbled.

"What's that?"

"I said, 'Not for the better, either.'"

"Pshaw. I've never dallied with a woman who wasn't willing."

Much to her chagrin, Sarah didn't doubt it. Glancing down at Daniel with an attempt at impartiality—the way his potential bride might—she surveyed his brawny shoulders, rugged upturned face and devilish dark eyes. At one glance, she knew his words to be true. Women *would* be willing to dally with Daniel.

Although not as fancily turned out as some of the dandies who came through Morrow Creek, he was, to her eye, more perfectly formed than all of them. He had a special quality about him, too. A quality that promised laughter and protection in equal measure.

To her, he also promised strength. Kindness. Affection. He had since they'd trod this same schoolroom together years ago—she in short skirts, he in mended britches.

"Well. Not all women are so easily influenced," she said.

"I've yet to find the one who isn't."

Instantly, a rebuttal jumped into her head. Sarah thought it best to leave her disagreement unspoken. After all, she could hardly count herself the exception to Daniel's charm. The fact that he was oblivious to his effect on her was probably for the best. It helped preserve her pride, at least. For a woman born into a family as exceptional as hers, pride was nothing to be taken for granted.

Apparently, neither was her friendship with Daniel.

Sarah didn't know what to do. She'd fancied him for so long, she'd half convinced herself he'd return her feelings eventually…once he'd finished sowing his wild oats, of course. But apparently Eli's arrival had set something new in motion.

Outside, the boy's movements caught her eye. He stomped in a pile of fallen oak leaves, scattering their rusty colors to the wind.

"It's getting colder outside these days," she said, welcoming the distraction from her troubling thoughts. "You should put a warmer coat on Eli."

"He won't give up that coat. He won it playing marbles."

She chose not to pursue that. "And a hat. And a scarf. And some mittens, too."

Silence. Then, "I'll just get busy knitting all that."

At his gruff jest, Sarah smiled. That was the Daniel she was used to. His teasing didn't daunt her. In this, she knew she was right.

Of course, she was right in her opinions of his wife-hunting plans, too. If she had anything to say about his choice… Well. Naturally, she'd have a say.

She only needed to regroup. He'd caught her by surprise. For now, Sarah determined, she'd finish working and handle this matter later.

That settled, she waggled her fingers in a no-nonsense way, gesturing for Daniel to hand up the last volume from her desk. As the book passed between their fingers, his regard fell upon her. A speculative expression crossed his face—almost as though he saw her for the first time. Which, given their long friendship, was hardly likely.

"*You*," he said, "would make someone a fine wife."

Or maybe it was.

Her heart pounded. She had to be hearing things. Her tendency to flights of fancy had finally gotten the better of her.

"*I* would make a fine wife?"

"I reckon so." A little of the revelatory manner left his voice. Daniel's tone grew surer. "Don't know why I didn't see it before. You're a fine schoolmarm and a practical person. You can see children without even turning around. You know all about warm winter clothes. You're perfect. You, Sarah Crabtree, would make an *excellent* wife."

This she hadn't foreseen. Daniel sounded nearly jubilant, too. That was never a good sign. He was as given to impulsiveness as she was to stubbornness. As proof, she looked to his reckless smile. It had grown twice as wide just now.

She needed time to think. Also, time apart from that charm-filled smile in which to do it. Drawing in a deep breath, Sarah made herself finish shelving the book in her hand. It was a volume on mathematics, clothbound and heavy. She frowned slightly, as though in concentration, but her mind flew.

"That's true," she agreed. "I *would* make an excellent wife."

After all, her feminine pride would allow nothing less.

But as she chanced another look at Daniel, she felt herself being pulled in even further by the force of his appeal. Like other men brandished crooked noses or blue eyes or bowed legs, Daniel wielded irresistible charm. It was a part of him. She'd never been very adept at ignoring it.

Until now, *she'd* been directing this conversation about wifely qualities—and Daniel's need for the same. Uneasily, Sarah felt her control of the situation slipping. She didn't like it. But Daniel quite obviously did.

He stepped away decisively, leaving her ladder to wobble.

"We're in agreement, then. Good. Will a week be enough time for you to plan?"

"Plan?"

"Our wedding." He gave her a smile, pleased as punch to have things settled. "Yours and mine."

She opened her mouth to…what? Disagree? This was what she'd wanted. Mutely, Sarah nodded. Lord, what was she doing?

"Good."

Daniel strode to the schoolhouse doorway, his shoulders lightened without the burden he'd carried when arriving. There he paused, glancing over his shoulder. Relief brightened his features. Clear enthusiasm shone in his eyes. In his every aspect, he was a man prepared to conquer the world around him—including his future bride.

For one wistful instant, Sarah let herself wonder how this moment might have passed, had theirs been a typical proposal…a true engagement. She envisioned Daniel smiling down at her, pulling her in his arms, murmuring promises and sweet words of affection. She imagined him touching her face, bringing his mouth to hers, kissing her with passion and love. Those were the things she wanted most.

But instead, Daniel's hearty, rumbling voice interrupted her daydreams.

"One more thing," he said.

"Yes?" Sarah lifted her gaze to find a peculiar expression on his face. Her heartbeat quickened once more. Was this it? The moment he'd realize the truth? Just in case, she prepared herself for him to stride across the room and take her romantically in his arms.

"You should know, Eli has a distinct appreciation for cabbage. Be ready to eat it at least three times a week."

Daniel watched her expectantly. Sarah had no idea how to respond. As it turned out, a response wasn't necessary. In the next moment, her bridegroom-to-be offered a wink, then disappeared from sight. Probably off to finagle himself a church and minister, Sarah thought in a daze.

Or more cabbages. After this day's surprises, she just couldn't be certain.

Chapter Three

The day of Daniel's wedding dawned clear and chilly, filled with cold sunlight. The mountain air fell to rest, leaving the pine and oak trees still. 'Twas a good day for a wedding—a practical day. As far as Daniel was concerned, the no-nonsense weather suited a no-nonsense arrangement. An arrangement like the one he'd come to with Sarah.

He figured he would enjoy being married to her. At least as much as he could enjoy being married at all. If a man had to get hitched, Sarah was a good prospect—sturdy, sweet and biddable. She fit his qualifications of being both amenable *and* experienced with children, and she'd be able to bring mischievous Eli in line right away. Hell, he reckoned she'd probably enjoy exercising her mothering instincts while she was doing it. Daniel was practically doing her a favor.

Feeling good about that, he tossed through his wardrobe for the pair of fine britches he rarely wore.

Made of sober scratchy wool the color of tree bark, they matched his only suit coat and were the best he could manage for a special occasion. In honor of that occasion, he also searched for a fancy shirt. Sarah deserved a bridegroom who arrived at the church looking a mite finer than Daniel usually did—fit for better than sweating over a hot blacksmith's fire all day.

He paused, considering what his bride might look like when she arrived. The furthest he could imagine was a billowy white dress—and even that was stretching things, given that Sarah generally wore the plainest clothes she could find. In fact, her whole appearance was plain. Ordinary brown hair scraped in a bun at her neck. Teasing eyes. And…what else?

Daniel squinted, trying to bring Sarah's face in view. All he conjured were the vaguest details. He guessed he'd never examined her closely. With a shrug, he dismissed the effort. That was probably the way Sarah wanted it. Anyone could tell that ladies like the dance-hall troupe *wanted* to be looked at. His longtime friend clearly did not.

As far as he could recall, though, Sarah did look serviceable enough that she wouldn't be an eyesore over bacon and eggs in the mornings. That would be right fine, Daniel told himself as he got dressed. There were more important considerations than whether or not Sarah made him question the architecture of her bustle.

Striding through his small house, Daniel paused at the kitchen table. Eli sat there with one foot bolstered on his chair seat, spooning up the leftovers of last night's beans and corn bread. Daniel ruffled the boy's sleep-rumpled hair, gave him an affectionate tickle under the arm, then moved on to stoke the stove. Maybe he'd borrow a flatiron from old Agnes Harrison next door and fancy up his and Eli's duds but good. Ironing couldn't be that difficult. Hell, Daniel handled hot metal every day.

After he'd wolfed down the rest of the corn bread and a quantity of honey, Daniel found his thoughts turning again to Sarah. Although she was a female, most of the time she was nearly as sensible as a man. He'd never known her to be anything less than agreeable, faithful and tolerant. And she shared Daniel's views—their simple marriage arrangement was proof of that.

He hadn't had to charm her, cajole her or engage in mush-hearted, untrustworthy nonsense like courting her, either. Truthfully, the businesslike nature of their arrangement had come as a relief. He was not a man who believed in giving over to sentimental pap—now, since Eli's arrival, more than ever.

Most importantly, Daniel assured himself, Sarah knew him. Since their days in the schoolroom together—he, copying answers from her slate; she, charitably allowing him to—they'd been inseparable friends. Uniquely among women, Sarah understood his fondness for late nights, good whiskey and masculine disarray. She wouldn't expect to change him. That was a quality he valued in her.

Not that he intended to cheat Sarah in this marriage arrangement. Frowning at the very notion, Daniel washed up, then stropped his shaving razor. It would be good for her, too. She wanted children. He now had a child, and he didn't mind sharing Eli one whit. The boy was too much trouble for one person. Even one person as skilled as Daniel ordinarily was.

Caring for an eight-year-old boy was more than he'd ever counted on. It would be unnatural for him to prove talented at womanly arts like cooking, coddling and making sense of sewing up Eli's tiny britches when they ripped through after a bout of snake hunting. Hell, Daniel hadn't been able to find a pair of clean socks for either of them for the past week. That proved something, didn't it?

Satisfied this arrangement would be right for everyone concerned, Daniel spent the rest of the morning preparing for Sarah's arrival. For the first time in his life, he wielded a flatiron—then gave thanks it would be the last he'd have to do with the puny thing. For the first time in weeks, he got Eli into a bath—then gave thanks Sarah would be the one to threaten, bribe and chase sixty-five pounds of slippery, defiant boy next time.

For the first time in recent memory, Daniel even tidied up. He counted it as a demonstration of how much he looked forward to the meal Sarah would doubtless cook for them that night. After a frowning perusal of the kitchen, he paid special care to sweeping a clean path between the cookstove and food cupboard. There. That was better.

All the while, he listened to Eli. The boy followed him from room to room, chattering about the clouds, the spider in the corner, the white horse he'd seen two days earlier, the candy he wanted in the mercantile…it went on and on. Ever since their walk home from the train depot on the night of Eli's arrival, the boy had rarely shut his mouth. Daniel figured he must have stored up lots of conversation on the train ride from the East. He could think of no other explanation.

"It's time to head out to the church," Daniel said, ending a debate about whether tadpoles were fish or frogs. "We don't want to keep Miss Crabtree waiting."

Eli blanched. "Church? Miss Crabtree?"

That was when, looking down into the boy's astonished face, Daniel realized the truth. In his haste to get on with his marriage by arrangement, he'd forgotten to do one thing.

Tell Eli about it.

* * *

In the Crabtree household, events were proceeding as per usual. Which meant that mayhem was the order of the day. Much bustling and chattering ensured it would remain so—at least until after the middle Crabtree daughter was safely wed.

Sarah sat in the midst of all the hubbub, contemplating the hurried days that had brought her here. She'd written invitations until her fingers were ink-stained. She'd mended and washed and ironed all the things she owned, along with a few items Fiona Crabtree had decided her daughter should take to her new household. She'd experimented with hairstyles, rebutted Grace's warnings about the patriarchal aspects of marriage and—most difficult of all—had done her best to hide from her family the true nature of her "arrangement" with Daniel.

They'd been surprised, of course. Especially by the haste with which Sarah and Daniel wanted to go forward with their marriage. But in the end, the Crabtrees seemed to conclude that Sarah and Daniel's longtime friendship had finally blossomed into something more. They'd not questioned her any further. Her father, in particular, had thrown his support to her wedding with as much enthusiasm as he'd shown her sister Molly's recent nuptials.

"I suppose matrimony is in the air now," Adam Crabtree had said, blinking at her through his spectacles. "Ever since your sister got herself married, I expected either you or Grace would be next."

Grace, passing by in her grass-stained bicycling costume and gloves, had only snorted. With their father the sole exception, everyone knew Grace had other ambitions. Marriage was the very least of them.

Daniel had wanted to tell everyone the truth of their convenient match. Sarah's pride hadn't allowed it. For once in her twenty-five years, she was at the center of life in her boisterous household. She couldn't bear to see her family looking at her with pity instead, for having accepted such an arrangement.

Especially her sister, Molly.

"Are you sure this is what you want, Sarah?" she'd asked, looking concerned. "I've never known you to be this hasty. Marriage is nothing to be rushed into."

"I'm absolutely certain," Sarah had said. Then she'd snatched another piece of gingerbread from the tray Molly had baked and munched heartily to forestall further questions.

It was true. As she sat in the parlor now in her finest Sunday dress, quietly arranging the lace on her sleeves, Sarah didn't feel the least bit concerned. She knew beyond a shadow of a doubt that she could make a marriage work between her and Daniel McCabe—and that, sooner or later, he would love her.

She'd conquered difficult challenges before. Getting herself appointed Morrow Creek's school-teacher certainly hadn't been easy, but she'd done it. She'd done it the same way she'd accomplished everything else in her life, with persistent effort and creativity. This situation with Daniel would prove no different. After all, he was only a man. How much of a challenge could he possibly be?

He was agreeable, for the most part. He was handsome, strong and reliable. Despite being male, Daniel was both considerate and even-tempered. Sarah had never known him to raise his voice to her—not even when she'd confided some of her most outlandish daydreams. He might not love her—yet—but he did understand her. She knew he wouldn't be the least bit surprised by any of the changes she intended to make once she'd settled in his and Eli's household.

Just as encouragingly, she hadn't had to charm him, cajole him or engage in silly flirtatious maneuvers to coax him into matrimony. It was just as well. Such feminine fripperies had never been her strong suit. With Daniel, they weren't needed. He already knew and appreciated her. Wasn't that why he'd issued her the proposal in the first place?

Indeed, if Grace was the independent, practical Crabtree sister and Molly the coddled, pampered Crabtree sister, Sarah had long considered herself the clever, creative—if overlooked—Crabtree sister.

Daniel probably valued her qualities of imagination and verve—two she'd forgotten, in her surprise over his quest for a suitable wife, to enumerate.

She'd simply have to do her best, Sarah vowed, to show them to Daniel at every opportunity. A man would never want a wife who bored him, she reasoned. She would make sure, above all, that their life together was filled with stimulating changes.

Soon she and Daniel would be sharing that life together, along with their days, their laughter...their marriage bed. At the thought, Sarah felt a frisson of excitement rush through her. Despite its unconventional start, soon enough their marriage would be real. From there, anything could happen.

In the foyer, the big grandfather clock chimed three. Instantly, everyone quit moving to stare in its direction.

"Heavens, we're late!" Fiona Crabtree cried. "Get up, Sarah, get up! There's no time now to indulge in those daydreams of yours. Daniel will be waiting for you."

Tying her hat ribbons beneath her chin, Fiona bustled into the parlor. She grabbed her reticule, then Sarah's elbow. An instant later, Grace was at the other side.

"Yes. You mustn't be late. Your life of domestic servitude awaits."

"Grace!"

Sarah didn't know how her mother could continue to be scandalized by Grace's unconventional views. She would have to have been blind—or to be sporting a *much* larger hat—not to have spied the women's suffrage posters, picket signs, political texts and other rebellious accoutrements in her elder daughter's attic room.

"Someday you'll be nicked by Cupid's arrow yourself," Adam Crabtree warned Grace as he entered the parlor. Absentmindedly, he fiddled with his necktie. "Love makes strange bedfellows, you know. Just look at your mother and me—"

"Adam! I resent that," Fiona protested, goggle-eyed.

"Or Molly and Marcus."

Molly gave a yelp of protest. Marcus Copeland, her husband of only a few weeks, gave his wife an indulgent smile.

"We need to talk. About that 'domestic servitude' idea." His grin widened. "I may be missing a prime benefit of marriage."

"Keep up talk like that," Molly returned archly, "and you'll be missing my next batch of cinnamon buns. Don't forget, Grace taught me how to properly stage a protest."

She whirled on her heel, first out the front door. Marcus followed. Soon, Sarah heard much laughter

coming from the front porch—along with the un-
mistakably intimate murmur of a couple in love. She
wanted to sigh with yearning. How long would it be
before Daniel used those same romantic tactics on
her?

Not long, she vowed, and swept toward the door.
It wouldn't do to keep her future love waiting.

Sarah looked beautiful.

Daniel blinked, but nothing changed. She still
looked the same—unusually pretty as she moved
toward him on Adam Crabtree's arm. They walked
beneath the paper garlands someone had decorated
the small church with, their passage setting the carefully cut flowery shapes aflutter. Piano music played,
courtesy of old lady Harrison. Bright territorial sunlight streamed in through the church windows.

Sarah's dress was not white, as he'd imagined, but
a pale blue the color of a summer sky, with lacy cuffs
and a big lace collar. He'd probably seen it a million
times before. But today it looked different—as different as Sarah herself did, all at once.

She held her head high, meeting his gaze directly. That wasn't different. She smiled at him, as
though they shared a private jest. That wasn't different, either. But the blush in her cheeks was new,
the sparkle in her eyes was new, and the intriguing

curve of her lips...*that* he'd never noticed before, either. Confused, Daniel tilted his head.

Then her father released her. Sarah stumbled slightly.

"Horsefeathers," she muttered, righting herself.

All at once, she became herself again. Daniel relaxed. Things were going to be fine.

A loud clunk echoed through the church. As one, the friends and family gathered in the frontward pews turned toward the sound. Without a shred of guilt, little Eli bashed his foot on the pew in front of him. Another *thump* was heard.

Daniel shot the boy his sternest look. 'Twas possible he should have given a better explanation than he had for the day's events. Especially if he expected Eli to behave himself. But it was too late now. Eli would just have to settle down on his own. The sooner he did, the sooner this would be finished.

Standing beside him before the minister, Sarah drew in a nervous-sounding breath. The bodice of her gown swelled accordingly. Again Daniel experienced that strange sensation. Never in his life did he recall having noticed Sarah's bosoms. Yet there they were—drawing his attention in a way he wholly disagreed with.

Clunk. Eli again. With relief, Daniel speared the boy another quelling look. Then, feeling more like himself again, he returned to the task at hand. He was about to marry Sarah. When the ceremony was done, *she* would doubtless know how to tame the little ruffian. Daniel wouldn't have to worry about it anymore.

A blessing and their vows followed. Feeling uncomfortable—no doubt due to his scratchy suit— Daniel answered in all the right moments. He even produced a pair of wedding rings. Gruffly, he held out his Irish grandmother's plain gold band, prepared to slip it on Sarah's waiting finger.

At the surprise in her face, he felt a curious warmth spread all through his chest. She liked it. He was pleased. She gave a small "Oooh!" and raised her gaze to his...but there were tears in her eyes, too.

Panicked, Daniel hesitated. Tears? He didn't know what was wrong. Would Sarah prove as blubbery as all women? Was she, despite all her schoolmarmish practicality, secretly sentimental? Misgivings assaulted him. If she expected their marriage to become more than it was...

Fortunately, Eli chose that moment to cough loudly. And repeatedly. Truly, he sounded as though he'd swallowed a pound of chalk dust and was determined to dislodge it. Despite the sympathetic pats the boy received, Daniel knew nothing of the kind was true. Not when Eli kept sneaking glances 'round him to make sure he was fully disrupting the proceedings.

By the time Fiona Crabtree had calmed the boy with a hanky and—Daniel would swear—the whispered promise of one of Molly's special snickerdoodle cookies, Sarah's weepy moment had passed. She straightened her spine and regarded Daniel expectantly. Again he felt reassured. At Eli's shenanigans, another woman would likely have gone all fussy. But Sarah was different. That was why this marriage arrangement was going to succeed between them.

Confidently, Daniel relaxed the taut muscles of his shoulders and neck. He slipped the ring on Sarah's finger. She admired it, briefly tilting her hand while Daniel waited for further instructions from the patient minister. He'd been to many weddings—everyone in Morrow Creek had. But he'd attended far more to the ale that followed afterward than to the boring ceremony itself. He had no idea what came next.

Sarah seemed to, though. Nervously, she again drew a breath. Wise to that trick by now, Daniel determinedly sent his gaze to the minister's dusty shoes. She would not catch him flatfooted more than once. He might not know marriage, but he did know women—and he decidedly knew Sarah. From here, things would go exactly as he expected.

Except they didn't. The minister droned on, describing the obligations, duties and wonders of marriage. In the midst of his talk, Sarah reached forward. She took Daniel's hand.

Her touch jolted him. He realized he'd never touched Sarah with anything but commonplace courtesy—or, more likely, teasing intentions. But now he felt her fingers twine with his, felt the steady pressure of her grasp, felt the smoothness of her skin… and the cool contact of their wedding bands. All at once, the reality of what they were doing struck him.

This was not a game. Not a prank. Not even strictly a convenience. This was a union between them. It was as plain as the ongoing *clunk* of Eli's little boots against that pew. Sarah regarded this as seriously as she did everything else in her life.

Belatedly, Daniel remembered how easily hurt Sarah could be when her various hopes and plans failed. How solemn she could be, in between jesting with him. How very earnest she was, and how everything she felt tended to show upon her face.

She'd never been able to so much as fib to him. Not even the time when he'd misguidedly grown a dandy's mustache and waxed it to within an inch of its scraggly life. She'd told him it looked as though his chin hairs had migrated north and received a terrible fright in the process, most likely from finding themselves in the shadow of his oversize nose.

Daniel reckoned it had been true. But Sarah had

been the only one who'd admitted as much to him—and the only one who'd urged him to his razor. He trusted her. And she, him.

Because of that trust, Daniel made himself a vow. No matter what happened, he would never hurt her. Sarah would never, he promised himself, have cause to regret marrying him.

He lifted his gaze to hers, determined to communicate his intentions to her. As the minister jabbered on, Sarah looked mistily back at him. She squeezed his hand reassuringly. Relieved, Daniel smiled. He was glad she understood.

She squeezed his hand again, harder this time. When he didn't respond, she cast a wobbly smile toward their wedding guests. She did her best to crush his fingers in her fist.

Confused, Daniel looked around as well. He didn't know what was wrong. For the moment at least, Eli seemed to have tired of causing trouble and had his head down studiously. That couldn't be it. He glanced down. His suit coat was still buttoned on, slightly singed at the edges but otherwise fine. That couldn't be it. The minister was…

…not talking anymore.

The silence felt somehow accusatory.

"Kiss me!" Sarah urged in a whisper.

Her command seemed nonsensical. Sarah was his

friend. Sarah was reliable, schoolmarmish. She was not a woman to be kissed, especially by Daniel.

"You may now," the minister intoned, "kiss your bride."

A rustle swept through the church. Daniel had the sense this wasn't the first time they'd heard that suggestion. People were waiting, wondering. In a minute, they'd be gossiping. He didn't care about that, but he did care about Sarah.

Resolutely, he lifted his free hand. He cupped her chin, marveling briefly at the unexpected warmth of her skin. Then he lowered his head. A small kiss would do to seal their deal, to finalize their marriage and satisfy everyone gathered there. Most likely, Sarah dreaded this formality as much as he did. For her sake, he'd finish this kiss as quickly as possible.

His lips neared hers. An uncommon sensation seized him…something akin to anticipation but more muddled than that. His heart pounded. Sarah's hand tautened in his. Quickly, quickly…

Something small and wet plinked his temple. Then his cheek. Then his temple again. Hastily, Daniel planted a kiss on Sarah's waiting lips. That accomplished, he swung his face 'round to see what had struck him.

Eli sat, defiant and surly, with his fingers at his mouth to withdraw the next spitball.

"I'll pound him," Daniel growled.

"No, Daniel. Wait." Sarah grabbed for him.

But she was too late. Daniel strode down the aisle after the miscreant boy. Widow Harrison took up a cheery tune at the piano. Everyone stood in their pews, looking confused. A scrabbling beneath one of the long wooden benches alerted Daniel to Eli's position. Scowling fiercely, he hunkered down.

One long sweep of his arm retrieved Eli, squirming, from beneath the nearest pew. His small suit was covered in dust and torn bits of paper. His round face wore a mulish expression.

"I don't care!" he said. "I got you fair and square."

"Fair and square has nothing to do with this. I already told you, you had better beha—"

"You didn't tell me *anything!*"

Sarah gave a startled sound. Daniel glanced at her, stranded beside the minister. Too late, he realized exactly what he'd done. Only two minutes married and already—one look at her face told him—he'd broken his promise to her. Judging by the narrowing of her eyes, she already had cause to regret their arrangement.

"Well," Adam Crabtree said heartily, blundering into the awkward silence that followed, "I'd say congratulations are in order!"

As though his words were a signal, the other guests began milling around, talking. As Daniel attempted to glare Eli into behaving, Adam stepped nearer with the rest of his family in tow. Fiona and Molly dabbed their eyes with handkerchiefs. Even stoic Grace looked a bit red around the nose. Although, Daniel reasoned, that might have had more to do with her dire views of marriage than with sentimentality.

Jack Murphy stepped nearer. "Shall we all toast the bride and groom?" he asked.

"Err…" Daniel glanced to Sarah, his grasp still firm on Eli. An ale sounded heartily good to him. But something told him that admitting as much wouldn't be wise. His demure new bride looked fit to throttle him. Or at the least, to dump a pint on his head.

"Yes, indeed!" she announced. "An ale sounds fine!"

Sarah hitched up her gown. Then, with a tilt of her head, she swept past everyone assembled, headed back to the Crabtrees' residence for the wedding reception. 'Twas the very last tack he would have expected her to take.

It was also his very first inkling that things might not go as he'd planned.

Most likely, though, Daniel comforted himself as he followed her with Eli dragging behind, this would be the last surprise Sarah dealt him. Between turning up beautiful—even temporarily—and *ordering* him to kiss her, she must have used up her ration of surprises. For a year, at least. She couldn't possibly have more held in store for him.

But if she did, he vowed, he'd be sure to be ready. Next time.

Chapter Four

Just as Sarah was beginning to appreciate the fine qualities of a good ale, Daniel fisted his hand around her cup and took it away from her.

"I'd say you've had enough of that."

Stupidly, she stared at the simple gold band adorning his hand. Although her brain commanded that she protest the loss of her ale, all she could do was stare. Stare at Daniel's big, rough, wonderful hand, so familiar and yet so changed. It was hers now, in a sense. Just as he was.

They were married. Well and truly married. Or at least they were, provided Daniel's hasty kiss had correctly sealed their union. Everyone had seemed to consider that meager peck to be adequate. Privately, Sarah had hoped for so much more.

"I have *not* had enough," she informed him. "Of ale *or* of kissing."

He arched a dark brow. Drat it. Had she said that aloud?

It didn't matter. Daniel was her husband now. He deserved her uncensored opinions. In fact, her free-thinking sister Grace would have encouraged as much. Aside from which, Sarah felt certain that kissing *and* ale must both hold pleasures she'd missed until now. From here on, she was determined to miss nothing more.

She shook off her reverie to reach, unsuccessfully, for her cup. "You've had four ales. That's only my second cup. Next to you, I'm a paragon of sobriety."

"That might be true. I am a scoundrel." Cheerfully, Daniel admitted the truth. "A slightly drunk one, in honor of the occasion."

He smiled at that, leaving her to wonder if he felt happy to be married or merely giddy at the prospect of not having to scrub behind Eli's ears anymore. Probably the latter, Sarah mused. She frowned. Making a proper and loving husband of Daniel McCabe would prove a challenge, to be sure.

"But *I'm* not the one who's been dancing, now, am I?" An unaccountable glimmer lit Daniel's brown eyes as he settled on the divan beside her. "With arm waving and skirt swinging and...what did you call that thing you were doing?"

"A fan dance." If he'd noticed *that,* she was making progress already. Heartened, Sarah leaned nearer. None too subtly, she whispered, "It's used for seduction."

"Seduction?" Her new bridegroom nearly choked on his next mouthful of ale. "What in God's name does a woman like you need seduction for? You're a mother now. And a wife."

Daft man. As if *that* summed her up in any way.

"I learned it from Molly." Sarah gave a blithe wave. "She had plans to become a gypsy once, you know. Before she opened her bakery. She can tell fortunes, too."

Daniel seemed unimpressed by her sister's versatility. "She doesn't need any of that now. She's a wife, too."

He said it as though that settled everything.

"Marcus doesn't mind Molly's interests." Offering Daniel a nudge, Sarah nodded to her sister and her husband. "He loves her just as she is. See?"

At the other end of the Crabtrees' parlor, Molly and Marcus engaged in conversation, smiling at each other. Unabashedly affectionate in spite of the family and friends gathered around, Marcus took Molly's hand and cradled it to his chest. He listened, then laughed at something she said. They both fairly glowed with happiness.

Seeing their togetherness, Sarah couldn't help but feel wistful. What was the matter with her, that her sister could make an effortlessly perfect love match, while she...*she* endured spitballs at her own nuptials?

Perhaps this was what came of marrying too quickly. And for all the wrong reasons. And to a man who did not know she was just the merest bit— desperately—in love with him.

Contemplatively, Daniel also surveyed the newly-weds, a move that offered Sarah the perfect opportunity to retrieve her ale—and to observe *him*. She hadn't been able to do so during their vows. Then, the sheer remarkableness of their marrying had occupied her every thought. Now, after a fresh gulp of ale, she peered dazedly at his dark suit, his necktie, his enormous feet in his laced-up dress shoes.

She'd married a prince, she thought in an ale-woozy haze. A colossal-footed prince, wise and poetic and handsome.

Daniel gave a dismissive sound. "We're lucky to be clear of all that hogwash. Romance. Bah." Companionably, he slung his arm over her shoulder. "Who needs it?"

I do, Sarah thought plaintively. *I need it.* But what she'd gotten, it turned out, was a man who embraced her with all the seductiveness of a fisherman hooking a trout. Only with none of the attendant prize-winning demeanor one would expect in the event of a catch.

She wanted to feel like a prize. Wanted to feel like a *real* wife, one who inspired conversation and smiles and tender touches. Not to mention proper kisses. Feeling overlooked—as Sarah sadly did now—was already familiar to her. It had worn out its welcome long ago, during her years growing up.

"Daniel, I have a suggestion."

He glanced back at her, impossibly appealing and woefully ignorant of how strongly she felt drawn to him. His expression looked open, his eyes clear, his demeanor happy-go-lucky. At any moment, he seemed liable to burst out with a hearty, "Look! My very own trout!"

Sarah stifled a sigh. Just then, she would have gladly sacrificed a month's wages—no, her most treasured arithmetic text—to see Daniel regard her with one-tenth the romantic affection her brother-in-law had for her sister. But since that wasn't likely to happen without some prodding, she knew she'd have to be clever.

"Let's dance." She stood, her skirts swaying, to urge him to his feet.

He resisted her efforts, his fist still curled around his ale. "*You* already have danced. After a fashion." Another grin. "For a schoolmarm, you've got a fair amount of vigor."

"I mean a proper dance." He owed it to her after that stingy peck of a wedding kiss. "A dance together."

Daniel eyed her suspiciously. "Are you turning sappy on me? Just because it's our wedding day doesn't mean—"

"Don't worry. I won't let the sentimentality of the day go to my head." Sarah rolled her eyes, then tugged his hand. "Just so long as you promise not to tread on my toes with those oversize feet of yours."

He grunted. "My feet go along with the rest of me."

"Yes. They're sized to match your big, fat head."

"Careful, wife. People might think you're not head over skirts for me."

Wife. At the careless endearment, her heart swelled. If only he knew….

"Or perhaps you don't know how to dance?" Pretending concern, Sarah propped her hands on her hips. She examined Daniel. "I've seen you flirt. I've seen you pour on your so-called charm with ladies visiting here from the States and beyond. I've even seen you parade through town with your britches split up the backside."

"A bachelor's not supposed to know how to sew."

"But I've never, it occurs to me, actually witnessed you dancing. Hmm…"

"Pshaw. I can dance." He gulped his drink. "Everyone can dance."

"Prove it."

"I don't need to. Sit, wife. Or make yourself useful and bring me another ale."

"Sweet heaven, I wouldn't have believed it." She gawked, shaking her head. "Grace was actually correct. Marriage truly *is* a step-and-fetch institution created solely for the benefit of men."

He scoffed. "What's the benefit in your carping at me? I said I can dance. That's that."

"Hmm." Sarah glanced to the couples near the parlor window, most of whom danced to the piano's tunes. She sighed. Elaborately. Then she nodded to another group. "Perhaps one of those kind gentlemen would partner with me."

"My cousins?"

She clucked at him, holding back a grin. "There's no need to turn red in the face. They're my family now, too. I believe George would make a fine dance partner."

"George has two left feet and a laugh like a whinnying nag."

"Frank?"

"Pickpocket. Leave your reticule with me."

"James?"

"Only if you don't mind his inviting you to pose nude for one of his 'sketches.' He claims to be an artist." A contemplative pause. "Wish I'd thought up that one myself."

My, but his family was a veritable rogue's gallery—those who lived in the territory at least. His parents and sister had moved east some time ago. Sarah tossed another glance to the cluster of jovial, ale-drinking McCabe men. "Nathan, then?"

"Nathan is more of a scoundrel than I am." Daniel shook his head—whether in admiration or consternation, she couldn't tell. "He has only to look at a woman and her skirts fly up."

"Really? Well. *That* would be inconvenient for dancing, now, wouldn't it?"

"Yes. It would." Wearing a dark look, Daniel finished his ale. He set his cup beside hers. "Behave yourself. Sit down."

"If I do, will you tell me what scandalous things happen when *you* look at a woman?"

"That grin of yours is not very wifelike."

"That doesn't answer my question."

For a long moment, he only gazed at their wedding festivities, probably lamenting the day he'd been born a relation to so many scoundrels. Then he lifted his suddenly somber gaze to hers.

"Doesn't matter anymore. Because none of those things will ever happen again." With a heavy sigh, Daniel stood. "How long will it take you to say your goodbyes? It's time we collected Eli and started home."

For a woman who was supposed to make a convenient wife, Sarah had so far proved herself anything but, Daniel reflected as he strode homeward. First she'd shown up inconveniently beautiful for her own wedding. Then she'd ordered him to kiss her, gotten tipsy and volunteered to dance with his idiot cousins. And now...

"You cannot have lost your own shoes." He frowned at her, disbelieving. "'Tis like leaving behind your ears."

"I have, Daniel." She shrugged. "I can't explain it."

"I suppose you can't explain your mother's sudden interest in corralling Eli for an overnight visit, either?"

Sarah blinked up at him with what he'd swear—if it weren't impossible—was a coquettish gaze. "I can't help it if Mama wants to be better acquainted with her new grandson. Or if she believes a bride and groom should spend their first night alone together. What should I have done? Refuse her?"

"Yes." He set his jaw. "I'll not be beholden to anyone. Especially not family."

"'Not family'? Don't be silly. My family lives and breathes for helping other people."

"For meddling, you mean. No need to put too fine a face on it. I've known the Crabtrees as long as I have you, remember?"

"Then you ought to understand they only have the best of intentions at heart."

"Intentions change." Darkly, Daniel shifted Sarah in his arms. When she'd lost her shoes, she'd insisted he carry her home. Fortunately, he was more than strong enough for the task. "So does your size. Damnation, woman. When I used to toss you up to that old tree we climbed, you were light as a feather."

She gave him a mulish look. "I was only ten years old."

"As I recall, you didn't mind walking barefoot then, either."

There'd been more than one time Fiona Crabtree had accused Daniel of being a poor influence on her daughter for that very reason. And others. She'd claimed he was turning meek little Sarah as wild as an Indian, and unladylike in the process.

Reminded of that now, he peered curiously at her lace-frothed form. By accident, his gaze nearly went to her bosoms. They rose cheerfully from her bodice in a way he couldn't quite countenance. Now that he noticed it, Sarah didn't seem especially lacking in female attributes. Even if they were usually shrouded in ugly dresses. Smugly, he decided he hadn't been such a poor influence after all.

"I'm not so very heavy, Daniel. But you are getting on in years, you know. Nearly twenty-eight. Perhaps your advanced age is making you weaker. Too weak even to carry little old me."

He grunted a denial. If he didn't know Sarah to be the gentlest, most sensible of creatures, he'd have sworn she was trying to bait him. Just in case, though, he flexed his arms.

There. Let her see the kind of man she'd married.

"Goodness!"

That was better.

"Do your arms hurt? You seem to be straining to carry—"

He gritted his teeth. "My arms are fine."

"If it would make you feel better, we could send for your cousin Nathan to carry me home." Solicitously, she patted his shoulder. "I'm sure he'd be willing."

"Maybe. But you wouldn't be."

She stilled, staring up at him. "I wouldn't?"

Why did she look so startled? So...hopeful? "No. You're far too sensible for the likes of Nathan. You're practical, Sarah. Once you find your shoes, I expect you'll make a fine and loyal wife."

She snorted. "You make me sound like a hound dog."

"Dependable, too."

"Or a trout!"

Now that just didn't make any sense at all. "You're not nearly so slippery as a trout."

Teasing, he squeezed her in demonstration. She laughed and squirmed against him. To Daniel's relief, no strange, unexpected feelings assaulted him in response—no revelations of Sarah's curvaceous figure or long, feminine limbs. Clearly he was cured of whatever malady had assailed him before.

Arriving at his house—their house—he stomped up the steps. On the threshold, he set down Sarah and opened the door. For some reason, she only stood there.

"What's the matter? The door's open."

She slanted him a meaningful, if completely undecipherable, look. A look as cryptic as any Daniel had received from a cardsharp over the gaming table. Frowning, he peered past her. The path looked about as clear as it ever did, barring a few mislaid shoes and some of Eli's playthings.

"I'm barefoot," she said. "I'll get a splinter."

"If you do, I'll pry it out. I've got a pair of black-smith's tongs handy someplace."

Sarah seemed unimpressed by his practical suggestion.

"Carry me over the threshold, Daniel."

"Why? It's four steps, maybe five at the most. You're an able-bodied woman. I've seen you corral three hooligans by the ear and drag them inside the schoolhouse all by yourself."

She didn't move.

He searched for more proof. "I reckon you can

throw a baseball nearly as well as any man in the Morrow Creek league."

A gasp. "You swore you'd never tell anyone about that!"

"I haven't. I'm the one who taught you to do it." After she'd pestered him endlessly when he'd joined the league himself. "But you're no weakling, and we both know it."

She crossed her arms over her middle. Arched her brow. "All I know for certain is that I begin to believe I've married the weaker McCabe. Next thing you know, I'll be wielding your blacksmith's hammer myself to spare you the exertion."

Enough was enough. "Fine."

He scooped her up in a flurry of lacy skirts and girlish squeals. Befuddled but determined—and slightly more deafened than he'd started out— Daniel carried her the few steps inside the house. He stopped with her still in his arms.

His burly, brawny, hammer-wielding arms. Blast it.

He glanced downward, keeping his expression fierce. His new bride needed to know that this order-giving of hers was a wedding-day exception. It would not be an everyday occurrence. He was the master of his own household.

Opening his mouth on a warning to that effect,

Daniel gazed at Sarah. At the shining look on her face, the stern words he'd meant to say flew clear from his head. Had he ever seen her look so pleased? So...pretty?

"*Now,*" she said, eyes shining, "I believe we're married."

"Just because I carried you inside?" It was the most outlandish thing she'd said to him today, short of "kiss me." Yet there was something about the look on her face....

He didn't want to think about it.

"Stop talking nonsense," Daniel said gruffly. He put her down, then rammed his hat on his head. "I'm off to Jack Murphy's saloon."

Her husband had gone carousing. On his wedding night.

Still smarting at the realization, Sarah kicked aside a pair of gargantuan muddy boots. They had to belong to Daniel. No one else possessed feet that big. Or an arrogance to match. Did he truly expect her to stay here alone while he tossed back pints at the saloon?

Frustrated, she raised her skirts and went to the window. Daniel was just disappearing around the bend, his shoulders broad and his manner carefree. She'd done all she could to make him stay with her, short of clamping herself on his leg and begging. She did have some pride. But he'd refused to linger. In the end, Sarah had decided that if Daniel didn't want her, she didn't want him.

Until she'd made him love her, of course.

Resigned for now, she released the curtain. As the fabric flopped in place, it raised a billow of dust. Sarah frowned at her hand, then rubbed her fingers together. They felt gritty.

Daniel's parting words came back to her.

"I tidied up this morning, on account of the occasion," he'd told her. "I reckon you won't have a thing to do while I'm gone but unpack all your dresses and whatnot."

He nodded at the belongings she'd had carried over earlier. With one sweep of his beefy arm, he indicated the appropriate chamber down the hall. It had been Eli's room, Daniel explained further, until he'd moved the boy's things.

"You and I aren't to share a bedroom?"

A frown. "Didn't seem quite right to me. Seeing as how we're only married on account of Eli."

"Oh. That's true. That's fine, then. An excellent idea," Sarah bluffed, not wanting him to know the notion bothered her. As near as she could tell, sharing a room was one of the cozier aspects of being married. She had—she was embarrassed to admit—looked forward to it. Dismayed, she peered down the hall. "But if *I* am in that room, where will Eli sleep?"

Clearly, Daniel hadn't thought of that. "I guess we'll likely take turns with my bed. Yep. That solves it."

Then he'd set his hat at a rakish angle, given her an unreadable look and stridden from the house as if his heels were on fire.

Sarah didn't understand it. Now, picking her way among the bits and pieces of his bachelor's household, she realized that while she had spent the past several days in frantic preparations, Daniel had… not. In fact, he didn't appear to have considered her arrival at all. Their marriage—a monumental event in Sarah's life—didn't mean anything to him beyond a means of solving his troubles with Eli.

She knew she should have expected as much. She'd gone into this arrangement with her eyes open, after all. Daniel hadn't tried to deceive her. But somehow, a part of her had still hoped things would be different.

"Why, Sarah!" Daniel was supposed to have exclaimed upon seeing her today. "You're beautiful! I don't know how I haven't noticed till now."

She'd have blushed prettily, glowing with his praise.

"In fact, now that I think on it, I've been in love

with you all along!" he'd have continued. "How could I not be? You're an ideal match for me. So lovely, so kind, so clever."

It would have been immodest to agree. She'd merely have smiled, linking her arm with his in a way that bespoke gentle, long-standing affection. He'd have chivalrously offered her a flower. A rare blossom, perhaps, like the ones from her mama's greenhouse. She'd blink back sentimental tears, planning to press the flower and cherish it always, and—

A clatter in the kitchen shattered her reverie. Jolted into alertness, Sarah glanced to the cast-iron cookstove. A tabby cat streaked from amid the handmade pots and pans scattered atop it, giving her a baleful glare as it slipped beneath a chair.

"Hello, there." Surprised, she stepped nearer. "I didn't know you lived here, too."

Frankly, Daniel had never seemed the sort to nurture a pet. Especially given how much of his time was devoted, of necessity, to blacksmithing. Perhaps the cat was Eli's.

She crouched, her skirts whispering, then extended her hand. "Come here, little kitty. I won't hurt you."

The tabby regarded her suspiciously, whiskers twitching.

"Are you hungry? I am. I didn't have a bite to eat at the wedding party." She'd been too busy trying to catch the eye of her new husband for anything so mundane as food.

Straightening, she surveyed the kitchen. *Her* new kitchen. It looked as if a pack of donkeys had been here last, attempting to rustle up a noontime meal with two hooves tied behind their backs. Open cans of tinned fruit littered the tabletop, along with crumbs, pieces of twine and paraffin-coated baker's wrap—the latter, more than likely, from Molly's bakeshop. Most unmarried men in Morrow Creek bought their baked goods from her sister.

To the left, scrubbed plates and bowls sat higgledy-piggledy on the worktable, beside a bag of green coffee beans and a grinder. Near the unused cook-stove stood a barrel of pickles—popular with the men of the household, judging by the blobby green trail of pickle juice on the floor nearby. Another barrel held oats, and a third, dried beans.

At least Daniel possessed some foodstuffs. He also had on hand at least a month's worth of the Pioneer Press newspaper—her father's broadsheet—and some cornmeal. The gritty stuff coated every hori-zontal surface in a fine dusting, as though a bag of it had exploded in here. Knowing Daniel and Eli, it probably had. There were tracks in the yellow meal here and there, as though someone had palmed up a handful to cook with and left the rest where it lay.

Ugh. Wrinkling her nose, Sarah left the mess for

now. Her bridegroom may have absconded, but she refused to spend her wedding night tidying up.

Minutes later, she'd prepared a simple meal of bread and cheese. Between bites—some of which she fed to the cat as she carried it in her arms—she wandered through the rest of the house. The front room held hardy furniture, doubtless handmade. Clothes lumped on the chair seats and served as draft-catchers in the corners; Eli's puzzles and toys had set up camp on the round braided rug. A cadre of blacksmith's tools occupied a prominent spot near the fireplace, apparently keeping company with the supply of cut and stacked firewood.

Although Sarah had come calling on Daniel and Eli many times, today their home held new interest. This time, it was partly hers, to do with what she pleased. In her mind's eye, she saw the windows stripped of their dreary, dust-clogged curtains and brightened with ruffle-trimmed adornments instead. She saw the chairs embellished with embroidered pillows and the floor scrubbed clean. Perhaps a new rug, as well.

"It's so homey!" Daniel would say when he saw it, reaching impulsively for her hand. His expression would shine with amazement. "You are a marvel, Sarah. No wonder I find myself more in love with you every day. I don't know how I ever lived without you."

Satisfied at the thought, Sarah smiled. Daniel truly did not know how lucky he was. She was going to have a marvelous time putting everything in order—including her new husband. She could hardly wait to start putting her own special stamp on their shared household.

But first... Feeling her heart skip a beat in anticipation, she sauntered to the other end of the house. The tabby purred in her arms, content with their makeshift meal. It seemed Sarah had made at least one friend here. That was good. She entered the hallway, her footsteps loud on the floorboards, and approached the private chambers there.

She stuck her head inside the first, an austere room with bare walls, a small bed and a row of pegs on the wall. One of her trunks sat beneath the single window. Another waited just inside the door. Clearly, this room was meant to be hers.

Frowning, she crossed the hall. Daniel's door stood slightly ajar, inviting her to investigate the room within. She'd never entered it before, of course. It wouldn't have been proper, even for two friends as close as she and Daniel had always been. But now... now they were wed. She was well within her rights to explore the entire house.

"I expect he'll want me in this room when it's time to clean it," she reasoned to the cat, giving it a gentle pat. "Let's have a look."

Inside, she found a brass bed covered with a patchwork quilt, a bureau with a washbasin atop it, several pegs hung with rough-hewn men's clothing and a braided rag rug. A sheet of muslin tacked over the window provided privacy; a lantern held the promise of light. It wasn't fancy, but it offered myriad possibilities...exactly like Daniel.

Arranged on the bed, a length of fabric caught her eye. Edging closer, Sarah lifted it. She gasped in surprise. 'Twas a fine lawn nightgown, trimmed in lace and finished with a deep ruffle at the hem. It was easily the most beautiful gown she'd ever seen—and the most seductive. In this, a woman would be nigh irresistible.

She would be nigh irresistible.

In that moment, Sarah realized the truth. She'd been mistaken about Daniel's carousing! That rascal. He'd left her, certainly—but only long enough for her to find the romantic gown he'd gifted her with... and for her to prepare for their wedding night. He was a simple man, she knew, given more to action than words. Leaving this gown for her was exactly the sort of thing he'd do.

Well. This made her new husband's intentions plain, didn't it? Daniel wanted their marriage to be more real than he'd first implied. This nightgown was proof enough of that. Doubtless, he couldn't wait to see her in it. Perhaps he was even waiting round the bend, eagerly anticipating her unveiling.

Excitedly, Sarah clutched the gown to her heart. When her new husband came home, there was one thing for certain. She'd be ready for him!

Chapter Five

The next morning, Daniel awakened with a curious sense of impending disaster. He couldn't reckon why at first. His head ached, but that was to be expected after a night at Murphy's. His mouth felt parched, but that would be easily remedied with a drink from his bedside pitcher. His bed felt lumpy, but that was because his mattress was occupied on the other side.

Occupied?

"Eli." Realizing what must be afoot, he cleared the hoarseness from his voice and tried again. "Go back to your own bed. Whatever bogeyman you're scared of is gone now."

"It's not Eli. It's me."

The mattress sagged. Sarah rolled over, a smile on her face. She got herself comfortable with both hands flattened on the pillow beneath her cheek, then regarded him steadily.

Daniel started in surprise, his heart pounding. He clutched the bed linens and stared back at her. His first thought was, *she looks angelic.* Which was daft. Then, less groggily, *what the hell is she doing here?* Which was better. He didn't remember having gotten in bed with her last night, but that didn't mean… Could he have sunk so low as to seduce Sarah?

A flood of feelings washed over him, led by remorse and tailed by…damnation, it felt almost like curiosity. What was the matter with him? Of a certain, he was a scoundrel. He freely admitted to that. But to have taken advantage of an innocent like Sarah? His friend?

With a mighty effort, Daniel managed to relax his grasp on the sheets. No matter how odd this was, he could not leap from the bed straightaway. That would only hurt Sarah's feelings. Clearly, she felt at home with…whatever had happened between them.

Hoping to figure things out, he risked a wary second glance at her. Yep. She gazed back at him as steadily and as trustfully as she ever had. Just as she had yesterday, when they'd…exchanged vows.

All at once, Daniel's wedding rushed back to him, complete with Eli's shenanigans, Sarah's prettiness and that disturbing thing she'd said after he'd carried her inside the house.

Now I believe we're married.

Hell. They'd really done it. This was what it was like to find himself hitched. Carefully, Daniel considered things. It turned out *he* felt more married upon finding a bride in his bed than he had upon acting as a pack mule yesterday. He guessed that was just one way he and Sarah were different. Probably the only way. Aside from the obvious.

Without his permission, his gaze went to her bosom. From beneath the quilt, he could just glimpse the top of her—

"Good morning!" she said cheerfully.

Daniel whisked his gaze upward, still feeling on the wrong side of the situation. Sarah beamed back at him, limned by the dawn—which explained the *angelic* notion he'd experienced upon seeing her. She fairly crackled with alertness, while he felt barely capable of scratching his beard stubble.

"Oooh, you're a slow riser. I wouldn't have guessed that. Especially given how early you must wake up to get to your smithy. And how active Eli is. Why, he must keep you hopping! You're probably busy from sunup to sundown, aren't you?"

He blinked. Lord, she was a talker. Was she always so...*awake* in the mornings? He'd seen roosters with less vigor, and they were responsible for waking folks.

"I've been awake for *ages*," she said, wiggling a little beneath the quilt. She sighed happily. "Waiting for you. After last night, I thought we'd—"

"I don't want to talk about last night."

At his hasty tone, her eyes widened. "Why not? It was ever so promising, until you—"

"Stop." Hell. What had he done? He had to fix it somehow. But in the meantime... "I need time to think."

At her abashed look, guilt swamped him.

"I mean, wake up. No more talking."

Wrinkling her nose in puzzlement, Sarah complied. Grudgingly. Her silence lasted approximately as long as it took Daniel to realize he was naked beneath the linens. Naked! With Sarah! Not that sleeping in the altogether was unusual for him, but... hell. He and Sarah spent their time talking and fishing and dunking each other in Morrow Creek. Not lying comfortably abed after a night spent...doing things he couldn't even recall.

"So," she piped up, "if you don't want to talk, what *do* you want to do?"

Immediately, several wicked suggestions leaped to mind. Ferociously, Daniel tamped them down. If Sarah had been an ordinary woman, things might have been different. He enjoyed a roll in the sheets as much as the next man—possibly more. But as it was, the two of them had a marriage to tend to. They couldn't muddle the issue by lolling abed and behaving like two people who were besotted with one another.

"I want to get up," he decided.

She looked stricken. For naught, as it turned out. Because no sooner had Daniel grabbed a handful of quilt to toss aside than he remembered. He was still naked. God forbid, Sarah might be naked, too! If he threw off the coverlet...

Tarnation. They might *both* need smelling salts.

He stayed put, frozen in the wake of Sarah's confused gaze. The bed shrank to a cozier size, making him intimately aware of their nearness. And the potential for swooning. Not that Sarah had ever been particularly delicate. Typically, she was sturdy and sensible and extremely handy with a bamboo fishing rod. But she *had* turned all weepy on him yesterday. There was just no telling what getting hitched might have done to her.

Forlornly, he missed the old Sarah. The one who made sense.

"We could have a walk along the mountain trail after breakfast," she suggested breezily. She snuggled deeper in the quilt, her unbound hair silky and tousled. "That would be nice. Of course we'll have to go to church with my family this morning, too. I told my mama we'd collect Eli after services are over. But until then..."

He'd have sworn she fluttered her eyelashes at him. Suggestively. With all the feminine allure of a dance-hall girl. Befuddled by the very notion of

Sarah doing something so unabashedly flirtatious, Daniel stared at her.

He'd never seen her with her hair loose like that, he realized. It looked nice. Soft. Touching it would be…

A mistake. Damn it. He had to concentrate. Unless his years of bachelorhood had made him incapable of ignoring a woman—any woman—in his bed.

She's Sarah, he reminded himself sternly. *Sarah.*

"How did you get here?" he asked.

"Why…it happened last night. Don't you remember?"

Was it his imagination, or did she suddenly seem to be hiding something? Frowning, Daniel tried to recall what had happened after he'd come home from Murphy's saloon.

He had a vague recollection of finding Sarah in her nightgown. Of turning away, his face burning, while she scrambled barefoot to her own room. Of realizing, belatedly, that he should have been clearer on exactly whose chamber was whose. Although, come to think of it, he'd thought he'd done a good enough job of that.

He recalled further that he'd felt Sarah crawl in bed beside him sometime later. That he'd decided it would be better to deal with her in the morning when he hadn't had quite so much whiskey. That he'd dreamed he'd felt her snuggle up to him sometime in the night.

That he'd dreamed he'd liked it.

"You told me we'd finish things this morning," Sarah said.

She looked expectant. Alert. And, he couldn't seem to forget, possibly naked.

"This morning. Right." Wondering what sort of *finishing* she expected of him, Daniel cleared his throat. He always *had* had a habit of putting off problems till they were nigh unsolvable, he admitted to himself. Look at his troubles with Eli. But this time, he knew he'd have to deal with Sarah straightaway. *"This* morning."

"Mmm-hmm."

He didn't know what to say. Or what to do. He and Sarah had an arrangement…didn't they? A businesslike agreement. Perhaps she was simply feeling extraordinarily friendly. Her family *was* a famously freethinking one, after all. She probably thought nothing of hugging her sham husband. In the dark. While they were both—he felt compelled to remind himself—completely unclothed.

Silence fell. Clearly, peacefulness was more than Sarah could stand. "I'll start, since we didn't have much time to talk last night. As you can see, I found your gift."

"Gift?"

"The nightgown." Shyly, she bit her lip. "I'm sorry I didn't thank you properly for it when you came home. It's beautiful."

The heartfelt gratitude in her eyes was his undoing. Daniel didn't have the will to argue. But the truth was, he hadn't given her any... "Nightgown?"

Sarah nodded. In demonstration, she allowed him a peek beneath the quilt. He spied lace over creamy skin, feminine curves swathed in white and one long leg bent at the knee before he forced himself to close his eyes. The image of her still swam before him. It looked as if schoolmarming did a great deal for a woman's...feminine assets.

Dry-mouthed, he opened his eyes again. He pointed. "It's, uhhh, hitched up. Right there."

"Here?"

She patted ineffectually at the wrong leg, doing nothing to end his view of her bare, curvy thigh. With any other woman, Daniel would have taken her movements for coquettishness, but this was Sarah. Sensible Sarah. She couldn't possibly be trying to snare him with a forbidden glimpse of her thigh.

She'd already caught him in wedlock, hadn't she? What more could a woman possibly want?

"Ahhh." She stretched, arms overhead. She offered him a brazen smile. "I slept splendidly. I guess we wore ourselves out, didn't we?"

He didn't know *what* to say to that. Agreeing with

her wouldn't quite put forward the no-nonsense marriage he'd hoped for. But despite that fact, Daniel couldn't help preening a little. He was good at satisfying a woman—most likely due to his enjoyment of the task.

Enough of that. He needed to get to the bottom of things. "When I came home last night," he said, "after you left here—"

"Oh, that," Sarah interrupted hastily. "Yes, I figured you needed some time to prepare yourself. To freshen up for our wedding night."

Freshen up? He arched his brow. For...?

"So I went to the other room to brush my hair, to give you some privacy. But by the time I got back..." Trailing off suggestively, she chuckled. "Well, that's neither here nor there, is it? A proper wife keeps her husband's secrets, and she keeps him warm at night, too."

Hmmm. Maybe he *hadn't* dreamed the feeling of her arms around him. What, exactly, had happened when she "got back"? For the life of him, Daniel could only remember stripping off his clothes, hastily washing, then collapsing on his bed, done in by the unusual events of the day.

"*You* clearly know more about being a good husband than you've let on, Daniel. I don't know where you learned it, but I'm glad." Looking contented, Sarah dragged the quilt over herself again. "A gift on our wedding night? So generous of you. I've never owned anything as beautiful as this nightgown."

He gave a noncommittal grunt. He was an honest man, and Sarah deserved the truth. He needed to tell her he hadn't given her that gown. But when she looked at him that way, all appreciative and sweet, he just couldn't do it.

"It's very lovely," she said. "Isn't it?"

It was. Especially on her. But it ought to have been in her own bed, along with the rest of her.

"It doesn't look very warm," he grumbled.

She smiled, her whole face shining with a mysterious sort of feminine wisdom. Likely she believed him to be teasing her, as usual. Daniel stewed.

He still couldn't figure out why Sarah wasn't across the hall where she was supposed to be. The question occupied most of his thoughts, leaving room for little else. Had he, in a whiskey-fueled bout of stupidity, invited her to sleep with him instead?

"Ahhh. I've just realized why you're so grouchy this morning." Sarah peered at him, apparently confirming her suspicions. "But you needn't look so troubled. I understand about last night." She offered him a gentle pat on his shoulder. "Mama warned me that some men have…difficulties when they've been imbibing."

"Difficulties?" He all but choked on the word. She

could only mean…no. *That* kind of talk absolutely couldn't continue. "I never have difficulties."

"Don't worry. There will always be…other occasions."

Her cheeks blushed pink, but she went on looking at him steadily. That was Sarah for him. Forthright to a fault. Still, this was a peculiar conversation, to be sure.

"Especially now that we've worked out this issue of whose bedroom is whose," she added. "We'll have plenty of other opportunities now that we'll be together every night."

Every night? "Your room is across the hall."

She didn't so much as blink. "But last night we decided to give Eli back his chamber, remember? He needs room to grow."

"Not *that* much room. Near as I can tell, he won't be man-sized anytime soon."

"Aside from which," she said blithely, just as though he hadn't spoken, "Eli needs to be assured our marriage is an honest one—something he can count on. The two of us sharing a chamber will only help in that regard."

Thoroughly confused now, Daniel frowned. Had he agreed to all this and then forgotten somehow? Sarah seemed so certain. And he felt so muddled.

She gave him a no-nonsense look. "Eli needs to see me as a mother figure, not a houseguest."

Reluctantly, Daniel saw the logic in that. Sarah was a schoolmarm, accustomed to dealing with children. It was possible she knew best when it came to Eli. Wasn't that one reason he'd chosen her for a wife?

Still...it bothered him that he hadn't foreseen this hitch in their new partnership. It made sense that their marriage would need to seem real, for Eli's sake. But sharing a bedroom? Sleeping beside Sarah every night? That would require more fortitude than Daniel had counted on.

He hoped there weren't any more surprises lying in wait for him. A necessity to call Sarah some nonsense endearment, as Marcus did with Molly, for instance. A requirement to pare back his time at Murphy's saloon or pick up his socks. Or, God forbid, a curtailing of his poker nights. Marriage was mighty inconvenient for some men, he knew.

On the other hand, none of those men had been wise enough to wed a practical woman like Sarah.

"It's all settled, then," she announced. "We'll stay here, and Eli will sleep in his own room." Smiling, Sarah clasped his hand. Her wedding band glinted in the sunlight, reminding him of exactly how deep this arrangement between them went. "It will be cozy and wonderful."

That's what Daniel was worried about. That, and the question of exactly what had happened last night. He obviously wouldn't get a straight answer out of his wife.

"If that's what we decided." He frowned, honestly unable to recall doing so. "I'll sleep on the floor. It won't take me long to make up a pallet."

"A pallet? No! Don't be silly. You don't have to—"

"Yes, I do. My mind's made up."

Otherwise, he'd inevitably hurt Sarah—even more than he had already. That was more than Daniel could stand. They were friends, first of all. Since he couldn't promise her anything so mush-hearted as love, he knew it wouldn't be fair to treat their arrangement of theirs as an ordinary marriage.

Gently he withdrew his hand, hard pressed to withstand the disappointed look she gave him in return.

"Last night won't happen again," he promised.

Glumly, Sarah looked back at him.

He couldn't let her dissuade him. Daniel McCabe was a man of his word. He knew what was best for them both. He had to keep their friendship in the fore, *not* whatever shenanigans had happened last night. If they didn't linger over it, they would both forget it. In time.

Vowing to keep his life with Sarah strictly companionable from here on, Daniel reached for the quilt.

"Now close your eyes, wife." Despite the peculiarity of their situation, he couldn't help but smile. "I don't want you to swoon when I get out of bed."

Chapter Six

Sarah did *not* close her eyes. Not when Daniel turned back the quilt that morning, and not when he rose from the bed, either. How could she? Her curiosity was simply too powerful.

She didn't feel the least bit guilty about sneaking a peek at him. Daniel was her husband, after all. Aside from which, she'd wager her last hunk of schoolmarm's chalk that the rascal had lingered for a moment in a patch of sunlight as he'd reached for his britches, all but *encouraging* her to look her fill of him. Without his cooperation, she'd never have glimpsed such a scandalous view of his backside.

The very memory of it made her feel hot, even days later. She had only to recall his tanned skin, his muscular back or his brawny arms, and she flushed all over. When she thought of his round-cheeked, jaunty posterior, she wanted to giggle aloud with delight. Who knew a man could have so appealing a backside? Or that the sight of it would make her feel so giddy?

Of course, she hadn't glimpsed anything...front-ward on Daniel. Even she—for all her vaunted open-mindedness—wasn't that bold. And despite her intimations to the contrary, she and Daniel hadn't shared anything more on their wedding night than a few inches of mattress and part of the quilt.

Something had gone wrong between her finding the nightgown he'd given her and his arrival home that night. How else to explain his surprise upon seeing her wearing it? He'd gone positively beet red in the face—*not,* she'd estimated, the reaction of a man delighted to see his bride in her finery.

Never one to be daunted by a setback, though, Sarah had simply regrouped. That was her way. She refused to be defeated. If one tactic didn't work, another was in order—it was as plain as that. So she'd bided her time, then slipped in bed with Daniel after she'd been certain he was asleep. It was only proper, she felt, that they spend their first married night together.

Admittedly, it had been somewhat devious of her to mislead him the following morning. They'd had no such discussion about Eli's room, and Daniel hadn't agreed to a thing regarding their sharing a bed. But between growing up in her unconventional family, reaching a spinster's age and teaching dozens of schoolchildren, Sarah had learned a thing or two about human nature. If a person insisted on anything staunchly enough, sooner or later everyone else gave in. It was only natural.

Besides, her tactics had been for the greater good. It was true that Eli—so recently arrived in the territory—needed stability. Surety. An openly false marriage would give him neither. And Daniel—his protestations to the contrary—*needed* love. For too long, he'd held himself apart from the more sensitive qualities in his nature, preferring to spend his time in decadent bachelor pursuits. Her taming of him was for his own good. In the end, Sarah didn't doubt he'd thank her for it.

Especially once he fell in love with her.

"Put down Whiskers and sit still in that chair, Eli." She nodded to the cat in his arms. "And please stop kicking the rungs. As soon as I get this in the oven, we'll start on your haircut. It's past time you looked respectable again."

The boy groaned in protest. Sarah slid a graniteware dish of beans in the oven, wincing at the blast of heat that greeted her. Over the past several days, she'd become adept at her new role, teaching during the days and caring for her family in the mornings and evenings. Now, on her first full Saturday with the McCabe men, she felt determined to affect some additional—and much needed—changes in their household.

This seemed a fitting time, while Daniel was busy at the smithy employing a new apprentice. In her experience, the least said about an intended change, the better. It only upset folks if they had too much time to contemplate progress. Wasn't the resistance Grace had encountered in establishing her new Morrow Creek Ladies' Bicycling Club evidence of that?

After a careful perusal of Eli's hair, Sarah picked up her shears and tackled the task at hand. She did a fine job on the boy's dark brown locks, she thought, especially for someone with her limited experience. Even if Eli's hair *was* turning out a bit shorter than she'd originally planned.

With a hearty greeting, Daniel entered the kitchen on a breath of chilly autumn air. The scents of dried leaves, wood smoke and tobacco came with him. He set down the armload of repaired cooking utensils he'd lugged home with him, then turned away to shuck his woolen coat.

Wistfully, Sarah watched his shoulders bunch beneath his shirt, his hands flex as he hung his coat on a peg. He had wonderful hands, big and strong and sure. Now that she knew what they felt like clasped within hers, she yearned for more. More touches, more embraces…more kisses.

The memory of the brief wedding kiss she'd shared with Daniel tantalized her still. What would it be like, she wondered, to feel truly loved? To feel cherished, like a proper wife? 'Twould be…

Daniel glanced her way. Caught gawking, Sarah hastily returned her attention to Eli's unruly hair. Her cheeks heated, though, and her heart took to pounding as well. Undoubtedly, Daniel had seen her mooning at him. If that didn't make him pull foot for the fireside with a mug of cider in his hand and an urgent need to be away from his wife, nothing would.

It proved awfully inconvenient, she supposed as she snipped diligently, when a man's wife showed signs of actually being in love with him.

To her surprise, though, Daniel leaned against the worktable with, it seemed, every intention of staying to watch them. Almost as though he'd glimpsed the yearning in her eyes, she fancied, and felt intrigued enough to study her further.

At his lingering there, Sarah couldn't help but feel her spirits lift. It was silly, but she couldn't help it. For the past few days, Daniel had done all he could to keep his distance from her. His insistence on behaving strictly as "friends"—despite their marriage— had driven her half mad. She'd imagined she'd be able to bring him round to her way of thinking—her *romantic* way of thinking—by now. But so far, he'd proved stubbornly resistant to her charms.

Not to mention her repeated invitations to join her in their bed instead of his pallet. Foolish man. She had half a mind to sharpen her washboard and "accidentally" shred his makeshift bedroll the next time she laundered their things.

"A haircut, eh?" Good-naturedly, Daniel peered at Eli, who sat with his arms stubbornly crossed. "Don't look so glum. That bald spot will grow back lickety-split."

"Bald spot?" Wide-eyed, Eli reached for his head.

"Hush." With practiced movements, Sarah stilled the boy's hand. She went on snipping. "You don't have a bald spot, Eli. And I wouldn't be so full of jests if I were you, *husband*. You're next."

He laughed. "That's what you think, *wife*. You'll have to tie me down first."

"Very well. If that's the way you want it." She shrugged, pausing to comb a cowlick. "Eli will help me. Won't you, Eli?"

"Yes, ma'am!"

"You'll help me get a rope? And tie extra-sturdy knots?"

"*Really* sturdy!" The boy guffawed.

At his laughter, warmth welled inside her. She truly did love Eli. He was a sweet, tenderhearted boy—beneath all the muddy shoes and frog-filled pockets. She didn't know how he'd wound up on that westbound train—especially *without* the chaperone who'd been meant to accompany him—headed for an indefinite stay with his uncle. She didn't know how anyone could have given him up. All she knew was that he was hers now—a part of her makeshift family of three.

"Give him a bald spot!" Eli crowed. "A big one."

"Hmm. I just might." Enjoying their banter, Sarah pretended to scout an appropriate place amid Daniel's thick brown hair. Using her shears, she pointed to a likely location. "Right there above his ear, perhaps?"

Daniel shook his head. "I get my haircuts—and my baths—down at Miss Adelaide's place. I don't need—"

"'Miss Adelaide's'?" Gaping in astonishment, Sarah clapped her hands over Eli's ears. "But that's practically a brothel!"

"Nothing 'practical' about it."

He grinned, a smile that probably came from remembering his *impractical* visits there. Or from recalling those occasions when he'd been illicitly "soaped up." As if they didn't have a perfectly serviceable washtub at home.

Sarah felt her blood boil. "There'll be no visits to Miss Adelaide's in your future. I won't have it."

He looked confused. "But you always knew I visited there. You used to joke about the place with me."

"I wasn't married to you then." Ignoring his puzzled frown, Sarah straightened as regally as she could. She resumed snipping. "It's different now. You have Eli. And…and me."

A grin. "Well, I didn't plan on taking you two with me."

"It won't do any good to argue." Her tone was a reasonable impersonation of her mother's, whenever Fiona took Adam Crabtree to task for sneaking a cigar. Sarah figured she was doing well, in a wifely sort of way. "I've said my piece on the matter."

Daniel, blast him, didn't seem the least convinced.

"I didn't ask for your 'piece.' Not that it matters now, anyway, because I don't need a haircut. That's *my* final word."

Did he truly believe a blustery statement like that would dissuade her? "Indeed you *do* need a haircut," Sarah insisted, feeling a need to stand her ground. On something. "*You* might fancy looking like a mountain man, but *I*—"

"But *you* can't handle my fine rugged looks?"

"Pshaw." That was too close to the truth. Could he tell? Hoping not, Sarah lifted her chin. "Your head is growing fatter by the minute. That's not what I meant at all."

"Come, now. You don't have to be coy. Admit it."

"I will not!"

With sham regret, he pursed his lips. "I'm simply too fine looking for your delicate sensibilities."

Daniel gave her a roguish wink, one she felt certain he typically reserved for dance-hall ladies and their ilk. She looked again, but he only offered her an even more dazzling smile. He must have momentarily lost his head, she decided, to have unloosed a portion of his charm on her.

"After all, you can hardly be expected to withstand so much manliness—" outrageously, he spread his arms in demonstration "—all in one place."

Sarah scoffed. "Don't be silly. You're not so very... manly."

She nearly choked on the fib. And Daniel obviously didn't believe her—not that she could blame him. This was the way it had always been between them—he, spinning ever more outlandish tales; she, secretly relishing every one. Daniel possessed an audaciousness Sarah had never found for herself.

The difference was, he'd never before used that boldness of his to suggest she fancied him. Why was he doing so now? Of a certain, that fatheaded grin of his was no clue.

"I want to be manly, too!" Eli piped up, suddenly switching allegiances.

Sarah gawked. "Eli!"

"We'll be a manly pair together." Daniel nodded assuredly. "You and me, Eli. How's that?"

Affectionately, he slung his arm around Eli's skinny shoulders. Thus united, the two of them faced her—dark haired, dark eyed and so alike in their man-size mulishness that Sarah actually wondered...had she been wrong all along? Was Eli truly Daniel's son in secret, as everyone in Morrow Creek suspected?

He'd told her the boy was his sister's, but looking at them now...

No. That way lay madness. Rather than wonder, Sarah decided to take what providence had given her—Daniel and Eli—and try to recapture some of the warmth they'd shared earlier.

With that aim in mind, she stuck her hands on her hips, then regarded the pair of them puckishly. "Are you two ganging up on me, then?"

They nodded. Solemnly, Daniel explained, "We men have to stick together."

Eli nodded. "Against the womenfolk."

"The 'womenfolk,'" Sarah pointed out, "are the ones who keep you clothed and fed."

"Pshaw." Daniel waved off the notion. "If by 'fed' you mean that mush you slopped out for us last night—"

"That was a perfectly good dish of barley and ruta-bagas!"

Fiona Crabtree had recently become a Grahamite,

in keeping with Sylvester Graham's revolutionary findings about the merits of eating whole grains and plenty of plant stuffs. Following her mama's example, Sarah had decided to try out one of the doctor's receipts. She'd wondered why Daniel and Eli had volunteered so readily to scrape the plates and stack them for washing.

"—then I'm happy with beans and bacon down at Murphy's."

"That's another thing." Reminded of Jack Murphy's saloon—and Daniel's habit of taking his meals there—Sarah prepared for another tussle. "Why haven't you been taking your noontime meals to the smithy with you? I leave out something for you every morning, nicely packed with a gingham napkin and—"

"—and *vegetables*. Green beans, corn, tomatoes." He made a face. "Those aren't foods fit for a man."

"Well, I can hardly scurry from the schoolhouse to cook you a beefsteak on your blacksmith's fire every noontime, now, can I?" Sarah arched her brow. "Mama gave me some things Cook had put up for winter. I thought you'd like them."

"But...they're vegetables."

At his aggrieved tone, Sarah grinned. As a girl, she'd helped Daniel smuggle his share of carrots and turnips from the dinner table and feed them to the neighbor's hogs. But things were different now. Pointedly, Sarah glanced at Eli.

"You're a grown man now. You have an example to set. That includes vegetables."

Daniel groaned, sounding markedly like Eli had when she'd originally suggested trimming his hair. Ignoring him, Sarah gave her charge one last comb-through. She unfastened the cloth she'd tied around his neck to catch the clippings.

With a hopeful face, Eli glanced up. "All done?"

At her nod, he hopped gleefully from his chair. "I guess I'll go read a book, then," he announced.

Daniel stared, diverted from his tirade against vegetables. "A book?" He turned to Sarah. "You *have* bewitched him."

She smiled, feeling satisfied. The change in Eli was no less dramatic than she planned for Daniel. Not that he needed to know the details yet.

"No mud pies? No mischief?" he prodded.

"Nah, I like my book." Eli nodded toward the other room. "Miss Crabtree got it for me from the News Depot."

Daniel frowned. "You mean your Aunt Sarah got it for you."

The boy shrugged. "No, Miss Crabtree did." He headed for the distant hearth, where his book waited on a chair.

Daniel held out his hand to stop him. A curious

tension emanated from him. "She's not 'Miss Crabtree' anymore. She's Aunt Sarah. That's what you're to call her."

"She's Miss Crabtree," Eli insisted stubbornly.

"You go ahead and read your book, Eli." Sarah stepped in, giving him a pat on his rigid shoulder. "It's all right."

He scampered away, clearly relieved. Sarah wished she felt the same. Something in Daniel's face alarmed her. Something dark and pained and very unlike him.

"It's *not* all right." Daniel peered past her, probably intending to call back Eli. His voice was a rumble of pure displeasure. "He'll do what I say, or—"

"Leave it, Daniel. Please. We can't force Eli to change the way he thinks of me. Maybe in time—"

"Maybe *you* can't force him. But *I* can." His mouth hardened. "Already you care for him more than his mother ever did. More than she ever will. You deserve—"

"I don't deserve anything more than he's ready to give." Sarah hesitated, wondering if she dared ask about Eli's mother. Why had she sent away her own son? But given the stormy look on Daniel's face, she decided another time would be better. "Honestly. I can be patient."

"You? 'Patient'? Ha." At that, Daniel gave her a skeptical look. "'Twould be the first time, that's for certain." Unexpectedly, some of the gloom left his expression. "Remember when you wanted to cross the creek on those stepping stones? You nearly drowned yourself being 'patient.'"

"I was only eleven, and I got tired of waiting for you to teach me, like you promised." Sarah folded her arms, willing to reminisce all morning if it brought back the happy man she was used to. "It's not my fault you couldn't tear yourself away from chasing girls and scribbling naughty pictures on the blackboard. You were *supposed* to be cleaning up the schoolhouse."

"Right. 'Supposed to be.' Even then *you* knew I wasn't doing it. I guess you were meant to become a schoolmarm." Another wink. "To keep rascals like me in line."

"Not hardly. There is no one else like you."

Wistfully spoken, the words slipped out before she could stop them. There *was* no one else like Daniel—at least not for her. That had always been true.

Not that he needed to know it. At least until he loved her back. Aghast at her slip of the tongue, Sarah fumbled for another rejoinder.

"Fortunately for me, that is. I have my hands full already, without a six-foot, fully grown student to deal with."

Daniel's brown-eyed gaze turned faraway. "I'll admit, staying late never was much of a punishment for me." He pinned her with an indecipherable look. "I stole my first kiss while sweeping the floors with—"

"Stop! I don't want to know who you debauched in your youth." Primly, Sarah brushed wisps of hair from the ladder-back chair. She shook out the neck cloth, then patted the chair seat. "We have haircutting to see to."

He scoffed. "You don't mean that."

"Oh, yes. I do."

"Damnation, woman. I was happy enough when you mended my shirts and boiled my socks clean. And when you sewed those new britches for Eli. If I have to, I can even live with the rutabagas. But uglifying me is taking things too far."

"'Uglifying' you?" Sarah couldn't help but smile. It would require more than trimming Daniel's overgrown locks to accomplish that feat. But telling him so would only feed his oversize ego. She heaved a mock-sorrowful sigh. "It's too late for that. I'm afraid someone else already beat me to it."

He gave her a frown. Then a considering look.

A half hour later, she'd had her way with his overgrown head. Proving once again, Sarah reminded herself, that persistence will out.

Stepping back with shears in hand, she surveyed her work. "Ahh. That's better. You look almost... handsome."

His suspicious gaze narrowed on her face. "Are you turning all spooney on me again?" he demanded.

"Again?" She opened her mouth in an undoubtedly poor imitation of astonishment. "When did I ever—"

"Yesterday," he said bluntly. "I caught you mooning at me over the dinner table."

Well. She couldn't be blamed for that. She'd married an impossibly appealing man, hadn't she? Besides, she'd thought she'd covered that quite adeptly.

"I told you. Your eyebrows are crooked."

He seemed less convinced by that explanation today than he had last evening. Then, the explaining of it had gained her a good fifteen minutes' time to moon over his features. He'd been none the wiser of her true motivation...unabashed longing.

Musingly, Daniel touched the tip of his finger to his bushy brow. Then he blinked like a man shaking off a dream.

"I warned you already, Sarah. We can't have any of that foolish cooing and fussing 'romantic' marriages have. Our arrangement is different." With a distressingly intent expression, he reached for her hand. He rubbed his thumb over her knuckles. "It's a practical trade. My name and protection, for your help with Eli and this household. We agreed."

Sarah barely registered the words, so caught up was she in the warmth of his fingers on hers. Truly, when she glanced to him in an attempt to better understand, she found herself entranced by the deep timbre of his voice, by the poetry of his mouth. Both were fine, masculine and familiar. Beloved.

He seemed to be waiting for a reply. To what?

She swallowed hard. Then…why not?…nodded.

"Good." He squeezed her hand, obviously relieved. "We have no need for 'love' between us. What we have is better. Affection. Mutual regard. Mended britches."

A ghost of a smile crossed his face. Sarah did her best to muster a similar response for him. Was he telling her he could never love her? That was impossible.

Needing to tell him so, she touched his face. Briefly, she cradled his jaw in her hand, savoring the feel of his warm skin, his emerging beard stubble… *him*. "Daniel—"

Something flared in his eyes. A kindred feeling? Or merely confusion?

"Found some stray hairs?" he blurted, brushing at his cheek as though that were the reason she caressed him. "Don't worry. Now that you've finishing your haircutting, I can clean up the mess myself."

With a brisk demeanor, Daniel stood, scattering shorn brown curls in his wake. He clomped his boots against the kitchen floorboards. In a trice, he'd scooped up all the mess in his wrenched-off neck cloth, which he bundled in his hands.

"See? Good as new," he declared. "Everything's exactly the way it was."

Sarah sighed. *Yes. Exactly the way it was,* she agreed as she watched him walk away. But if she had anything to do with it, that wouldn't be true for long.

Chapter Seven

Holding up the rock drill he'd been firing, Daniel peered at it to gauge its heat level. Straw yellow. Nearly the ideal temper for the tool. Signaling for his apprentice, Toby, to work the bellows, he fired the drill again before plunging it in his water barrel. Steam issued forth, hissing and spitting in the cold autumn air.

Despite the coming weather, winter would be one of his busiest times at the smithy. His neighbors would be by with garden tools and wagon wheels and things they'd put off repairing till after the harvest. Broken chains, axes, plowshares and sleigh runners would need mending. Horses would need outfitting in studded winter shoes for protection on the icy roads. By springtime, he'd wager he'd have seen most of Morrow Creek—animal and humankind alike.

"Have you got those tools, McCabe?" Marcus Copeland strode into the smithy, his usual hat and fine suit in place. With a smile, he clapped his new brother-in-law on the back. "I've got timber to fell and boards to saw, you know."

He nodded to the pile of axes, crosscut saws and felling wedges belonging to his lumber mill. They'd been brought to the smithy earlier in the week, awaiting sharpening and repairs.

To an outsider, the newly formed stacks probably looked a mess, Daniel knew. But to him they were as orderly as the piles of scrap metal, broken iron and other odds and ends he kept stacked all around his blacksmith's shop, inside and out. He never knew when a cast-off piece might come in handy.

He grunted an affirmative. "Took longer than I thought. I had to make new ax heads and reshape some of the wedges. Job's finished now, though. Your men can start hauling things out."

Marcus nodded, busy examining one of the axes. With the practiced motion of a trained lumberman, he tested its edge with his thumb. "This looks good. Fine work, as always."

He nodded to the workers who'd arrived with him. In pairs, they started carrying crosscut saws to the wagon parked outside the smithy's open double doors. It wouldn't take long for the task to be accomplished. In the meantime…

"I reckon I'll see you for poker this week, as usual?" Daniel raised his water for a drink, then wiped his mouth with his sleeve. He grinned. "O'Neil has fat pockets this time of year. Ripe for the picking."

Marcus grinned, too. The butcher was a terrible poker player, but a good sport and an even better friend.

"Not this week. Molly wants a trip to Prescott."

"Prescott?" The neighboring town was an after-noon's ride away. "What for?"

"Damned if I know. She says it's supposed to be a picnic."

Daniel scratched his head. "You can picnic here." He jutted his chin at the mountainous landscape and pine trees surrounding them. "It's nice down by Morrow Creek, ever since the oak leaves turned color."

"That's what I told her. Didn't work."

"What do you mean, 'didn't work'? You told her no, right? That should have been the end of it."

"Well…" Tugging at his hat, Marcus glanced to the men laboring at the other side of the smithy, almost as though he wanted to make sure he wouldn't be overheard. "She *looked* at me," he confessed.

There had to be more. But there wasn't. "And?"

"That's all." A goofy smile spread over Marcus's face. Truth be told, he didn't seem put out by the situation, as would have been fitting. "She just looked at me, in this way she has. I'll be damned if I could tell her no."

Daniel scoffed. He could tell anybody no. Except maybe a pretty dance-hall girl. But that was all behind him now.

Shaking his head, he picked up a worn hoe, preparing to hone its blade. "Trouble with you, Copeland, is you're a damned pushover. I ought to have known it, I reckon. Fancy suit-wearing Eastern type like you—"

"Go to hell, McCabe," Marcus said cheerfully. "You married Sarah. You must know what I mean."

Determinedly, Daniel shook his head. "I won't be led by the nose by any woman. 'Specially all the way to Prescott."

A guffaw. "That's a hoot, coming from a man who married a Crabtree."

Daniel frowned. It almost sounded as though Copeland knew something *he* ought to know—about being married.

But that couldn't be. Daniel might not wear highfalutin suits to work in, but he did know people. He understood human nature. *His* nature compelled him—unlike Marcus's, he guessed—to be the master of his own household. Besides, his arrangement with Sarah was unique. So what if he'd found himself enjoying her company more than he'd expected to? Their togetherness was companionable. Comfortable. It was right and fitting.

Although sometimes, like when she showed him

her new nightgown or cupped his face in her hand...
sometimes Daniel thought there might be something
more there. Something sweet and hot and needful.
Something beyond his experience.

But maybe not beyond Marcus's experience. Had
Sarah ever looked at him, Daniel wondered suddenly,
in a *Molly-like* way? Had he already succumbed?

"You'll see." Wearing a dead-certain expression,
Marcus held out some bills in payment for Daniel's
blacksmithing work. "One of these days, Sarah will
ask you to do something you'd never in a million
years thought you'd do. And you'll say to yourself,
'No. I'm not doing that. Hell, no.' And the next thing
you know, you'll be doing it."

Alarmed, Daniel stared at him. Damnation. Could
it be true? Could a woman make a man do whatever
she decided he ought to? The notion was chilling.

It didn't matter, he told himself staunchly. Because
Sarah was meek and gentle and sensible. She was his
friend. She wouldn't ask him to do outlandish things.
Why would she? He'd wed himself the choicest
Crabtree woman, to be sure.

Mustering a smile, he counted the payment and
pocketed it. "Maybe," he said. "I guess I'd better be
on the lookout."

He offered a handshake, then they said their goodbyes. But just before his brother-in-law took his leave,
Daniel thought of something else. He didn't want

to bring it up, but he didn't have anybody else to ask—at least not anybody who wouldn't laugh their fool head off at the question.

Frowning, he stepped nearer. "Copeland. One more thing."

Marcus turned, midway through adjusting his hat. He raised his brows in question.

Damnation, this was ridiculous. But still, Daniel had to know. Especially given the conversation they'd just had.

He cleared his throat. Then he just came out with it.

"Do my eyebrows look crooked to you?"

After dismissing her students from the schoolhouse, Sarah met Molly at her bakeshop. She sat on a pretty wirework chair at her sister's counter, sampling an apple fritter and enjoying the company of someone who didn't swear, spit, play with toy trains or scratch under their arms with utter abandon.

"Sometimes it's hard living in a household of men," she confided to Molly. "They leave their things all around, blind to the hamper or the drawer. They scatter crumbs on the rugs, wandering through the house like horses following a strung-up carrot on a stick. They belch! Sweet heaven, Moll. I never knew."

Molly nodded. "Mama's done an excellent job of

taming Papa. That's why you didn't realize what you were in for."

Thoughtfully, they both took bites of their fritters. It occurred to Sarah that growing up with two sisters and a mother—clearly creating a skewed female-to-male ratio where their papa was concerned—might not have been her best preparation for marriage. Especially with a small boy in the mix.

"So...how is married life?" Molly asked.

"Splendid! Although my corn bread is still a little dry." Sarah thought about it some more. "Also, we need new curtains in the kitchen, and I may have caused Daniel to believe he couldn't fulfill his husbandly duties on our wedding night."

Molly choked. Goggling at her sister, she reached for a glass of water. She sipped till her throat cleared. "*What?*"

"It was an accident. I told him he'd imbibed too much at Jack Murphy's saloon, and he believed me. He honestly couldn't remember the truth. That's how much of an impression his wedding night made on him!"

"Oh, Sarah. I'm sure there's a reasonable explana—"

"Daniel doesn't want me...*that way*," Sarah confessed. "He is wonderful in every fashion, but he doesn't yearn passionately for me. Not really. Not, you know, the way a flower yearns for the golden kiss of the sunlight."

Molly gawked, her fritter halfway to her mouth. She shook her head. "You have read too many romantic novels. Daniel is hardly a flower. A giant oak, more likely. With shaggy bark."

"That's solved now," Sarah said absently. "I trimmed his hair the day before yesterday."

"Well, then." A smile. "Problem solved."

"No, it's not. I want a husband who is affectionate!"

"And Daniel is not? Perhaps he isn't a demonstrative man."

"Oh, he's demonstrative, all right." Sarah made a churlish face. "I've seen him flirt with four women at once."

"But that's not the same as being married," Molly pointed out. Tactfully, she refrained from commenting on Daniel's scandalous past. "Most likely, Daniel is merely being respectful of his wife. Some women would appreciate that."

"Perhaps." Morosely, Sarah chewed a cinnamony bit of apple. "Or perhaps this is all my fault. I *never* should have climbed trees and gone fishing and built rock forts when I was a girl!" Over the past week, she'd given the matter grave thought, trying to reason out a solution. "I believe I may have stunted my feminine wiles," she said seriously. "They don't appear to have developed properly. And now I'm paying the price, with a husband who won't look twice at me."

"Oh, Sarah." Molly looked about to laugh. "I'm sure your feminine wiles are fine. Do you know, at one time I believed mine might be damaged, too? But everything turned out all right in the end."

"Really?" That was difficult to believe, given how very feminine Molly was. She flirted as easily as pie, and she was sociable enough for three. Still, Sarah found it a great relief to learn her sister had faced similar troubles and overcome them. But on the other hand...

"That's easy for you to say. You always were more feminine than me. So is Grace, for that matter, and she's done all manner of mannish things. But I'm a great hulking woman! Sized nearly to fit a man."

"A puny man, perhaps." Molly covered Sarah's hand with hers. Consolingly, she offered a squeeze. "You are fine. And beautiful! If a tad bit prone to letting your imagination get carried away with you at times."

Sarah shook her head. "I am *not* getting carried away. It's the truth. For instance, I'm as strong as an ox. An ox! Papa's always said so."

"Only when he wanted you to help Cook carry heavy pots in the kitchen instead of him, so he could go on reading his book. You know that."

But Sarah couldn't listen. Now that she'd begun unburdening herself, she had to go on.

"An ox certainly isn't feminine. No wonder Daniel and I are having…problems. Also," she offered as further proof, "I wear only practical dresses, not pretty ones, and I have no notion how to fashionably wear my hair. Or a bonnet."

She flopped in misery, laying her head on her sun-browned arm. The sight of it reminded her that she hadn't managed to give up her beloved sojourns out-of-doors, either.

"You loathe bonnets," Molly reminded her. "And hats of all kinds. You say they're unnecessary frippery."

That was true. But Sarah wanted Daniel to love her, blast it. And soon. She was going daft waiting. If her lack of bows and geegaws and foolish flounces was keeping that from happening…

"That's why I told Mama not to bother with your trousseau overmuch," Molly went on. She finished her fritter, then went back to rolling out a batch of cinnamon buns on the work counter. Her stylish bustle swayed to and fro as she labored. "Your Sunday best needed trimming to serve as your wedding gown, of course, but that fancy nightgown Mama made—"

Sarah perked her head up, suddenly alert. "Nightgown?"

"Yes. You know, the white lawn gown with the

Belgian lace at the collar and sleeves." Noting Sarah's baffled look, she specified. "With the double ruffle and ribbon trim at the hem."

"You may as well be speaking Greek." Sarah cupped her chin in her hand, saddened at this further proof of her lacking femininity. "You know I don't pore over the fashion plates in *Godey's* the way you do."

"The nightgown. The fancy nightgown that Mama, Grace and I left for you at your new home as a surprise wedding gift."

The nightgown! "I thought Daniel had given that to me."

"No. We did." Turning her dough, Molly sprinkled it with cinnamon and sugar. She didn't glance up to see the shocked look on Sarah's face. "Otherwise, you might have sported that tattered old flannel thing you wear. We couldn't have Daniel seeing you in *that* on your wedding night, now, could we?"

When Sarah didn't say anything, Molly did look up. Her previously puckered expression turned to a more aghast one.

"You *did* wear the flannel! Oh, sweet heavens—"

"No, no. I wore the new gown."

"Good." Molly beamed. "Grace will be glad. Do you know, she even lowered herself to stitch on some of the lace? Of course, she muttered something about women getting stuck with all the most trivial work while men did the exciting things as she sewed…but you know Grace."

Sarah did. Her sister was an avowed suffragette, a devoted advocate of the work of Elizabeth Cady Stanton and Susan B. Anthony. She'd organized a number of ladies' aid organizations in town, and served on several committees, as well. She bicycled, picketed and even engaged in amateur ornithology. There was nothing traditional about her elder sister. But then, that was expected of a Crabtree woman. Their parents had allowed them the freedom to pursue their own interests.

Returning to the subject at hand, Molly smiled. "We decided every bride should have a lovely night-gown. Most especially our Sarah."

Lost in thought, Sarah murmured an agreement.

Molly jabbed her with a floury finger. "Well? Tell me! Did you like it or not?"

"Oh! I'm sorry. Yes, very much. It was lovely."

Considering this new information, Sarah wiped her fingers on a napkin. That the nightgown had been a gift from her family explained a great deal. About Daniel, about their wedding night…about the morning she'd awakened beside him.

A terrible thought struck her. "Molly, I displayed myself to Daniel in that nightgown. Like a brazen hussy!"

Molly looked at her as though awaiting further

information. When none was forthcoming, she put her hands on her hips.

"Yes? And?"

"What do you mean, 'yes, and'? I behaved like a common—"

"Wife. Certain liberties are allowed once you're married, you know. Or did Mama forget to tell you that? She did forget to tell me. There were a rocky few weeks, indeed, after Marcus and I were wed."

Sarah peered at her. "Then why are you smiling over remembering them?"

"Because we found our way." Briskly, her sister fit cinnamon buns in the waiting pan. "I have no doubt you and Daniel will, too. It's only a matter of time."

Pondering that, Sarah watched as Molly slid the pastries in her big work oven. Daniel had known he hadn't given her that nightgown. So he *hadn't* been tacitly inviting her to join him on their wedding night by leaving it out for her. Yet when they'd awakened the following morning, he'd allowed her to stay. That had to mean he *did* yearn for her…at least a little bit.

The notion gave her far more hope than she'd had till now.

Heartened for the first time in weeks, Sarah reached for another fritter. The door to Daniel's heart had cracked open! Just a wee bit, it was true, but that would have to be enough. From here on, she only needed a wedge to widen the gap further.

Feeling grateful for her sister's encouragement, Sarah glanced to Molly. There was still one more thing she needed to know, and her sister was the likeliest source.

"Moll, when you want Marcus to do something, how do you accomplish it?"

"Hmm?" Streaked by sunlight from the bakeshop window, Molly glanced up. She dusted her floury hands on her apron. "Accomplish it? Don't be silly. I simply ask him." She shrugged. "That's usually all that's required."

"Excellent. That's all I needed to know."

Long past dark, Daniel confronted his wife.

"What's this?" he demanded.

Innocently, she blinked at the clump of fabric he'd dropped on the kitchen worktable. "Hmm. Is this a quiz?"

"A what?"

She gave him a cheerful look. "My papa used to instigate games of charades in the parlor after dinner, but we never—"

"Sarah. Don't fiddle with me. I'm in no mood."

"Oh. In that case…" She set down her flatiron and regarded the fabric. "It looks like a pile of rags. Hurrah! What do I win?"

"This isn't a game! What's the matter with you? You've been in strange spirits all day." And here it was dark outside, with Eli tucked safely in his bed.

"I'm just happy, that's all. Optimistic." Sarah traded her cooling flatiron for another, then hummed as she set to work on one of Eli's shirts. "Today I'm glad just to be alive."

He peered at her suspiciously. Grunted. He guessed this mania was what came of allowing her to visit her sisters. Those Crabtree women were an uppity lot. They were prone to all sorts of oddball ideas promoted by their freethinking family. Doubtless, Sarah had learned a new way to darn socks and was overcome with joy at the prospect of trying it out.

Which mattered to Daniel not a bit. Socks were socks. Fighting for patience, he moved the lamp closer and pointed to the thing he'd brought with him.

"That," he said, "is my pallet!"

"Well." She smiled at him, her demeanor exceedingly reasonable. "If you knew that already, why did you ask *me?*"

"Because this household is your business. It's up to you to make sure things like this don't happen." Daniel shook the rags—*his pallet*—in his fist. "Explain yourself."

"I don't have an explanation. Other than it's difficult for me to get to all the housework, given my duties at the schoolhouse. If I had a spare pair of hands, maybe—"

"Stop talking nonsense. It's unlike you."

"Hmm. How do you know that, Daniel? Perhaps there are other sides to me. Sides you haven't noticed before."

Resuming her humming, Sarah pressed the flatiron over Eli's shirttails. She seemed beyond self-satisfied to him. And something else, too, something he didn't understand. Daniel goggled at her. He considered himself a patient man, but this tried his fortitude.

He tried again, ladling some sweetness in his voice. "Does one of your 'sides' know what happened to my pallet?"

She smiled. With a graceful gesture, she tucked a strand of hair in her knotted braid. "It might have been my rogue washboard. It's come dangerously close to shredding things lately. I've noticed a few snags."

"Fine." That was settled, then. "I'll have a look at fixing it. Should be an easy enough thing to do."

"Or I suppose…it may have been Whiskers who did it."

He was losing his mind. "Whiskers?"

"Your cat."

"I don't have a cat."

"Of course you do. It's your pet."

For a moment, given the surety in her voice, he

almost wavered. Did he have a cat? Then he caught himself. "You mean that old tomcat? The mouser that prowls around here?"

"If that 'old tomcat' has beautiful fur and a regal demeanor, then yes. That's the one." She folded Eli's shirt, then plucked a wind-stiffed pair of britches from her basket and started ironing them. "I'm afraid he has something of a mischievous streak."

"You and that stray cat have a lot in common, then."

She blinked at him. Impishly. "Meow."

Daniel couldn't believe his ears. Or his eyes. Something was wrong with her—something serious. How else to explain that his sensible Sarah was *meowing?*

She caught his expression and laughed. Laughed!

"Don't look so horrified, Daniel. I'm making a jest. It's what we do together, remember? We share jokes."

Yes, but...usually *he* was the one teasing her. This was different. This time he didn't seem to have the upper hand. It did not feel right.

Daniel folded his arms. "You named my cat?"

"I thought you said you didn't have a cat."

"Well, I refuse to have one named something so chowderheaded as 'Whiskers.' That's for certain."

"Oh. What's your suggestion of a name, then?"

"I don't have one. Cats don't need names. I've been

trying to be rid of that one for weeks. It can barely catch a field mouse. It's useless."

Sarah looked aghast. "It's lovable!"

"I suppose you fed it, too."

She rolled her eyes in a way that he suggested he was daft to entertain any other notion. "Yes, beefsteak. Morning, noon and night."

"Now we'll never be rid of it," he groused. Frowning, he flung down the useless tattered pallet. "Look! That cat destroyed my bed. Where am I supposed to sleep now?"

A smile curled the edge of her mouth. "We have a perfectly serviceable bed. It's large enough for two. We can share it."

"Share it?"

"You know." She flipped over the britches, ironed the final wrinkled leg, then folded them. "Lie side by side, sleeping. Share the bed. Your bed. *Our* bed."

"Humor is unbecoming on you, wife."

"Oh? Then why are you smiling?"

Daniel slapped his hand over his mouth. 'Twas true. Beneath his beard stubble, a grin stretched his face. He could not find this feistiness in her attractive. Nor could he be interested in sharing a bed with her. She was his wife!

More importantly, she was Sarah.

"Fine," he heard himself say. "We'll share it."

What? That wasn't what he'd meant to say at all.

He frowned, done in by the devilish part of him that had agreed to this terrible idea. Daniel had never in his life slept chastely beside a woman. Never. At least not knowingly. He damned well didn't intend to start now.

Unaware of his slip of the tongue, Sarah nodded. Placidly, she went on ironing. For some reason, her lack of a more interested reaction irked him. Daniel didn't understand it.

"But only until I make another pallet. Is that clear?"

"Perfectly." She traded her flatiron for another she'd heated on top of the cast-iron stove, then licked her fingertip and tested the new iron's heat. "But I can't promise good results, Daniel. After all, your pallet is on the floor—well within Whiskers's reach. As you said yourself, he is an exceedingly mischievous cat."

"Then tame him."

"If only it were as easy as that." Sarah gave a gusty sigh. "I fear some creatures are simply unpredictable."

Why did he have the sense she spoke of more than one mangy cat and its mischief? Fiercely unsettled, Daniel stared at her.

"The cat is part of this household. He's your responsibility. Do something."

"Very well. I will."

With a nod, Daniel turned. That was settled, then. Good. Then another thought struck him. "I *don't* mean spoil that cat any further," he warned.

"You worry overmuch, Daniel. I said I'll take care of it." Contentedly, she ironed a pillowcase. "Speaking of which…since we're discussing the household anyway, I have a proposition for you."

What had this to do with an irksome cat? He didn't know, but he decided to humor her. "A proposition?"

Nodding, she reached for the final item to be ironed—that blasted lacy nightgown of hers. Beset by a sudden recollection of the way she'd looked in it, all womanly curves and soft skin, he could not, for a moment, quite remember where he was.

"Yes. My suggestion is this." Sarah didn't seem to notice his distracted state. "I do a great deal of work in this household. Work *you* benefit from. And I'm doing a fine job of it, too. Wouldn't you agree?"

"Yes."

She glanced at him, clearly startled. Daniel didn't know why. He was many things, but grudging with the truth wasn't one of them. "You've done an excellent job. Aside from the rutabagas."

"Well, then." Not taking his bait, she raised her chin with dignity. "I'd like to suggest a trade."

"We've already fashioned a trade between us."

"Yes, but it needs amending. In return for my

continuing wifely duties, I think it's only fair that you give something to me. Some...husbandly duties."

Ahhh, hell. Steeling himself, Daniel asked the inevitable question. "What husbandly duties?"

"Oh, you know." Seeming almost indifferent, Sarah gave an offhanded wave. "Your arm in escort when we're out together. A kind word here or there about your meals. Even..." She paused, swallowing hard. "A few kisses whenever you leave or come home. Inconsequential husbandly things like that."

Daniel thought about it. He pictured himself touching her the way she'd suggested, praising her cooking...kissing her at least twice each day, morning and night.

"You'd hardly notice any of those things," she urged. "But they'd mean a great deal to me."

Considering the merits of it, he looked at her. In the lamplight, Sarah's face glowed, framed by curled wisps of hair. Her cheeks were flushed, pinkened by the exertion of ironing. And her eyes...her eyes gazed into his with a hopefulness and an affection so real, he could have looked into their depths all night long. He wanted to make her happy. Wanted to touch that wayward curl at her temple and curl it round his finger. Wanted...

Damnation. She was doing it to him! 'Twas the look Marcus had spoken of. Daniel knew it. With a jolt, he snapped himself out of it.

"Impossible," he said. "Our deal stands as it is."

His refusal came not a moment too soon. Another instant and he might actually have caressed her hair. Her hair! Like a lovesick schoolboy!

With a feeling he'd narrowly escaped something better left uncontemplated, Daniel left Sarah behind. He headed for bed, only pausing to look back once... and to wonder if he really knew the woman he'd married at all.

Chapter Eight

Stymied in her attempts to make Daniel treat her as the wife she wanted to be—rather than the convenient seamstress, washwoman and preparer of bacon and eggs she was—Sarah decided a few days' regrouping was in order. Perhaps Daniel was fearful of change. Perhaps he did not enjoy husbandly kissing. Or perhaps he merely liked things as they were. In any case, Sarah did *not,* and she knew one more thing for certain.

For a moment that night, Daniel had wavered.

She'd seen it in his eyes as she'd awaited his answer to her proposal, sensed it in the subtle movement of his hand as he'd lifted it toward her face—likely without even being aware of it. She knew that Daniel was beginning to see those other sides of her she'd mentioned, and that was all the encouragement she needed. Fortified by it, Sarah sailed through the days that followed in very good spirits.

Her marriage would *not* be a repeat of her time at

home, she vowed, with her overlooked by her family—overshadowed by her more noticeable sisters. That had been painful enough the first time 'round. She couldn't bear to be overlooked by Daniel as well. Besides, she reminded herself, it was only a matter of time before he loved her. How could he not?

Sarah kept that heartening thought in mind as she traversed the path to the schoolhouse each day, with her books in hand and Eli running and jumping and picking up sticks alongside her. She reminded herself of it as Daniel greeted her each night, with a smile on his lips and a silly story to make her smile. She thought of it in the mornings, when she awakened to find herself snuggled securely in Daniel's arms.

In his sleep, he wanted her unabashedly. It was only when he awakened that the problems began.

But as she found herself in bed with him for the third morning in a row, Sarah decided to set all that aside. Being held by Daniel was simply too wonderful to quibble about. So what if it ended abruptly whenever he woke? For now, she'd simply enjoy it. Judging by the faint pink sunrise outside, there was time for that aplenty.

Stifling a sigh of pleasure, she closed her eyes again. Daniel lay behind her, his front cradling her back, one massive arm holding her waist. Her nightgown bunched around her knees, baring her legs to brush against his hairy calves. His breath whispered warmly over her shoulder. The intimacy of it all thrilled her.

Thank heaven she'd had the gumption to shred his silly pallet and end that nonsense of them sleeping apart.

Cautiously, Sarah put her hand to Daniel's forearm. It felt hard with muscle, warm and masculine. He didn't stir. Emboldened, she pulled his arm more firmly against her bosoms, then wrapped his other arm around her as well. She wiggled her backside, getting comfortable. There. That was better. Now they were truly cradled together, like two matching spoons in a silver drawer. Satisfied, she smiled.

In no time at all, she drifted asleep again.

Confoundingly, Daniel awakened with an armload of woman.

He blinked himself into alertness. Thus roused, he took stock of the situation. Even with the quilt kicked off in the night, his body felt hot and ready. Nothing unusual there. His left hand enjoyed a palmful of—if he wasn't mistaken—partially bared bosom, and his right hand had fallen asleep. A woman's dark, soft hair obscured his view of anything more. Curiously, he angled his head sideways against the pillow, listening.

A soft snore met his ears.

A soft *wifely* snore.

Blast! It was Sarah, snuggled up to him just as she had been for the past three mornings straight. He needed to move, to get up as he'd done every other time he'd found her like this. It was for her own good. But against his will, Daniel noticed that she felt warm and good, and he decided to stay put. Just for a minute.

Carefully, he eased backward enough to free his tingling hand. Then, driven by a mad urge he didn't dare think about, he swept his other hand very lightly along her side. Sarah was curved in all the right places, he observed, womanly and yet strong all over. No frail miss was she, he thought on a burst of ridiculous pride. She was strong enough to haul in firewood, to tighten the rope bedsprings, to carry Eli all on her own. She did those things uncomplainingly, too. He'd always admired that about her.

Safe in the comfort of his bed—a comfort he enjoyed in spite of his resolution to construct a pallet the damned useless cat wouldn't shred—Daniel considered Sarah. He thought of the situation they'd made for themselves. In some ways, his marriage was exactly what he'd expected. In others, it might well be his most foolhardy decision yet.

Generally speaking, he did not ponder things overmuch. Daniel was a doing kind of man. He saw something that needed doing, and he did it. Plain and simple. But this time, he wondered if his tendency toward straightforward action had been a mistake. If it had been too hasty, after all.

From what Sarah had said while ironing, she wanted more from their marriage arrangement. She wanted "husbandly duties." The other night, he'd refused her in no uncertain terms. Now, though, lulled by comfort and that contented place between sleep and full wakefulness, Daniel reconsidered.

Would it really hurt matters to give Sarah what she wanted? At least a little bit of it? He knew it would make her happy. She was his friend; he wanted happiness for her, of course. If it came at but a small cost to him…

Experimentally, Daniel smoothed a hank of hair from her shoulder, just above the neckline of her gown. With her skin bared to him, he listened again to her breathing. She still sounded like a snoring buffalo buried in a foot of deep mud. Good. Satisfied that Sarah would be none the wiser to his actions, he decided to experiment further.

He took a breath. His heart pounded strangely, no doubt due to the rattling effects of her snoring. Puckering his lips, he hesitated, then pressed a soft kiss to her shoulder.

There. Kissing was a "husbandly duty," according to Sarah. Now he'd tried it. Holding himself still, Daniel waited for something to happen. She did not stir, and his heart did not stop pounding. Curious.

But since he didn't feel unduly roused by the action, he tried it again.

This time, he made his kiss more lingering. Her skin smelled of lavender, he recognized. That, and the castile soap she bought at the mercantile and forced on him and Eli at all-too-regular intervals. Smiling faintly at the memory, Daniel dared to conduct a second test, this time with his free hand. This would serve only, he assured himself, to discover exactly what offering those "husbandly duties" of hers might cost him.

He glided his palm more firmly down her body. Her waist felt compact, covered by the soft finery of her nightgown. *The* nightgown. The one that had haunted his daydreams since he'd glimpsed it. Moving lower, he felt her hip, lush and firm, exactly as feminine as any he'd ever touched. He skimmed his hand to the top of her thigh, as far as he could reach.

Sarah stirred, giving a little moan.

Daniel stopped, breath held.

Damnation, he was a fool. What would he tell her if she discovered him this way? Touching her all over? Kissing her shoulder? Pressing himself—he realized too late—intimately against her backside?

Everything below his beltline felt pleased enough with the attention, especially after weeks of neglect. His body fairly leaped with eagerness, wanting to arrow closer to her softness. But Sarah might have a different, less favorable view of his lustful grinding against her. Tensing his muscles, Daniel held himself rigidly still.

His breath rasped in the stillness. When had it quickened that way? He didn't remember being aware of it. He'd been rapt with attention at Sarah's hardy feminine figure, so full and so...he noticed now as he peered closer...freckled. There, on her shoulder where his mouth had been. Unreasonably, he found those freckles adorable. Even though he had spots of his own and thought nothing about them at all.

She snuffled and rolled over suddenly, one arm flung above her head. Daniel found himself with a full view of her sleeping form. To his surprise— and with the likely help of that sinful nightgown— Sarah seemed almost pretty. Her face looked relaxed in slumber, her brows smoothed without their usual furrow of...concentration? Determination? Dyspepsia?

He didn't know what the hell made her look like that most of the time, it occurred to him. Possibly her eyes hurt from reading all those books she'd lugged to his house when they'd married. Sarah read an uncommon amount—while she stirred the soup, while she waited for Eli to finish bathing, even while she fixed her hair. That habit, like much about her, was a mystery he hadn't expected.

He'd honestly never pondered what went on in her illogical female brain. He knew that a great deal did; her schoolmarming was proof enough of that. But Sarah was unlike any other woman. She climbed trees as competently as she baked biscuits. She threw a baseball as enthusiastically as she scrubbed a floor. She fit in with the menfolk as easily as she guided her students, and somehow she made it all seem natural. Sarah was uncommon. That was why the two of them got on so well. And now she was snoring again, fit to raise the roof, leaving him free to finish his wanderings.

Daniel considered what he'd learned. So far, these "husbandly duties" of hers didn't seem all that taxing to him. Of course, he did want her. Right now. He wanted her the way any man would have wanted a woman he woke up mostly naked next to. That was only natural.

But when he touched her, when he kissed her shoulder, when he felt her curves fit beneath his hand, he didn't experience any untoward sentiment. He didn't feel prone to burst into song, or write a love poem, or forsake his own family. Or, overall, to indulge in any of the twaddle folks "in love" seemed to do.

Relief swamped him. "Love" made a person foolhardy. The very *last* thing Daniel meant to do, by everything he held dear, was fall prey to it. It was a view he hadn't explained to Sarah. Truly, he probably could not have done. But more than most, he understood the ruinous nature of that emotion. He'd be damned if he'd inflict it upon anyone he cared about. He had only to glance at Eli to remind himself of that fact.

And to deepen his resolve.

He could not love Sarah, he reminded himself now, frowning at the thought. It would only hurt them both.

Innocent of his meanderings, she lay flopped beside him, one hand curled on the pillow. She let fly another resounding snuffle. At the sound of it, Daniel grinned. Given all the caterwauling she did about the occasional belch in this household, a man would expect not more than a peep from her. When she woke, he ought to tell her so. He ought to start calling her Buffalo Sarah. He ought to belch freely and manfully, whenever he chose, and not stifle himself as he had been. But first…

Continuing his explorations, he slid his hand up her arm. She squirmed when he reached the tender crook of her elbow, but did not awaken. Too late, it occurred to him that she'd always been ticklish. He'd have to take care. Inciting a round of her carefree guffaws, as much fun as that would be, was *not* what he had in mind. He didn't want her to wake up. If she pinned him with another of her bewitching Molly-ish gazes, he knew he wouldn't have the fortitude to do what he knew he must.

Kiss her fully. On the mouth.

Nothing else would be a true test of his "husbandly duties." Any man could kiss a shoulder. Pshaw—that was nothing. But to kiss a woman on the mouth…that was enticing. Intimate. A pathway to other things. Contemplating his next move, Daniel studied Sarah's mouth. He'd never noticed before, but her lips were a lovely shape. Perfectly full. Their deep pink color would have tempted any man to action.

Well, 'twas fortunate he was a doing kind of man, then. Keeping that excuse—no, rationale—in mind, he levered himself up on his elbow. Carefully, he placed his hand on her jaw, holding her steady. Sarah slept on, so he cradled her face in his fingertips and lowered his mouth to hers. Slowly, silently, he brushed his lips the merest degree over hers.

Kissing her felt strange. Different than he'd expected, yet invigorating. At the contact, his whole body stiffened, confusion and desire washing over him in equal measure. *This is Sarah,* a part of him prodded. A larger, stronger part of him urged him onward. *Yes. It is Sarah.* A new Sarah, to him. And he did want her, even more than before. But that was only natural. It was a man's way. It didn't mean a thing.

Feeling more certain, Daniel kissed her again. Yes.

He could cope with this kind of kissing. He could manage those "husbandly duties" she wanted without breaking a sweat. Smugly, he raised his head and regarded her. He would do it. A lesser man might have weakened, but not him. He knew exactly what he was about.

At that moment, Sarah opened her eyes.

Daniel froze. Surely she would wonder, would want to know why he hovered over her this way. Needing an excuse, he searched his brain for a reason why he might be here with his face only inches from hers—with his mouth poised over hers. But then Sarah lifted her gaze to his, and there were no questions in her eyes. Only happiness.

Happiness that was his undoing.

Smiling, she reached for him. "Daniel," she murmured.

It was the way she said his name—so huskily, so joyfully, so damned hopefully—that made him realize the folly of what he'd done. Kissing Sarah while she was insensible to it was one thing. Kissing her while she looked at him, full of trust and affection, was something else entirely.

He could not do it. Already he'd begun to see her differently. Already her laughter made his heart turn over strangely. Already her smile meant something new to him—made him long for things he never had before. How much worse would it be, Daniel

wondered savagely, if he gave in? If he found himself
in the grasp of some foolhardy "love"?

He could not risk it.

"It's past time to get up," he announced with a
frown. Then he grabbed for his britches and got out
of bed.

Later, Sarah traced many of Daniel's most peculiar habits to that morning. For instance, beginning
that same day, he took to sleeping every night in his
clothes. Shirt, britches, braces, socks—everything
but his boots. She found it idiotic and told him so. For
one thing, it made a mockery of her ironing, since
Daniel came home, bathed, dressed in clean clothes
and then slept in them, wrinkling them beyond recognition for his new day at the smithy.

Also, it make him so overwarm that he inevitably
hurled all the linens on *her* at night, forcing them
both into dark, sleepy tussles. Thirdly…well, she just
plain didn't like it, and she figured that was good
enough reason for him to stop doing it. Nevertheless,
despite her reasoned arguments to that end, the daft
man persisted.

Sadly, his woolly layers of garments deprived Sarah
of the thrilling feeling of his bare skin during their
morning cuddling. That was the bad news. The good
news was that their cuddling continued. She didn't
dare exult in that fact when the overly clad Daniel

was around, but she enjoyed it immensely, all the same. Because to her, his inability to stop waking with his arms around her had to mean that he loved her a little.

Eventually, he would tell her so, she assured herself. Eventually, he'd quit leaping out of bed, swearing imaginatively every morning, and give her the words she longed so much to hear from him. Then everything would be right in their world.

Until that time, Sarah persevered with her campaign to turn her scoundrel into a husband. She made great strides, too.

Daniel complied—if grumpily—with everything she suggested, save husbandly duties and falling in love with her. She successfully got him to eat all his vegetables, to pick up his socks and to play poker with wagered buttons instead of money—as an example to Eli. She persuaded him to quit making new pallets, with the reminder of Whiskers's supposed ferocity. She even got him to demonstrate fine manners on pretense of teaching them to Eli. Daniel tipped his hat to her and escorted her round the front room with an imaginary gentleman's cane, and he was, as she'd known he would be, absolutely charming.

She fell in love with him a bit more that day, she thought.

As a thank-you for that last, Sarah sneaked into

his smithy when Daniel was delivering plowshares by wagon and arranged everything tidily for his return. The task occupied an entire Saturday afternoon. Oddly enough, Daniel seemed less than overjoyed by all her hard work—with Toby's help—on that account, complaining that if he'd wanted his metals displayed by shape, size and color, he'd have damned well done it himself. But Sarah knew that, deep down, he appreciated her assistance. Because after all, no sensible person could have accomplished a good day's work amid that kind of disorder.

Thus encouraged, she became indefatigable on behalf of her husband and Eli. She sewed them both handsome new shirts, made them their favorite dishes—including cabbage for Eli—and lit Daniel's cheroots. She smiled at her husband's ribald jokes. All the while, she kept up with her schoolteaching, difficult as it was.

Daniel joshed that their whole house was chockablock with uppity female, but Sarah didn't mind. At least that meant he *saw* her. Most people in Morrow Creek only saw her dazzling sisters, Molly with her sociability and Grace with her rabble-rousing. It did not pay to be the middle daughter. But for once in her life, Sarah felt at peace with that fact. Because now she had Daniel on her side.

Eli, too, prospered under her care. He took to reading even more, to listening to stories before bedtime and keeping track of his oft-missing shoes. He even performed better with his schoolwork. But part of that was due to Daniel's influence, Sarah felt sure. Because if she'd never noticed it before, she did then—Daniel was a wonder with the boy.

Sitting in the Crabtrees' parlor to pay a call to her family, Sarah held a cup of coffee on a saucer on her lap. While she visited, she watched Daniel on the floor with Eli. Unbothered by the conversation swirling around them, the two of them worked at one of Adam Crabtree's prized jigsaw puzzles, their identical dark heads bent in concentration.

"After all," her papa had said when he'd handed over the heavy wooden puzzle, "Eli is our first grandchild, in a sense. It's our duty to spoil him, isn't it?"

Fiona had laughed and agreed, and they'd both gazed fondly on the boy. Then Sarah had felt truly special. Because her whole family loved Daniel and Eli. And as soon as those stubborn McCabe males grew accustomed to Grahamite cooking, they would love her family right back.

While Sarah discussed the recent Chautauqua, Daniel and Eli's puzzle steadily took shape. Every once in a while, Daniel would offer a bit of encouragement. He'd point out a spot Eli had been searching for, then tousle the boy's hair in congratulations when he fitted the proper piece. He'd murmur about the picture they were making, or use a funny-shaped piece to trot over the whole works as an imaginary steed, neighing with complete abandon. Every time, Eli laughed.

Sarah did, too. But seeing them that way felt almost painful, all the same. Because she knew that Daniel and Eli didn't truly need her. Not yet. Right now, they'd do fine on their own, whether they realized it or not. The thought filled her with resolve to do more, to try harder, to make sure that she earned her place in their lives.

"Oh, Daniel!" Fiona said, breaking a momentary silence in the openhearted way she had. "Before you leave, I simply *must* give you some cuttings from my greenhouse. Sarah won't accept them—"

"Mama, you know I don't have your green thumb."

"—but if I present them to you as a belated wedding gift, then your wife can't very well refuse them, now, can she?"

Daniel grinned. His rapscallion's gaze shot to Sarah, brimful of certainty. "Well, now. I'd say your mama is someone who knows how to deal with you. I should pay a call on my own sometime, to gather hints from this wise woman. Tell me, Mrs. Crabtree, how do you make Sarah stop spinning tall tales? I swear she has a whopper for me every night at the dinner table."

He turned his attention shamelessly to Fiona,

lavishing his charm on her and on everyone present. When she laughed and swatted him with her handkerchief, Daniel pronounced their deal as sealed. He proclaimed that Fiona had captivated him, then hornswoggled him into accepting half the flowers she grew.

"Likely," he said, "I'll be too burdened to walk home. I'll have to hire a wagon and team just to carry the posies."

"You silly man." Fiona wiped tears of laughter from her eyes. "No wonder Sarah loves you so."

An awkward silence fell. Sarah stilled, her coffee cup partway to her lips. Horsefeathers, but her family was forthright. What would Daniel say now?

As it turned out, nothing. He merely sipped his coffee. Perhaps everyone would believe him to be exceedingly thirsty, Sarah thought in a dither. Perhaps they would believe he found his deep and abiding love for her too personal to share.

Or perhaps they would guess the truth.

It fell to Molly to save the day.

"Yes, no wonder," she agreed, calmly arranging her skirts. "We all are so happy you've joined our family, Daniel."

At that prompt, the conversation resumed. Talk turned to the weather, the new millinery in town, the possibility of a circus troupe coming through from the East. Sarah cast her sister a grateful smile. She

didn't dare look at Daniel, fearful she'd see specula-
tion in his eyes.

Fiona spoke up again. "Oh, dear. I nearly forgot.
Daniel, I'd be much obliged if you would also write
down your dear sister's direction for me, please,
before you leave. After all, we're family now. I would
very much like to send Lillian my wishes for a full
recovery."

Daniel looked up. "Recovery?"

At his stony expression, Mama blanched.
"Well...I...yes. I'm sorry. I thought surely she must
be ill, to have sent Eli here to stay with you..."

Uncertainly, Fiona glanced to Adam, then to Grace.
Both of them watched Daniel with interested expressions. Near the piano, even Molly and Marcus had
stopped their conversation.

"My sister recently remarried and is on her wedding trip." Daniel's voice sounded firm, almost harsh.
"In Europe, I hear tell. Italy, by now. She won't get
your letter."

Curiously, Eli glanced up from his puzzle.

"Oh. Her...wedding, you say?" Fiona floundered.
"I...my goodness. Isn't that unexpected? Of course,
I knew she'd been widowed some years ago." A sor-
rowful glance to Eli. "We all did, but I'm afraid I'm
not quite..."

Grace, seeing her distress, offered a protective
squeeze. "It's all right, Mama." When she faced

Daniel, it was with her ablest, most intimidating expression. "I assume Lillian *will* receive her mail eventually?"

"Hard to tell." Daniel met Grace's direct gaze with an unswerving look of his own. There was something of a warning in his expression—not that headstrong Grace would be likely to heed it. "I didn't get her letter about Eli coming here until after he arrived."

"All by myself," Eli piped up proudly. "I wasn't s'posed to, but my chaperone missed the train."

"Still," Grace persisted, showing all the doggedness of a born crusader, "it wouldn't hurt to give Mama the address."

He inclined his head toward Fiona. "I'd hate to give you false hope of a reply, Mrs. Crabtree," he said gently. "Lillian is not the woman she once was."

What in the world did *that* mean? Sarah wondered. She knew about Lillian's remarriage, of course. Daniel had told her that much. And she knew the rudimentary details of his sister's voyage overseas, also. But how, exactly, had Lillian changed?

When the McCabes had lived in Morrow Creek, she and Sarah had been too far apart in age to share more than a passing acquaintance. But now they were family, as her mama had pointed out. Surely Sarah deserved to know more.

In the awkward silence that filled the parlor, Eli

tugged Daniel's sleeve. "Where's Italy?" he asked. "Is it far away? As far as I came on the train?"

Innocently, he scrunched his nose, awaiting a reply. None was forthcoming. Daniel merely fitted another puzzle piece, appearing to ponder the question. His reaction both concerned and annoyed Sarah. Had Daniel actually neglected to tell Eli where his mother was? It would be like him, she realized, to skirt the issue. After all, this was a man who'd failed to announce his own wedding.

"Yes, it's very far away," he said at last. He ruffled the boy's hair affectionately. "Eli, why don't you go see if Cook has any of that honeyed milk you like? Maybe you can have a glass, if you ask the way I told you to."

A mischievous gleam came into Eli's eyes. "With a big smile and a little wink?"

"That's right."

Sarah shook her head. It just fit. Daniel had taught the boy to be a rascal like himself but hadn't explained the facts of his new life to him. Her husband was a scoundrel for more reasons than mere flirting with the ladies in town.

A grin. "All right. Cook! Hello, Cook!"

Filled with childish enthusiasm, Eli ran to the kitchen. His skinny shoulders bobbed beneath the shirt Sarah had sized with room to grow—one of her earlier stitchery attempts. The door slammed behind him.

Daniel saw her face. "What's the matter? Charm comes naturally to him, I swear it."

Her family exchanged telling glances.

Sarah was having none of it. "You didn't tell him?"

Daniel gave her a brooding look.

"*Lillian* didn't tell him?" Sarah pressed. Heedless of their surroundings, she rolled her eyes. "Heaven help us. Hardheadedness runs in the family."

"Sarah, that's enough."

"But what does Eli believe he is doing here? *Visiting?*"

"We'll talk about this later."

His ominous tone stopped her. Of course, it was all well and good for him to be mysterious. But she wanted answers.

Frustrated, Sarah looked to her family for help. To a person, they suddenly became engaged in other pursuits. Molly and Marcus scrutinized their sheet music, Papa adjusted his spectacles and Mama polished her silver coffee service. Even Grace pretended absorption in the plain piped trim on her dress.

That was when Sarah knew she'd seriously overstepped her bounds. Grace didn't give a fig for fashion. If even *she* were embarrassed by this conversation…

Well. She'd simply have to wait till later to uncover Daniel's secrets. And Lillian's. It was as plain as that.

"So." Awkwardly, Sarah folded her hands in her lap. "Would anyone care for a game of charades?"

Chapter Nine

"I don't know what to do," Sarah told her sisters.

They'd met at the town mercantile, ostensibly to shop for a holiday gift for Mama. In reality, they'd planned this occasion immediately after Sarah's visit to the Crabtree household. She'd pleaded with Molly and Grace to meet with her privately, to help her decide what to do about Daniel and Eli.

"I'm at my wit's end. I buttonholed Daniel after we came home, but I could get nowhere with him!" Sarah picked up a pretty thimble set and turned it over. "He says he's already told me all he knows about Lillian."

Molly nodded. "Perhaps he has."

"No, he hasn't. He's told me the facts of how Eli came to him, certainly. On the train, bearing a letter, and so forth. Also a bit about Lillian's new husband—a wealthy Philadelphia businessman somewhat older than Lillian. But Daniel's told me none of the important things. How he *feels* about it all, how it affects him, how he hopes it will turn out."

Her sisters nodded in understanding—Grace a little less readily than Molly.

"I'm his wife!" Sarah replaced the thimble set with a frown. "I need to know what's in Daniel's heart."

"You can never know anything about a man," Grace opined, "because they don't know anything about themselves. Why, just yesterday I had a set-to with that irritating Jack Murphy, and—"

"Are you still on about him?" Molly looked surprised. "I thought the two of you had come to some sort of an agreement."

Grace and the saloonkeeper shared space in the same building at the edge of town. Grace wanted it for conducting meetings and rallies and ladies' aid society projects; Jack Murphy wanted it to provide men with boardinghouse rooms in addition to the whiskey and ale he already offered. Both sisters' sympathies naturally lay with Grace.

"I'll never come to an agreement with that man!"

"Yes, yes. We know." Sarah moved to a display of painted trinket boxes, uncomfortably aware that her sisters had clearly forgotten her presence. Again. "But in the meantime, I have a real problem."

"Daniel's silence on this issue is not that much of a problem," Molly said reassuringly. "He is your husband. Eventually he'll tell you everything. When he's ready."

"Or he won't," Grace put in. "Because men only ever do what they want to do. It's the natural outcome of our patriarchal society."

Sarah didn't feel prepared for one of her sister's suffragette lectures today. She sighed. "I did learn one thing of interest. Do you know why Daniel's family moved away from Morrow Creek all those years ago?"

"I was young when they left," Molly said. "I can hardly remember it. But I assume they missed the States?"

"Or couldn't make a go of their business?" Grace added.

"No. It was neither of those things." Sarah leaned closer to keep her news private in the overstuffed shop. "Lillian's first husband didn't like Morrow Creek. He'd just been passing through when he met Lillian, and he wanted to return to the States. He told her to choose between living here with her family or returning east with him—"

"And she chose him?" Grace asked, disbelieving.

"Over her own family?" Molly looked appalled.

Sarah nodded. "'Without blinking twice,' Daniel said. I'd say he's still upset over the matter…except he insists he has no feelings on the subject."

Just remembering their fruitless conversation upset

her all over again. Why was it that Daniel claimed utter honesty when she *knew* he was holding things back?

"That doesn't explain why the entire McCabe family left here, save Daniel," Grace pointed out. "Lillian could easily have gone alone."

"I know. But according to Daniel, his mother always had a taste for finery. Moving to Philadelphia suited her."

Molly shook her head. "I don't understand it."

"I do." Grace seemed thoughtful. "But then I've always wanted to travel. Any excuse would do." Her eyes shone. "There's so much more to be seen, to be tried, in this world than can be contained in Morrow Creek."

Sarah and Molly stared at her.

"Merely as a point of interest," Grace clarified, shelving her enthusiasm along with a pair of knitting needles. She moved to a tumble of crochet yarn, examining the varied colors. "Mama would enjoy these, don't you think so?"

They chose a few, eventually placing them in the basket on Molly's arm. No harm in actually accomplishing some errands, Sarah reasoned, while she poured out her frustrations.

"Does Eli talk about his mother?" Grace asked.

"At first he did. Quite a lot," Sarah confided. "Daniel told me so. But now..." She paused, considering it.

"Now he seems busy with other things. He mentions his mama rarely—but happily, when he does."

"That's because Eli is a good boy, glad to have you to care for him," Molly said loyally. "He knows you love and provide for him, and that's all any child needs. In time, things will get easier."

Sarah hoped so. "I still don't understand about Lillian, though. Daniel said she's changed...but what would make her send away Eli?"

"I can't imagine," Molly said staunchly.

"Only one person knows that," Grace said. "And she is all the way in Italy. Let it go, Sarah. I know your flights of fancy probably have you imagining all sorts of unlikely things, but the truth is, you have a life of your own—one that includes Eli and Daniel. One that's moving forward! *You* must move forward with it. Stop dwelling on things you can't help."

Discontentedly, Sarah added a skein of wool to the basket. Perhaps Grace was right. She'd already done all she could about the situation between Daniel and Eli, short of dragging the answers she wanted from her husband by force. Likely, he would tell her the rest in his own time. What she *hadn't* yet taken care of, and what *still* remained in her power to affect, was her marriage. She could *definitely* help that.

While merely asking Daniel to cooperate with her wishes hadn't proved satisfactory, that didn't mean there weren't still other tactics to be tried. With her sisters' help, it was still possible Sarah could get through to the man she loved…and make him love her back. Possibly, once that happened, everything else would fall in place, too.

"All right." Brightening, she looped her arms with her sisters'. She steered them all toward the clerk, ready to be finished with the mercantile. "I'll try to be patient. *For now.* But while I have you both here, there's one more teeny thing I need your advice on…."

When Daniel had agreed to marry Sarah, he hadn't expected his life to change much. He'd figured things would go on nearly as they had been—except for getting help caring for Eli, of course. But as it turned out, getting hitched had changed his whole life in unexpected ways, both large and small.

That fact became real to him as he stood on the fringes of the Morrow Creek annual winter social, a mug of hot mulled cider in one hand and, oddly enough, no woman on his arm. That in itself was a change—and not much for the better. Raucous fiddle music played, lamplight gleamed and snow piled outside at the darkened windows. Inside, though, it was warm. All around him, his friends and neighbors swept past in pairs, dancing. They talked and laughed, gussied up in their finery.

Feeling surly and alone, Daniel squinted overhead.

Evergreen boughs—provided by the Copeland lumber mill—brightened the space. Each bore a bright, tied-on ribbon, courtesy of the ladies' auxiliary committee. Those ribbons were a daft notion, as far as Daniel was concerned. If ponderosa pines were meant to flash gaudy silks and satins, they'd grow bows on themselves and have done with it. But the greenery seemed popular with those present—almost as popular as the cider.

Daniel took another sip, feeling the hot brew spread pleasurably through him. Privately, he felt his contribution to the yearly social was best. Without his enormous metalwork chandeliers overhead, none of the other decorations would have been visible. Each November, he spent part of his chilly days repairing and seeing to the creations, the only fancywork ever to come from his smithy. Each fixture, created in a Spanish style, held multiple lamps, their chimneys polished to a high gleam that showcased the brilliant wicks inside.

They were fine workmanship. Even if he was the one to say.

Feeling unaccountably restless, Daniel shifted to the right. He went on watching the dancing. He'd been coming to this shindig, he reflected, since he'd been old enough to know what a lady kept beneath her bustle. At first, he'd been a gangling boy, all elbows and shoulders and big sloppy feet. Then he'd been a man, all brawn and sweet talk and enough certainty for ten of himself. Now he was a husband, with a child in his care and a wife in his keeping. Somewhere along the way, his certainty had gotten away from him. Where once he'd known and understood and loved many women, now Daniel felt confounded and bewildered and riled up by a single one. Where once he'd arrived with a beauty on each arm, now he escorted just a solitary freckled female. Where once he'd felt wanted and talented—and yes, damn it all, *sated*—before the night ended, now he wondered if he'd ever stop feeling hungry and confused and annoyed.

'Twas all Sarah's fault, blast it. She was up to something new. This time, Daniel didn't have a clue how to cope with it.

Across the room, he glimpsed her. His stupid heart skipped a beat, forcing him to frown and gulp more cider. If only the damned stuff had some kick to it. But Grace Crabtree's Women's Temperance Union had gotten here first and declared the whole social a teetotaler's haven. There wasn't a spot of whiskey to be found anyplace. How, Daniel wondered, was a man supposed to make merry under those intolerable circumstances?

He glanced to Sarah again. She'd arranged her hair in a fussy style, with fat curls cascading down her back. When he'd teasingly tugged one earlier, she'd actually slapped his hand away for fear of spoiling them. Remembering it, Daniel shook his head. This, from the same woman who'd caught frogs with him at the edge of Morrow Creek? Less than a year ago?

Limned by the lamplight of *his* chandeliers, Sarah was the very picture of decorum now. Not like when they'd run laughing to grab those frogs—him with his britches rolled and her with her face flushed and her skirts hitched up. Then, she'd been carefree and understandable. Now, she perplexed him.

Sarah strode at the edge of the dancing to meet a friend. Moving with her characteristic vigor, she was a sight to behold, all strong female and damnable... certainty.

She talked and laughed in the group of women she met, waving her arms and making the bustle sway on her favorite green dress. It wasn't even a fancy dress, Daniel groused to himself. It didn't have shiny silk or ribbon trim, like the dance-hall ladies' gowns did. It didn't offer a single glimpse of scandalous petticoats beneath it, nor did it display so much as a hint of bared bosom. But it did, unfortunately, stir his interest.

Confounded, Daniel finished his cider. He didn't want to feel his gaze drawn to Sarah; didn't want to feel pulled to join her. She was his wife, not some piece of skirt he needed to coax and cajole and flatter. She was his already. So why did it feel as though she slipped further away from him each day?

Hell. He stared into his empty cider mug and felt his frown deepen. Flattery wouldn't have helped anyway. Not with Sarah. With Sarah, Daniel was neither the most affable man in the territory nor the most handsome. He wasn't the strongest or the bravest. He was only himself. Her husband. The man who slept chastely beside her in his bed—*their* bed—the bed that turned *less* comfortable every night.

Why that bothered him these days, he didn't know.

He had to find Murphy, or even Copeland. One of them would know where to wrangle a drink with some spirit to it. Tonight, of all nights, Daniel needed it.

"What is wrong with Daniel?" Grace peered across the room to the spot where Sarah's husband stood. "He is positively glowering."

"I know." Excitedly, Sarah hugged herself. Then she remembered she was attempting to behave like a lady tonight, and demurely folded her hands at her skirts. "Isn't it wonderful?"

"Wonderful?" Molly peered closer. "He looks fit to chew the decorations and spit them out. You call that wonderful?"

Sarah nodded. "I do."

Looking jointly perplexed, her sisters examined her.

"Because your strategy is working!" Sarah announced triumphantly—and a trifle impatiently, too. Didn't they know how important this was? "It's working!"

"To capture Daniel's attention?" Molly asked.

"To gain his cooperation?" Grace wanted to know.

"Yes." Smugly, Sarah fanned herself. "To both questions."

She'd never seen such expressions of awe on their faces. Not even when she'd passed her tests to become a schoolteacher.

"My goodness," Molly said. "That's wonderful."

"Excellent!" Grace raised her cider. "To Sarah's imminent victory!"

With her cup partway raised, Molly cast her sister a disapproving look. "It's not a battle, Grace."

"Oh, yes. It is indeed a battle." With her usual conviction, Grace nodded. "Sarah wants one thing, Daniel another. By my reckoning, that makes it a battle."

"Only because they are a man and a woman," Molly argued. "You think every relation between the sexes has to be a battle."

"It *is* a battle, whether we wish it or not. That is the nature of social conflict."

"But that suggests there can only be one victor." Catching the eye of someone in the crowd, Molly waved. "When I know from my own experience that both parties can prevail."

Curiously, Sarah glanced in the direction of Molly's greeting. Marcus stood beside Daniel now, joining him at the cider bowl. Ahhh. Molly had been waving to her husband.

Imitating her, Sarah tried to catch Daniel's eye. While Molly and Grace volleyed arguments, completely forgetting her existence, she waved her fan. She wiggled her fingers, tossed her hair...even puckered her lips in an attempt to blow a kiss in Daniel's direction.

All her efforts failed.

Dispiritedly, she rejoined the conversation.

"Mmm. Quite," Grace was saying.

Oddly enough, she displayed a distinct lack of enthusiasm for her argument. In fact, she seemed to be *agreeing* with Molly now. Taken aback at this unprecedented event, Sarah stared. Then she glanced over her shoulder and squinted.

Was it her imagination, or had Grace's attention turned squarely on Jack Murphy, all of a sudden? The tall Irish saloonkeeper stood near the cider bowl with Daniel and Marcus, his head bare and his suit finer than most. He tossed back his dark head and laughed, then slapped Marcus on the back.

Surreptitiously, Sarah peeked at Grace again. Her sister seemed transfixed. Curious. Especially since, only yesterday, she'd called Jack Murphy "a loathsome excuse for a whiskey-besotted layabout, with no regard for common decency *or* a hard day's work *or* a woman's right to enrich herself."

Oblivious to the drama playing out beneath their noses, Molly turned to Sarah. "I guess if you're feeling victorious, my advice did the trick for you. I see you fixed your hair. Did you try some of the other things I suggested?"

"Yes." Sarah decided to put aside the matter of Grace's feelings for Mr. Murphy, at least for tonight. "I tried the lavender water you gave me, and the beauty cream. Also, I used the hot iron to make curls in my hair, but I fear I've singed off a portion in the back. See?"

Daniel had very nearly touched those heat-crisped hairs earlier, when he'd jokingly tugged one of her curls. She'd have died of mortification if he'd encountered her mistake. Most women knew how to wrangle beauty implements, Sarah knew, but she'd always been discouragingly lacking in that department. She didn't want Daniel to think less of her.

She only wished he hadn't looked so hurt by the tiny whack she'd given him to warn him off. She hadn't seen brown eyes that big and surprised since she'd told Eli he'd have to spend part of tonight being cared for by one of the young ladies from town.

Molly examined the spot, displaying all the expertise of a woman born to wield hot hair tongs. "Don't worry," she said with a comforting pat. "You can hardly tell the difference. And anyway, you'll learn the way of it soon enough. Before long, beautifying yourself will come naturally to you."

Grace snorted. "You can't honestly believe a little powder and paint and perfume has led to Sarah's victory?"

"I certainly don't think it's hurt," Molly said.

"Ridiculous. I gave some advice, too, you know. *Useful* advice."

"Useful, you say? Honestly, Grace. If you think—"

"Stop, you two. I haven't won *anything* yet," Sarah demurred, casting a nervous glance to her husband. Had anyone else seen him steadfastly ignore her greetings from across the room? "I only meant I've made some progress. I'm heartened by that, of course, but still…Daniel remains fairly resistant."

With a carefree wave, Grace dismissed that obstacle—just as though it *weren't* six feet tall and packed with brawn…not to mention a devastating knack for humor. And a skill for morning cuddling.

"Just continue with your protest plans," Grace counseled. "You'll have your conquest soon enough.

Those tactics always work for me. Speaking of which, did you change your mind about the signs?"

"I don't need picket signs in my own home."

"You may well, yet. Men are a stubborn lot, dead set on having their own way. It takes imagination and vitality to make inroads against them."

"*With* them," Molly specified primly. "Cooperation is key."

At her sisters' differing philosophies, Sarah rolled her eyes. "You wouldn't know it, to hear the two of you go on. It's as if you've never heard of cooperation." She addressed her younger sister. "Molly, I'm primping and fluffing, just as you said. In fact, I aired out this fancy gown from mothballs, especially for tonight."

She grabbed its folds and curtsied. She didn't even wobble in the unfamiliar movement, thanks to the agility and strength all her tree-climbing and rock-skipping had given her.

"And Grace, I've officially gone on strike, just as *you* suggested," Sarah went on. "After hearing your advice, I issued Daniel an ultimatum. Until he gives me a few husbandly courtesies—"

"They're not courtesies," her sister interrupted resolutely. "They're your due, as part of the unspoken contract you entered into when you married him."

"—I won't be doing his washing, cooking his meals or mending his woolens." Sarah meant it. This tactic was nigh on her last hope, else she wouldn't have tried anything so drastic. "No matter how smelly, hungry or tattered he gets. I won't be doing anything 'wifely' of any sort."

Aside from lying abed beside him, she amended privately. Waking next to Daniel had been something she'd been unwilling to give up, even for the sake of hog-tying him into loving her.

Sarah knew her lack of resolve was shortsighted. But she just couldn't help it. She'd loved Daniel even before marrying him. Becoming his wife had certainly done nothing to dim her ardor. In fact, when faced with his rough-hewn charm, his general good humor and his alarming knack for making her weak in the knees with a single one of his smiles— *every blasted day!*—Sarah knew she'd only fallen further.

Drat it. Why did Daniel refuse to love her back?

"Poor Eli, then." Molly crossed her arms, giving Sarah and Grace similarly dismayed looks. "What's he to do during all these shenanigans? He's only a little boy! He can hardly cook a meal or wash his own clothes."

"I still take care of Eli, of course." Sarah could not believe her sister would suspect otherwise. "*He's* done nothing wrong. He's wonderful, and I love him dearly. In fact, I think I've become something of a hero in his eyes for finagling a place for Whiskers in the household."

She explained about adopting the cat, about Daniel's insistence the mangy feline was not a pet at all and about Eli's fondness for the furry tomcat. He slept with Whiskers—well-scrubbed now—curled up on his bed and talked to him in the mornings while he prepared for school. In the evenings, Whiskers was the first one Eli greeted.

"Very well." Molly seemed reassured. "Still, I'm not convinced about these tactics of yours. Mark my words—sooner or later, Grace's radical ideas will lead to trouble."

"They have not led to trouble yet. At least not an unmanageable quantity of it." Grace sipped from her mug, then slanted a sideways glance to the men at the cider bowl. "But judging by the conspiratorial looks of *those* three, I think something…inconvenient just might be afoot yet."

Chapter Ten

"Stop laughing, Murphy," Daniel growled. "You might hurt yourself. Or *I* might hurt you *myself.*"

"I can't." Weakly, the saloonkeeper swabbed at the tears in his eyes. His brogue had deepened, as it always did during those rare moments when he let down his guard. "My damn side hurts, too. Ahhh, the pain."

"It *is* a laugh, McCabe. Admit it." Marcus struggled to speak, his usually somber face alight with mirth. "It's not every day a man's wife—"

Unable to finish, he dissolved into laughter. He leaned on Jack Murphy's suit-clad shoulder for support. The two of them guffawed like loons.

"—goes on strike!" Murphy gasped. "Ha, ha! Strike!"

They collapsed together, their dark coattails flying as they spun drunkenly beside the cider bowl. Uttering dismayed cries, several fan-flashing ladies stepped backward. A few men aimed disgruntled looks their way. Farther out, the music continued, muffling the sounds of their hilarity-fueled scuffle.

This was getting him nowhere.

Scowling, Daniel grabbed the flask Jack had secreted into the social. At least the man was good for something. He added a hefty slug to his cider, then drank. It tasted vile, but it gave him a satisfying warm glow. He needed it. Especially tonight, when his two nearest friends found his predicament hilarious. He shouldn't have mentioned it at all.

But he had to do *something,* damn it. Sarah had her dander up. Her head was filled with contrary ideas—ideas doubtless put there by her suffragette sister—about "husbandly courtesies" and marriage agreements and other nonsense. Because of them, she'd issued him an ultimatum. Him! An ultimatum!

It had been bad enough when Sarah had served up those Molly-like wifely looks of hers—although by now Daniel knew what to look for where those were concerned. He'd nearly learned to withstand them. But this refusal to act as a wife was different. 'Twas a horse of a different color—one he damned well refused to ride.

He sampled another mouthful of liquored-up cider, then sadly admitted the truth to himself. He hadn't learned to bear up under those affecting looks of

Sarah's. He hadn't. But he had learned to avoid them. That was something.

Yet this latest…abomination of hers. It was daft. Going on strike? Only railway workers and coal miners resorted to such measures. They weren't for a simple woman with a simple husband. But who could tell that to Sarah?

The state of things was dire. His dirty skillets were mounting. He couldn't find any socks. And he couldn't afford to send out his clothes to a laundress—not now that he had two additional mouths to feed on his blacksmith's earnings. Aside from which, he missed Sarah's roast chicken. 'Twas a sight better than any of the sorry grub down at Murphy's place.

Truth be told, Daniel had gotten to *like* having her fuss over him. Buttoning up his shirts, arranging his dinner plate just so, turning his face this way and that in the mornings to examine his shave. Smiling at him, touching him…even just being there waiting for him when he came home to his now-bustling household at the end of a hot, hard day.

There were a million little things Sarah did for him, he realized now. He'd be damned if he didn't miss them all. Even the ones that had aggravated him at first, like her tendency to starch his shirts so stiff they all but stood up by themselves. He missed her caring. He missed her laughter. He missed *her.*

Hell. He should have known *marrying* a woman would ruin her somehow. He felt heartily sorry to have done such a thing to Sarah. But his back had been against the wall.

The two of them had never quarreled before. And even though this…he refused to say the word…*thing* was not an official set-to, it had gotten itself wedged between them, all the same. Daniel did not like it. He refused to accept it. Just feeling the limp way his shirt hung against him—lacking any starch at all, since he hadn't known how to brew it up himself—stiffened his resolve. He had to solve this.

"Look at them." He pointed to Sarah and her sisters across the room, gaily laughing and swishing their skirts. "See how they look so happy? That's probably because they're plotting the downfall of all mankind."

Marcus laughed.

Jack choked on his drink. When he'd recovered, he looked uncommonly sober. "Possibly. *Particularly* Grace."

"Oh, ho. Do I smell trouble with your cotenant?" Marcus's ears all but perked up at a hint of business talk. "I thought you and Grace Crabtree had come to some sort of an agreement about your property dispute."

Jack frowned. "I'll never come to an agreement with that woman!" he swore. "Never."

But his expression, when he gazed across the room, told a different story. A story likely to end in something sweeter and fierier than a simple union of commerce.

"Keep your word, then," Daniel advised glumly. He hefted his drink again, then loosened his necktie, feeling overwarm at the crowded social. "Save yourself now. Before it's too late. Elsewise, Grace might start *looking* at you."

Marcus cocked a brow, an all-too-knowing look on his face.

Grumbling, Daniel did his best to ignore it. At least the man had quit chortling over his misfortune. So what if he might suspect Daniel had fallen prey to a woman's coy look?

So what if—once or twice—he had?

"So," Marcus said, offering Daniel a slap on the back. "Sarah's done it to you, as well." Shaking his head, he swallowed some of his liquored cider. "Fine, then. At least we know what we're dealing with. Besides, I knew it would happen. Sooner or later, every man falls."

"Oh, no. Not I!" Jack vowed, his brogue still deeper.

"Nor me," Daniel agreed, appalled at the very notion. "I may have married, but I refuse to let a woman dictate the terms of our life together."

As though that were somehow humorous, Marcus's

mouth quirked. "You may not have much choice in the matter. Sarah has already refused to act as your wife, hasn't she?"

Until you grant me a few husbandly courtesies, I'm afraid I won't be doing your washing, cooking your meals or mending your woolens. No matter how smelly, hungry or tattered you get.

Glumly, Daniel nodded. "She said she won't do anything 'wifely' of any sort." He looked up. Frowned. "Hold, now. What are those damned smirking looks for?"

"Nothing 'wifely'?" Marcus prodded, eyebrows waggling.

"Nothing?" Jack prompted.

Their meaning struck him. He refused to discuss it. So what if he and his wife lay virtuously beside one another each night? It was no business of theirs.

The important thing was, for the want of his kiss and a few sentimental words, Sarah had gone to outlandish lengths. She'd gone on strike. *That* was the fact of the matter and the problem before him. Hell. If Daniel had known this was coming, he might have mustered the fortitude to dole out her "husbandly duties" when she'd first requested them.

"There must be another way," he said, sidestepping the issue of sampling Sarah's "wifely" pleasures. "Or another explanation. I cannot believe Sarah would wage this…this cockeyed battle of wills with me."

He shoved his hand through his hair in frustration, doubtless leaving it standing on end. He didn't care. "I thought she was sensible!"

Marcus shook his head. "She's a Crabtree, isn't she? That explains it all."

Looking beleaguered, Jack Murphy nodded. "Crabtree women are unlike any other women. In the territory *or* the States."

They fell silent, triply contemplating the mysteries of womankind. Across the room, the Crabtree sisters gossiped and laughed. Grace even had the gall to stare boldly back at the men, then whisper something more to Sarah and Molly.

"Still," Marcus mused, "there may be a loophole here."

Ahhh. *Finally.*

"Trust a businessman to spot it." Feeling more hopeful, Daniel turned to him. He *hadn't* entrusted his friends with this issue for nothing, after all. Eagerly, he rubbed his hands together, beyond ready for a solution. "What loophole would that be?"

"I can't talk about it here."

Marcus tipped more whiskey into their mugs. After glancing at the nearby revelers, he angled his head to the corner of the crowded room. The three men retreated there, where it was a sight quieter and a little more private.

"Your reluctance to discuss it says it all," Jack

blurted, plainly unwilling to wait for Marcus to speak. His face shone with the damnable cockiness of an unencumbered bachelor. "I think I know what it is. I can't believe I didn't come up with it myself."

"Indeed." Marcus nodded. "It's simple."

Yes. So simple both of those lunkheads could see it, yet Daniel could not.

He gritted his teeth. "Come out with it, or I'll pound you both."

Jack smirked. "I cannot believe the legendary Daniel McCabe is stymied by a mere woman." From the depths of his suit coat, he retrieved another flask and uncorked it. Irksomely, he raised it toward Sarah in a toast. "Here's to the woman who's outfoxed McCabe."

"Hear, hear," Marcus echoed, raising his own drink.

"Stop it, damn it." Daniel cast Sarah a nervous glance. "She'll see you."

"What if she does?" Grinning, Jack sampled his liquor. With mock sorrowfulness, he shook his head. "I never thought I'd see the day a female had *you* tied up in knots, McCabe."

"Nor I," Marcus said, "which is what led me to my solution. After all, what man in town knows more about women than Daniel?"

"No one." Everyone agreed with that, Daniel reasoned. Even Sarah. "What are you driving at?"

"Only this." The lumberman hunkered closer, keeping their conversation between the three of them. "For some reason or other, when it comes to this problem, you are ignoring your hardiest asset—your ways with women."

Jack snorted.

"You know it's true, Murphy," Marcus insisted. "Who has charmed more of them, *bedded* more of them—"

"Make your point." Daniel crossed his arms. "I'm a married man. It's not fitting to talk about my conquests."

"'Not fitting'?" That earned a laugh from Jack. He elbowed Marcus knowingly. "There's his problem, Copeland. He's gone all prissy on us since getting married. Damnation. Next he'll be wanting smelling salts or the like."

More guffaws. Daniel scowled warningly at him, but said nothing more. He didn't want to risk distracting Marcus from his supposed plan. With admirable patience—he considered—he resisted the urge to drag it from the man forcibly.

"All you have to do," Marcus announced, his entire manner suggesting it was obvious, "is *charm* Sarah. She is a woman, after all. Therefore, she should be no trouble for you."

"Mmm-hmm. 'Tis just as I thought," Jack said happily. "A good tactic. Seduce her. Charm her, befuddle her and then end this nonsense of a strike. Once you've worked your magic on her, Sarah will do whatever you want."

"*Seduce her?* This is my wife we're talking of." Daniel frowned, hoping the meaning of his words was plain. "My friend. I won't hear this kind of talk about her."

"Oh, put away your scowls, McCabe," Marcus said cheerfully. "You know it as plain as I do. It's the only solution. You must use your best skills and abilities in fighting this matter, and see it ended once and for all."

"Take a stand, man," Jack agreed heartily. "For the good of all mankind! You said it yourself—you're engaged in a battle of wills. Do you want to win or not?"

Truthfully, what Daniel wanted was for none of this to be necessary. But since it was…

"You know you have a skill with women," Jack urged. "God only knows why, but they seem to find you not too repulsive."

"Apparently, appealing to women is your primary talent," Marcus added. "So you may as well use it. Females *love* you. Sarah loves you. Go on and bring her to heel."

"With seduction?"

Both men nodded. Although they were well drunk by now, they seemed dead certain of this tactic and more than a little self-satisfied for having come up with it.

"Is that the method you use on Molly?" Daniel asked.

Marcus frowned. For the first time he seemed uncertain.

No matter. It was Daniel's only option so far. At his wit's end, he considered it. Looked at in a certain light, it seemed sensible. After all, his scandalous past proved his appeal to women. Evidently, he was simply *that* irresistible to Sarah, as well. He should have seen it brewing. Could he truly blame her for falling where other women had?

Now that he thought on it, in fact, Sarah's nonsensical maneuverings seemed less of an inconvenience to him and more of an inevitability. Of course she'd want him! Of course she'd want his kisses and his attention. How could she not?

But could he safely *seduce* her, as Murphy had suggested?

Pondering it, Daniel risked a glance across the room. He could only glimpse Sarah in profile now, with her nose tilted proudly and her fancified hair spilling down her back. Despite his recent... confusion...about his feelings for her, he had known Sarah all their lives. If he'd been meant to go sweet on her, he reasoned, it would have happened long before now. Therefore, wooing her must be safe.

Relief swamped him. At last, a solution!

He would endear himself to his wife and restore her wifely duties. He would use whatever charm lay at his disposal, and all the masculine attributes he'd been endowed with, and he would gain Sarah's co-operation. This problem between them would end, doubtless before Daniel had much more to do about it than kiss her good-night.

Squaring his shoulders, he looked to her once more. He grinned. Sarah didn't know it yet, but things between them were about to turn interesting. If it hadn't been a damned necessity, in fact, Daniel might have sworn he looked forward to the whole endeavor.

Wistfully, Sarah gazed across the crowds of friends and neighbors surrounding her. This was likely her tenth winter social, but nothing much had changed since her first foray here.

She still stood at the edges of the dance, trying to seem optimistic that a gentleman would ask her to take a round with him. She still put on her most interested face, with hopes that she'd appear captivated by the dance steps—whether she ever experienced them herself or not.

She still felt alone.

This time, she'd thought things would be different. After all, she was a married woman now, presumably with an escort for every last waltz. But Daniel had

disappeared into the far reaches of the room with
Marcus and that rascally Jack Murphy quite some
time ago. Thanks to him, Sarah was as good as the
wallflower she'd always been.

She folded her arms across her middle. Then, feeling self-conscious, she assumed a more ladylike
pose. Truly, it was wearisome to be delicate. She'd
much rather have been skipping along to a reel or
grabbing a fiddle herself. Standing still was not her
way—in partygoing or in life.

Some years, Sarah recalled, she'd refused to attend
the winter social. She'd claimed herself too caught up
in a book she'd been reading or too somber overall
for silly revelries.

But the truth was, Sarah loved a party. Even if
no one would have guessed such a fondness lay beneath her starched and buttoned exterior. She loved
the promise of it, the fancifulness of it, the possibility that—at any moment—she could find herself
whisked away on the arm of a handsome stranger.

Caught up in the notion, she tapped her toes, imagining herself approached by a wonderful princely
gentleman. Her make-believe admirer bore a striking
resemblance to Daniel, but Sarah didn't dwell on that
discouraging fact. In her mind's eye, she smiled and
flirted and chatted with him, and in no time at all
he twirled them both to the center of the dancing.

Somehow, her second-best green gown wove itself

into a dreamy spangled creation, like something from a fairy tale. Her steps were light, her hair *un*singed, her manner easy. As she and her spellbound prince went on dancing, all the townspeople would gradually drift aside, whispering among themselves about how lovely Sarah was. She'd be in the center of everyone's admiration, especially that of the dark-eyed man who'd claimed her. She'd dance trippingly, witty to the last, and he would smile at her forever.

"You look so enthralled. I must be missing something."

Daniel's deep voice dragged her from her reverie.

Startled, Sarah glanced up to find her husband standing beside her, resplendent in the same suit he'd married her in. She was embarrassed to have been caught daydreaming. Again.

"If you keep that up, you'll make me a jealous man for certain."

He smiled, possibly at her expression of astonishment.

Daniel, jealous? Of her? *You'd have to fall in love with me first* leaped into her mind, but before Sarah could blurt out such a telling comment, Daniel belied every one of her fears by holding out his hand to her.

"Dance with me. I deserve a chance to prove myself, at least, before you decide on another man to replace me."

Replace him? She gawked. Where had that mischief in his eyes come from? She'd swear that look on his face was the same one he gave to the women he fancied—the one that always made them blush. Lord knew, Sarah had watched him often enough, always with her heart in her eyes, to recognize it.

She gathered her wits. Daniel could not be flirting with her. This was simply her fanciful nature running away with her, as usual. Her family had warned her of as much.

"Don't be silly," she said lightly. "You never dance. Have you forgotten our talk on that very subject after our wedding? When I all but begged you to dance with me?"

Daniel gazed directly into her eyes. He shrugged, as though her protest were of little consequence. "I remember you looking beautiful," he said seriously. "I remember not wanting to embarrass myself by acting a clod in your parents' parlor."

Her mouth gaped. He'd worried about seeming silly…to *her?* He'd wanted to impress…*her?* Sarah could not believe it. Daniel always seemed so certain of things. Most especially her.

Suspiciously, she wrinkled her nose. "Then what's different tonight? You don't fear dancing anymore? This place is a sight bigger than my parents' parlor, but you may still trample my toes, after all."

"Ahhh." Grinning, he placed his hand over his heart. "You wound me."

He teased her now? Sarah arched her brows, still feeling off-kilter. This was not *quite* the princely sweeping away she'd dreamed of. But it came closer with every tender look her husband gave her. It was hard not to be affected.

"I wound you? *You* delay," she teased, hoping to restore some of the usual bantering between them. Hoping to feel comfortable, easy...*in charge,* as she had since her strike had begun. "This is all a jest, isn't it? You don't mean to dance with me at all, do you?"

"Try me." Catching her hand, he flattened it beneath his own, against his chest. "Say yes. Dance with me, Sarah."

When she hesitated, overcome with the surprise of finding herself touching him so intimately, he cocked his brow mischievously.

"Do you feel how my heart is pounding? That's how afraid I am that you'll say no to me."

She laughed at that. "No one ever says no to you."

"*You* do."

His hoarsely spoken words jabbed at her conscience. Yes, that was true. She had said no to him. But now, with her senses brimful of Daniel's warmth, his hard muscles, his curiously limp shirtfront...now,

Sarah found that prospect beyond difficult. *This* Daniel was not easy to refuse.

She must, she thought, but couldn't remember why.

"You won't say no to me tonight. I won't have it."

Daniel dropped to one knee at her skirts. Pleadingly—but with an uncommon amount of maleness, all the same—he held her hand in his. She'd barely recovered from the shock of finding him there amid her ordinary green taffeta when he smiled anew. Almost as though he knew something she did not.

That she could not countenance.

"Get up." She gestured frantically with her free hand. What if someone should see them like this? "Get up! What are you doing?"

"I'm acting as your husband." His tone sounded surpassingly reasonable, particularly for a man on bended knee. "The husband I ought have been to you from the start." Daniel's straightforward gaze met hers. "I saw you standing here alone and realized what a fool I've been."

Well, that made sense, but… She felt giddy. Truly. As though she might swoon. People around them were beginning to stare, to whisper behind their hands. To smile knowingly.

Flustered, Sarah smoothed her hair. She bobbed

lower. "Merely *seeing* me here incited you to drop to your knee?"

He nodded, a lock of dark hair falling against his brow. "I'll stay here till you agree to dance with me," he vowed.

He could not be serious. But when she looked down at him, at his callused hand holding hers and his somber expression, Sarah knew she could not refuse him. She could not refuse *herself* a taste of this new, courtly Daniel.

"You're being outrageous," she said, buying time for her knees to stop quaking before she agreed. "Outrageous."

She tried to make her voice sound stern. She had some experience with that; years spent wielding influence in the schoolroom should have lent her that much authority, at least. But Daniel, contrary as usual, seemed unaffected.

"I'm being husbandly." He turned up her hand and kissed her palm, his gaze never leaving hers. "I'm being dutiful. Exactly the way you wanted me to be."

He...he'd kissed her! She couldn't quite bring herself to believe it, but as proof her hand tingled where his lips had been. Still feeling light-headed, Sarah considered his words. She had wanted him to behave this way, that was true...but she hadn't quite dreamed up *this* much acquiescence!

Then it occurred to her. *Husbandly. Dutiful.* He was making a concession—a concession to the "husbandly duties" she'd requested of him. Of course. She was still winning. She was getting what she'd asked for at long last. The realization gave her the courage to accept his invitation.

"Very well." She could hardly suppress a smile of sheer excitement. "I'll dance with you."

The people nearest them made way, smiling wider. With Daniel as chivalrous escort, he and Sarah moved to the center of the dancing. He smiled at her, then took her in his arms. He began to dance. It was, she realized with a secret smile, exactly the scenario she'd envisaged in her daydreams.

Even while accommodating her untried abilities, Daniel executed the steps with surprising ease. He held her in his arms and moved to the music, and she realized that she'd never been held by him this way before. Not truly, not out of bed, not with purpose and gallantry.

Looking up into his intent, handsome face, Sarah found it easy to understand why ladies clamored for his attention.

She realized why and foolishly blurted it. "You make me feel as though no other dancers exist."

At his raised brows, dismay raced through her. Her statement was true enough, to be sure. But still…

Now Daniel would tease her. He would ruin this unusual, special togetherness between them.

"There are other dancers here?" He pretended to scout for more, then shook his head. "I only see you. You are the only woman I could ever want."

To prove his point, he twirled them both to a slightly more private spot. Just being there with him, Sarah felt scandalous. It was a new and pleasant experience.

Daniel's arms felt strong, his steps light. So brawny a man should have been clumsy or hesitant, but her husband was neither of those things. His hand on her waist felt possessive; his grasp on her hand, assured. Dancing with him was a heady occurrence. Indeed, Sarah hadn't known what she'd been in for. Another minute and she'd be swept away for certain.

She needed to converse. It was either that or continue mooning over the breadth of his shoulders and the brilliance of his smile. In a stilted voice, she tried an opening gambit.

"The decorations are lovely, aren't they?"

"Your beauty puts them all to shame."

"And the…the mulled cider is delicious."

"No more than your smile."

Oh, my. "Pish. A smile cannot be delicious."

He pretended regret. "You caught me. I wasn't thinking of your smile, after all. Beautiful as it is."

She shouldn't inquire, but she had to know. "What were you thinking of, then?"

"Your figure." His gaze swept lower. "*It* is delicious. Round and soft and made just right for my hands. *Here.*"

Shamelessly, he tightened his grasp on her waist. Sarah squealed, her whole body aflutter with having him touch her so purposefully...so manfully.

"Quiet, now." He gave a devilish grin as several dancers glanced their way, then murmured to each other. "You'll let everyone know I can't keep my hands from you."

She goggled, then let him spin her round the floor. "You've been able to well enough till now," she couldn't help but point out.

He gave a thoughtful sound. "I intend to remedy that. Starting tonight. And every night after."

Curiosity quickened within her. Exactly what did he mean?

"I won't take no for an answer, wife," he warned.

She wanted to squeal anew. Goodness! His mock sternness set her heart astir. Although, given her present state of mind, she wasn't likely to offer him "no" for an answer to anything, now, was she?

After his outlandish attentions tonight, it was hard to remember he was Daniel, *her* Daniel, the same man who'd awakened beside her this morning, raced from their bed and stubbed his toe in his haste to be away. She didn't know what the change in him owed itself to.

Contemplatively, Daniel gazed at her. "I meant to tell you before...I like your hair that way." His voice lowered intimately. "It makes me want to take it all down and run my fingers through your curls."

The image of that struck her. She, with her head tilted back in enjoyment; he, with his deft hands caressing her. Curiously enough, in her mind's eye, they weren't dancing at all. They were alone someplace, someplace cozy and candlelit.

Nearly carried away by the idea, Sarah shook her head. She had to reinstitute her common sense. It wouldn't be wise to let Daniel know how well his charm was working on her. Now that she held the upper hand, she meant to retain it awhile. He'd already set her off-balance enough.

"Oh, no. Doing *that* would only ruin the style."

He looked as though he knew a secret. "I would make sure you didn't care about that."

"Oh?" She affected a carefree demeanor, even though her pulse raced. "How would you do that?"

"Can't you guess?" A smile. "*I* can imagine it well enough."

At the naughty tone in his voice, she glanced up at him, wide-eyed. They went on dancing, spinning to the music, but Sarah didn't have a mind for tunes.

All she could think about was Daniel…Daniel, and his sudden interest in her.

"I would kiss you." He leaned close to her ear, giving her a sampling of his clean-shaven jaw against her skin. His breath whispered past her earlobe. "I would kiss you until you begged me to never stop. You," he promised, "would forget you had a hairstyle altogether."

Her heart pounded. The images his words gave rise to were tantalizing enough, even without the added incentive of his husky, masculine voice. She wanted his kiss—*had* wanted it, ever since their hasty wedding peck. She wanted it still.

Hesitantly, Sarah leaned back, searching his expression. Their bantering had done its work on her, but she had no notion if he felt the same. It would be awful if Daniel didn't mean it, if he were only teasing her. But all she glimpsed in his face was a curious sort of intensity, and hopefulness.

She swallowed hard. Met his gaze directly, with a bravery she hadn't known she possessed. "And if I did beg you to never stop? What then?"

For an instant, he seemed taken aback. Then his usual certainty returned. Daniel spun her round, his body naturally paired with hers and his grasp steady.

"Then I never would. I never would stop."

"I am glad," Sarah announced with certainty, just

as the song ended. "Maybe we will reach a compromise yet."

Smiling, she offered him a curtsy. She straightened to meet his befuddled expression.

"I'm offering more than a compromise," he said.

"And I am considering accepting it," she told him.

Keeping Grace's tutorials—and her own long-term goals—firmly in mind, Sarah excused herself. She made herself walk from the dance floor, then headed for the cloakroom. Right now, a long walk in the swirling snow sounded just the thing—although she had a feeling she'd be remembering Daniel's look of surprise the entire way.

Chapter Eleven

Guided by the moonlight, Sarah stepped between the snowdrifts to the sheltering cover of a stand of pine trees. Behind her, the winter social carried on in all its festivities, but she could not dance and laugh and mingle. Not the way she felt just now, so confused and overheated and so…alive.

A giddy giggle rose inside her. Daniel wanted her! If she hadn't experienced it with her own senses, if she hadn't felt his arms around her and his whispered words in her ear, she would not have believed it so. But somehow Daniel had been snapped to, made to see his buried feelings…*something*. Something had made a difference in him.

For now, she wouldn't question it. How could she, when she'd wanted this very thing for so long?

In the end, she thought she'd done quite well, she decided as she snuggled more deeply into her hastily thrown-on coat. She congratulated herself on her wit—what there'd been of it. On her dancing—insensible as she'd been to her moving feet. On her mustering the will to leave when she ought—reluctant as she'd been to do so. Thanks to those actions, Daniel probably didn't realize exactly how...affecting...his invitation had been, how stimulating his talk and his touch and his dancing. Sarah had done her best to keep her reactions to herself. She thought she'd succeeded admirably.

Had she succeeded admirably? She sighed, suddenly fearing not. His roguish talk had been so rousing! She didn't know how she would remain sensible in the face of more of it, if he continued. Likely she would manage somehow. She'd lived with her feelings for him for years, keeping them safe and secret inside her. She didn't dare let them out fully yet. But if in the meantime Daniel wanted her...

I would kiss you until you begged me to never stop.

Oh, yes. He certainly *seemed* to want her.

Beset by curiosity, Sarah considered exactly what such a kiss might entail. She couldn't quite reason it out. She'd experienced kisses before, of course. At the advanced age of twenty-five, she seen her share of masculine advances. She'd even possessed enough scholarly interest to sample one or two kisses. But never once had she felt moved to actually beg anyone. For anything. The very idea seemed preposterous.

Doubtless, that was only Daniel's natural arrogance

coming to the fore. Likely, he fancied himself a connoisseur of kissing and wanted her to believe the same. Well, Sarah decided magnanimously, she would allow him the opportunity to persuade her. But until that time arrived, she'd retain her skepticism.

A creak sounded behind her. Music swelled as a door opened. It receded again, replaced by the crunch of heavy footfalls through the iced-over drifts. Sarah stayed beneath her snow-frosted boughs, letting whoever had decided to leave the social pass by her. She wasn't in the mood for mannered conversation.

"I warned you already," came Daniel's voice. "I won't take no for an answer."

Sarah whirled to face him, ridiculously pleased that he'd sought her out. Deliberately, she made her voice light.

"An answer to what?"

He approached purposefully, wearing his coat and flat-brimmed hat, his face shrouded in the moonlight. All around them, the air felt still and crisp. The revelry seemed distant, a mere tune from a tinny music box. All at once, their solitude felt complete. Her heartbeat clip-clopped at a faster pace.

"To what?" He arched a brow, as though the answer to that should have been obvious. He brought his gloved hands to her cheeks. Briefly, sweetly, his smile flashed. "To this."

He lowered his mouth to hers, warming her with

his breath in the instant before their lips touched. The world swam beneath Sarah's suddenly unsteady feet, all her attention centered on the unbelievable event that was occurring. Daniel's mouth felt good, she observed dizzily. Firmer than hers, and plainly more experienced, but a perfect match between them.

Uttering a low moan, he angled her head sideways. Her cheek fit in the haven of his palm as though it were meant to be held there. His mouth covered hers again, this time in a kiss more insistent than the last. Eagerly, Sarah puckered back with all her might, letting him know she wanted this...wanted *him*.

Their kiss went on and on, surpassingly wonderful and engrossingly right. It was chaste but potent, simple but necessary. It was their much-delayed wedding kiss, she realized with delight, and therefore it was meant to be savored. When it ended, Daniel reared his head back, staring at her.

Surprise etched itself in the hard angles of his face. His brows lifted. For a moment he looked a stranger, someone both thrilling and darkly dangerous. But then he smiled, and Sarah recognized the devil-may-care slant to his mouth as well as she did her own indrawn breath.

"I like your kiss," he announced, looking perplexed.

"You needn't sound so astonished. It's not polite."

"I'm not concerned with politeness."

To prove it, he pressed another kiss to her waiting mouth, this one with an experimental flavor.
Sarah rose on tiptoes to get closer, grabbing fistfuls
of Daniel's coat with both gloved hands. She needed
to be next to him, she decided with some urgency.
Next to him from knees to forehead. This kissing
was remarkable stuff. She wanted it to go on and on
and—

Aaagh. Sarah broke off their kiss, staring at him.
"Was that your *tongue?*"

He seemed affronted. But humored, too. "You
needn't sound so dismayed. It's not polite."

"I'm not dismayed." In truth, she was. A little. She
didn't want to seem unsophisticated, but the shock
of finding another person's tongue inside a different
person's mouth would have that effect on the hearti-
est individual, she suspected. "I'm merely—" She
hesitated, contemplating it. "Uncertain."

"Uncertain?"

"Whether I like it. Perhaps I need more experience."

He watched her, not complying. Why did he look
so amused?

"You'll need to cooperate," she instructed with
some impatience. "I already know what my own
tongue feels like, and it's fairly unspectacular."

At that, he actually laughed. The scoundrel.

Sarah crossed her arms. "Stop it. You are ruining

the magic of the moment. Hurry up and kiss me again, or the wonder of it will be lost forever."

"The 'wonder'?"

"Yes." She nodded. "Oh! And use your tongue again."

"All that?"

"Faster."

"I cannot believe *you* lecture me on propriety."

She felt a smile coming on. "Please."

Ahhh. She'd always known that word was magic. At her very utterance of it, Daniel moved closer again. He lost the irksome grin on his face and regarded her seriously.

"All right. But lean against that tree behind you. I don't want you to swoon."

Was he delaying *again?* "You're overly concerned with my potential daintiness. I never swoon."

"You will before I'm done with you."

"Promises, promises."

"Have it your way."

His mouth descended over hers again. Just when she reckoned he would swoop in with another tongue-like surprise, though, Daniel defeated her expectations. He offered up a series of gentle kisses, each one sweeter than the last. He covered her mouth from corner to corner, trailing those kisses along sensitive places she hadn't known she possessed.

She squirmed. "You're not doing it properly."

Fractionally, he raised his head. "You don't like it?"

"I may," she hedged. She did. So much so that it left her breathless. "If I ever receive a proper sampling."

Rising to the challenge, Daniel pressed still nearer. In the shadows of the snow-shrouded pine boughs, he held her with one arm round her middle. With his free hand, he thumbed up her chin. "If you swoon, you have no one to blame but yourself."

"Psha—"

The sound was stolen from her by his next kiss. This kiss was different from the others. More purposeful, more exciting, more...*more*. Light-headed beneath its influence, Sarah swayed and clung to him. She offered herself up for another, and this time when Daniel urged her to open her mouth beneath his, she did so knowingly. Curiously. Enthusiastically.

The invasion of his tongue still felt strange, but a part of her liked it. The wicked part, most probably. Her toes curled inside her boots, and Sarah leaned all the way against Daniel, proving she didn't need a silly tree. She didn't need anything except him.

Wholeheartedly, she gave herself over to kissing her husband. *I love you,* she thought before kissing him again. *I love you, love you.* She caressed his broad shoulders, his sturdy jaw, everywhere she could reach. It was all a part of loving him...making sure he knew she appreciated every part of him, every muscle, every inch. It was the least she could do. After all, he made her feel special merely with the touch of his lips.

Too soon, their mouths parted.

She couldn't seem to catch her breath. Daniel was similarly afflicted. He stared at her with eyes gone dark and mysterious, his whole body hardened beneath her hands.

"You," he said, "are never what I expect."

Absurdly pleased, Sarah smiled. "I hope I never am."

At that, he rolled his eyes. "God help me. I didn't know you were doing it apurpose. That explains a great deal."

"It does not explain why you've suddenly decided to kiss me," she mused, but then another thought struck her. "Although perhaps this owes itself to the social. Perhaps you are a secret romantic at heart. Just like m—"

"Stop talking. I need to think."

Daniel's brow furrowed. The fervor of their kiss had knocked his hat askew, and its angle made him look like one of the clowns from the traveling circus. She considered telling him so, then decided against it. His arrogance wouldn't have survived it.

He examined her, toes to nose, as though trying to reason out some blacksmith's device or a tricky repair. "You *do* look beautiful. Maybe that's it."

His statement confused her. "You said so already."

She knew, because it had been a moment she would cherish forever. *Your beauty puts them all to shame.*

"Yes, I know. But tonight you look...uncommonly so. I wonder...?" Daniel gathered her hair in one of his big hands. His knuckles brushed her nape as he bundled her curls behind her head in a style more similar to her everyday chignon. With a determined expression, he surveyed the effect. He shook his head. "No. Even that doesn't change it."

Her hair swung back in place. "Change what?"

"My feelings about...kissing with tongues."

She had the sense he wasn't telling her the entire truth. Still, his lighter demeanor relieved her. "Mine are beginning to be revolutionized, though. Let's try it again. I do believe I am getting the knack of it."

"It is not supposed to be this way."

"What way?" A thought struck her. "Look. I'm leaning against the tree. See?"

Sarah offered what she hoped was an alluring pose.

Daniel glanced at her. His gaze meandered to her hips, then her lips. He seemed bedeviled all over again. "Stop it! I can't think when you're doing that."

Deflated, she straightened. Perhaps "alluring" simply wasn't in her repertoire. To be sure, "fanciful" was. Also "ridiculously hopeful." More than likely, asking the magic of this night to continue was simply too much to wish for.

A moment passed while Sarah officially allowed him time to "think." In the meanwhile, the wind whispered through the pine trees, shaking loose the snow on the boughs. It drifted down upon them like fairy dust, enchanting their hiding place.

"We're going home," Daniel announced.

Something inside her dwindled. Possibly it was her hope this night would change something between them.

"But I want to stay here." When he didn't reply, Sarah repeated herself. "I *insist* upon staying here."

He groaned. "Damnation. It's not working at all!"

Which seemed a fairly mysterious thing to say.

"What's not working?"

"Nothing." Grimly, Daniel straightened his hat. "'Tis only a matter of time before it does. I know it."

He held out his hand. Sarah took it. After a backward glance at the lights gleaming from the social, she permitted him to walk her toward their neighbors'. Eli was being cared for there, along with the smallest Morrow Creek children.

"That kiss," she mused as they passed the darkened

mercantile building. "Was that the one meant to make me beg?"

Her inquiry elicited a grunt. Perhaps he didn't understand what she meant.

"To beg you to never stop, I mean," she clarified. The only sound was the muffled thump of his boots. Then, "No. When I give you *that* kiss, you'll know it."

"Oh." Somehow, she doubted it. He could be frustratingly cryptic at times. "That's good to know, then."

She still felt disappointed, though. Also, alive with interest. What would that never-ending kiss feel like?

A few more steps. "*How* will I know it?"

"Sarah, enough."

"Will I be able to make *you* beg, too?"

He exhaled. "Yes. I beg you to stop chattering."

Fine. Hurt, Sarah shut her mouth. She walked faster, daring him to keep up with her strides. If he wanted silence, she would give him silence. Loads upon loads of absolute quiet. Stillness so complete it would make his ears ache for a whisper. Soon Daniel would beseech her to speak to him, to utter the merest peep in his direction.

Or not. Because as they strode past her father's *Pioneer Press* offices, another troubling thought occurred to her. Sarah could not contain it. Even as the snow squeaked beneath their boots, she dared another look at Daniel's thoughtful face.

"Daniel? Are you disappointed with my kissing? Is that what's bothering you? Are you imagining a lifetime of inadequate marital relations? Are you contemplating methods of tutoring me? Or perhaps you mean never to try again?"

Fearfully, she watched him. If he said he *was* disappointed in her, she didn't know what she would do. Search for an instructional manual on the topic of marital kissing, perhaps. Ask Molly or her mother for advice. Or even, heaven forbid, inquire anonymously within one of the etiquette columns so popular these days. The one in *Beadle's Magazine,* perhaps.

"No."

She waited. He couldn't seriously mean to leave it at that. A single syllable did not form a proper response.

She told him so.

He sighed. For a heartbeat, the old Daniel returned, with his friendly eyes and familiar smile.

"You're already launching plans and schemes, aren't you? I can see the machinations in your head. If I say 'yes,' that I am disappointed, then you'll waylay me at every turn for practice. Practice, practice, practice."

She thought about it. Nodded. "Probably."

"Then my answer," he said with a newly determined grin, "is definitely yes."

Over the next several days, Daniel applied himself diligently to the matter of seducing Sarah. He made himself lie abed beside her in the mornings, enjoying the kind of warm togetherness he knew she liked. He made himself kiss her hello and goodbye, observing the husbandly duties he knew she liked. He even made himself court her, talking and laughing with a flirtatious tone he knew she liked.

The devil of it was, *he* liked it, too.

He liked finding her in his arms. He liked seeing her smile. He liked viewing her, after all these years, as a woman—a woman both desirable and confounding. Sarah had a well-developed sense of wit, he discovered, along with a hearty enthusiasm for kissing and a pert backside made just right for squeezing. She squealed when he did that, but her blush told him she liked it. Daniel would have had to have been much less of a man not to have felt the same.

He took every opportunity to touch her. When they passed in the hallway, he made sure their bodies met in the middle. When he pulled down a heavy tin of beans from the pantry for her, he stole a kiss at the same time. When they tucked Eli in bed each night, he blew out the lantern and then drew Sarah into his arms for some of that dancing she liked, humming a tune himself. And all the while...*he* liked it, too.

The fact of that worried him. Was he developing feelings for Sarah? Falling in "love" with his wife would not do. Daniel knew he had to hold fast to his convictions and merely seduce her instead. Otherwise, there was no telling the dangers that awaited them both.

Just look at what had happened to Lillian.

It was worth the risk, though. Daniel knew he must be making progress, must be close to achieving a proper husbandly influence over Sarah. She had not yet resumed doing his washing or his cooking or his mending, but she had resumed laughing with him. That made him feel better than any clean shirt ever could. It gave him hope, as well.

Aside from seducing her, there was still the matter of needing her help with his household. Daniel pondered on that for a while, then remembered what Sarah had said to him. *It's difficult for me to get to all the housework, given my duties at the schoolhouse. If I had a spare pair of hands, maybe...*

Privately, he paid a visit to the school board. Its members were his friends in the community, people who brought him their sleigh runners and skillets for repair, who brought him their horses to be shod. Daniel figured they would listen to him when he explained about Sarah's heavy duties—when he asked that they hire an assistant schoolteacher for her. Getting help with her schoolteacher's work would lighten her load overall, and it would make her happier, too.

Although he did not receive an answer right away, he left with the feeling that he'd done his wife a favor. She would be pleased and surprised when his request came to fruition. And she would have all the more vigor for their kissing practice, too.

Indulging in that last was badly done of him, he knew. Just carrying on with "practicing" lent proof to the idea there was something lacking in her kiss, when Daniel knew nothing was further from the truth. But after their encounter outside the winter social, Sarah had insisted she needed "practice." Who better than himself, he reasoned, to provide it?

"Just hold still," he told her, late of a night when Eli was sleeping. Their bedroom was quiet and cozy and lamp-lit, perfect for the things he had in mind. "This is an advanced technique. You'd better let me demonstrate first."

Eyes wide and beautifully blue, Sarah nodded. "All right."

Clad only in his britches, partially buttoned shirt and braces, Daniel sat beside her on their bed. The mattress dipped beneath his weight, then settled. He arranged himself so that he faced her. In the lamplight, Sarah's unbound hair fell over her shoulders, making her look young and trusting and pretty.

Strange, that the notion of a "pretty" Sarah did not take him aback these days. Likely, that was the result of his seduction techniques, Daniel told himself. He'd bewitched *himself,* plainly enough, even if not her. Not entirely.

To begin with, he kissed her, delving his hand in her hair to hold her to him. 'Twas only a warming kiss, a starter for the practice to come. But across the short space of mattress dividing them, they both leaned in yearning. They both touched hands, both moaned with pleasure, both relaxed into the kiss.

She felt good, Daniel thought. She felt right. Now that the first oddity of finding himself kissing Sarah—*Sarah!*—had passed, he'd come apace with the notion. He'd even grown to like it. He loved her enthusiasm and her ardor, her willingness to learn and even, strangely enough, her bossiness. It told him what she liked. That was invaluable information for a man in the throes of seducing his wife.

Otherwise, he reminded himself firmly as he trailed his kisses from the corner of her mouth to her neck, he would never have clean mended socks. He had to remember that. He had to think about skillets and holey britches and roast chicken.

Oddly enough, he thought of Sarah instead. He

thought of her warmth next to him, of her curves beneath his hands, of the thrilling sound she made in the back of her throat whenever she especially liked something. She liked being kissed just where her earlobe met her neck, Daniel learned just then. She liked a brief bite to that tender lobe, liked a subtle caress of her shoulder as he licked, then kissed, her neck. She liked to wriggle beneath him as he returned his mouth to hers.

"Hold still," he warned. "This is tricky stuff."

She did not succeed in following his instructions. That made him glad, because it forced him to teach her a lesson by continuing his kiss...by deepening it until they both panted for breath. Sarah's body tautened under his hands, round and firm beneath her layers of dress and chemise and petticoat. Soon he would show her his mastery of ladies' undergarments, Daniel told himself, a skill of which he felt justifiably proud. But for now...for now he could not remember exactly where he was.

He opened his eyes and blinked. His gaze trailed from the disordered strands of Sarah's hair to the twin mounds of her bosom, displayed to advantage by her partially unbuttoned dress bodice. When had that happened? Daniel could not recall having laid his fingers there, but plainly...

"Why are you frowning? Was that kiss not a good one? I tried to hold still, but it's so difficult." Sarah placed a gentle hand to his jaw, coaxing him to look at her. "When you're kissing me, my whole body wants to get closer to you."

Her innocent words were his undoing. Groaning, Daniel kissed her again. "It was good," he assured her. Momentarily, he rested his forehead against hers, enjoying the closeness it engendered, even though closeness was not the goal of this night. "Very good."

"But not terribly advanced." She wrinkled her nose, looking charmingly put-out. "I daresay we've kissed that way before." A pause. "Are you staring at my bosoms?"

He was, he realized. They were entrancing.

Daniel cleared the hoarseness from his throat. He was playing with fire. It would be better to sound masterful here. Prepared. Especially since Sarah seemed entirely too proud of *his* brief lapse of control.

"The advanced part of this kiss," he told her sternly, "is that you must remain entirely still. No matter what I do—"

"No matter how much you beg?"

Her brow arched knowingly. The minx.

"—you cannot move. Understand?"

"Of course." She wiggled, arranged her skirts, then regarded him impatiently. "I'm ready."

Her zeal made him smile. It also made him hard

and hot and ready to move their lessons forward a mite. But that was not the point of this night. The point of this night was to prove his mastery over her and begin to assert his husbandly command. Elsewise, he would be eating his own poorly cooked meals forever. That would not do.

"I'm going to kiss you again," Daniel warned softly, "but all the while, I'm going to have my hands right here."

Gently, he placed both hands over her breasts. The blissfulness of touching her that way nearly made him moan. Ahhh, but she felt good. Beyond good. Better than he might have dreamed.

Sarah started, her whole body quivering. With quiet deliberateness, she stilled herself. She gazed at him through surprised eyes…eyes that grew darker and needier with every minute.

She wanted him, Daniel understood then. He felt shocked to the core by the realization. Somehow, he'd never quite considered what being wanted by her would feel like.

He knew in that moment he needed more of it.

"Very good." How he formed words, he did not know. "You feel very good. Very soft and warm and—" a small moan escaped him "—very, ahhh, good." Damnation, this was more difficult than he'd planned. He swallowed hard. "Are you ready?"

She bit her lip. Nodded. "Yes."

Crazily, he wondered if *he* were ready. All at once, it seemed possible he might have tackled more than he'd known.

But then his natural dominance asserted itself. The moment he moved, everything turned right side up again. Daniel leaned nearer, his vision momentarily blocked by a hank of hair falling across his brow. He sensed Sarah's eager presence, felt the mattress tremble beneath them both, inhaled the delicate fragrances of soap and lavender that clung to her. He wanted her, wanted her....

This kiss was hungrier than the last and far less controllable. Lost in it, abandoning himself to it, Daniel kissed her again and again, holding her in his palms all the while. Her nipples peaked against his hands, lifted by her corset and straining hard against her sheer chemise. Again and again he stroked her there, testing the wonderful roundness of her against him. He could not get enough of feeling her. Sarah was wonderful to touch.

Her bodice parted. Clearly, his fingers had more of a say in his actions than his sense of resolve did. No matter. His only thought was to delve deeper against her, to cup her more fully. Her bare breast slipped in his hand as though it had been made to be there, and Daniel kissed her even more deeply in response. He needed more. So much more.

"Oh, Daniel." Sarah trembled, her head tipped to the shadowed ceiling. "I need—"

"I know." With a single deft movement, he carried her back against the quilt. Let his plans be damned. This was more compelling by far. "Give me more, Sarah."

She nodded. He pinned his knee between her spread thighs, battening her skirts to the mattress. He found more buttons and worked at them avidly. He wondered how she would feel against his tongue, imagined the tender pucker of her nipples in his mouth. That was what he needed. *She* was what he needed.

Panting, Daniel kissed her anew. He paused to sample that forehead-to-forehead movement again, driven to it by an impulse he cared not consider any further. Comfort and need engulfed him, leaving him bettered by their influence. Slowing himself, he stroked Sarah's hair carefully from her face. He cupped her cheek, feeling, in that moment, beset by caring. He did not know why, and he refused to think on it. Not while she lay sprawled beneath him, not while they both teetered on the verge of something entirely new between them.

"What do you want from me?" she asked breathlessly. Her fingers caressed his cheek, traveled over his whiskery stubble. "Tell me. What do you want me to do, Daniel? Whatever it is, I'm ready. I want to make you happy."

This is it, a part of him dimly realized. The acquiescence he'd been waiting for. All he had to do now was push a little further, to tell Sarah how overjoyed he'd be with a patch for his worn coat or a warm knitted scarf. She would do it. She would do it, and he would win.

He *had* won.

"Let me love you," he heard himself say, inexplicably. Yet the rightness of it overwhelmed him. "I only want to love you."

"Oh, Daniel." All at once, Sarah looked about to weep. Her eyes turned misty and her lips wobbled at the corners, exactly the way they had during their wedding ceremony. "Oh, Daniel." She pressed a fervent kiss to his mouth, surprising him. "You *do* love me! I knew you would!"

Her words penetrated the fog surrounding him. He raised himself on his forearms, staring at her. "Love you? I did not say—"

"But of course you love me!" Gleefully, Sarah flung her arms to the side, the very picture of a delighted woman. "You said so yourself, just now."

Beaming, she hugged him. Her embrace threatened to overwhelm them both. Happiness radiated from her. Happiness and certainty.

How in the devil had this happened? It would not do.

"I do not love you," Daniel said. "I care for you, of course. I want you, and soon. But love…Sarah, that is not possible between us. You know that."

She stilled. All of a sudden, holding her was like canoodling with a hunk of pine. There was no life there at all.

Confused, he squeezed her, trying to bring back the woman he'd wanted so much. Who'd just wanted him. But all that happened was that Sarah shoved at his chest and sat up. Head down, she pushed herself away and crowded against the headboard with her knees to her chest. Jerkily, she yanked her skirts over her legs.

Daniel stared at the silky dark tangle of her hair, wanting to glimpse her face. He could not. She was shuttered from him.

"Damnation, Sarah! Don't be this way."

Silence. Then a snuffle.

Regret assailed him. He'd hurt her.

Daniel softened his voice. "All I want is for things between us to be good. To be—"

"To be the way *you* want them?" she interrupted. She raised her flushed face to his, eyes flashing. "With me ironing and mending and cooking?" Her expression sharpened. Saddened. "You've been so nice to me these past days. All because you want me to end my strike."

"No." She didn't understand. "Not…entirely."

But Sarah only glimpsed the part of it. She only saw that he wanted something from her and was not above using his body—and hers—to get it.

"Sarah, I want you." Beseechingly, he raised his hand to touch her cheek. He encountered only a stray length of hair as she stubbornly turned her head. "You want me. We're already wed. There's no reason we have to be apart."

"There is." She raised her face to his. With dignity, she regarded him. "It's called love. Until you can give me that, we'll always be apart."

Daniel didn't understand. "I…care for you. That should be enough."

"You expect that's so just because you say it is, don't you?" She offered him a wistful smile. "I'm afraid this time you're wrong. It's not enough. I want you to *love me,* Daniel."

Frustrated, he shoved his hand through his hair. "What do you think we were doing just now? I was ready to love you."

"I want you to give me the words."

Ahhh. That was the way of it, then. Seriously, he studied her. She deserved the truth. "I don't believe in them."

She shook her head. "You can't mean that."

"I do. 'Love' turns people to fools. It ruins lives." He saw her skepticism and went on. "For the sake of 'love,' my sister abandoned her only child," he said savagely. "She sent Eli away so he would not interfere with her new marriage. That is how much Lillian 'loves' her second husband. If that is love, I want no part of it. Ever."

Sarah stilled. "Is that true? Is that what she wrote in her letter to you?"

At her round-eyed expression of disbelief, Daniel looked at her squarely. "Do you believe I would lie about such a thing?"

She hesitated. "I believe you might be misled. Misinformed, or confused or—"

"No. I'm not. Eli has been hurt once already. Do you think I will let myself fall prey to some addle-headed idiocy and risk hurting him again?" Daniel shook his head. "I am his only family now. I won't take that chance."

"There's no saying you'll behave as Lillian did. You're a different person. A man! A *strong* man." She leaned forward, put her hand to his arm. "You would never abandon Eli."

He met her gaze, feeling restless. "No. I would not."

Pain lodged itself near his heart, defying all his

efforts to ignore it. He wanted Sarah, but couldn't have her. He needed to protect Eli, but only grasped at knowing how. He was only a man. An ordinary man. How had the gap between what he wanted and what he would allow himself widened so deeply?

"Then there is hope for us," Sarah said firmly. "Because if you won't abandon Eli, there's reason for *me* not to abandon *you*."

Daniel scoffed at that. "I don't need caretaking."

"I'm talking about loving."

"Then stop it." He frowned, further pained by her persistence, by her cockeyed beliefs. "The only love I can give you happens right here. In this bed."

For an instant, her eyes widened. She understood him.

But she wasn't afraid.

"The only way *that's* happening is if you let yourself love me first." Gently, she spread her hand over his chest, atop his heart. "Right here."

He shook his head. They were at an impasse.

"I can convince you differently." Daniel knew it was true. Another kiss, another caress… She would come to see reason. She would accept their arrangement eventually. "You're a sensible woman, Sarah. Don't tell me you're holding out for some romantic dream. It's not like you."

"Oh, but that's where you're wrong."

Of a sudden, Sarah looked as though she knew something he did not. The sensation discomfited him.

"It's very much like me. If it's the last thing I do, I intend to make you realize that."

"Don't be—"

But she wouldn't listen. She stopped him with a hand to his mouth, obstinately shaking her head. "Do you think I've made this life for myself only to give up now?"

With a quirky half smile, Sarah watched him. He could feel...something...building inside her, growing stronger with every moment. Something bullheaded and naive in equal measure. 'Twas a dangerous combination.

"I expect you'll give up on me eventually," Daniel said. "You'll have to."

"Then that's where you've misreckoned." She pushed from their bed with a businesslike air, smoothing her skirts. Her final words came tossed over her shoulder. "I intend to make you *see* me, Daniel McCabe. To see the truth between us. And there's nothing you can do to stop me."

God help him. He feared she was right.

Chapter Twelve

At Molly's bakeshop, Sarah plunked a handful of coins on the counter. "Hello, Molly! Are you there?"

Her sister came around the counter, wiping her hands on her apron. She tucked a stray lock of tawny hair behind her ear. As she did so, her gaze fell on the money.

"All that? You were serious about your order, then?"

"Yes." Firmly, Sarah nodded. "All two dozen."

"Very well." A few minutes later, Molly had everything prepared. She slid a box of spicy-scented, plump cinnamon buns onto the counter. "Are these for your students, then?"

"No. Just for me. Thank you!"

Box in hand, Sarah stepped past the dainty wirework chairs, carefully keeping her skirts from being caught. She'd nearly reached the door when Molly stopped her.

"Exactly *why* do you need two dozen cinnamon buns?"

"Errr…because they're so delicious, Moll. Bye!"

"Stop."

Reluctantly, Sarah turned. She'd hoped to dodge this conversation altogether. She faced her sister's expectant look.

"I need them because of Daniel," she admitted, deciding to have done with it once and for all. She'd save herself the further trouble of hiding it. "Your advice—and Grace's—worked too well! For nearly two weeks now, Daniel has been after me."

"After you?"

"Day and night. Night and day. Cornering me in the hallway, where we're bound to be…close to each other. Kissing me. Bringing me little gifts. Paying me outlandish compliments. Plying me with flattery. I'm at my wit's end!"

"Yes." Molly crossed her arms, her sleeves floury. "I can see where an excess of husbandly romancing would be wearisome."

"It is! Moll, I mean it." Beset by doubts and confusion, Sarah crossed the empty bakeshop again. It was a good thing there weren't customers thronging the place. She sidled closer, hardly daring to meet Molly's eyes. "If you must know, Daniel seems intent on…*seducing me*."

Falsely aghast, Molly gave a cry.

"I'm serious." She gave her sister a playful whack. "It's very hard to deal with. I can't think straight anymore! And it's wreaking havoc on my strike, too. Yesterday I nearly served Daniel a biscuit. *With* honey."

Molly's eyes widened. "Grace will be appalled. All her notions of connubial disobedience, spoiled by breadstuffs."

"Stop laughing! I should have known this would happen."

Distraught, Sarah put down her cinnamon buns. By force of habit, she smoothed her dress. Lately she'd begun finding it partially unbuttoned at the oddest moments, thanks to Daniel's continued courting of her—and her own blasted weakness when it came to him. The man was a scoundrel, through and through. Not even sturdy wool worsted could stand between him and a solid, manly grope.

Despite what had happened between them when he'd told her about Lillian's abandonment of Eli—and the woman's astounding excuse for it—Daniel remained persistent in his pursuit of her…in his charming of her. Sarah didn't understand it. It was almost as though, by refusing his advances, she'd fired up his ambition to bed her properly. These days he *definitely* would not take no for an answer.

But Sarah, more than ever, felt determined to give it. He was close to loving her. She was convinced of it. Until Daniel gave her his heart, she'd promised herself, she would not surrender her body.

If only her pledge weren't so dreadfully difficult to keep! She didn't know how long she could continue to keep her long-held, embarrassingly unreciprocated feelings for Daniel a secret—especially when he seemed so determined to lay her bare...in every way.

Partially, she blamed her sisters.

"Your persuasive counsel on 'dressing prettily' was too much for my husband, I fear," Sarah told Molly. "Now Daniel can't keep his hands from me."

"But...that's good, isn't it?"

"Not for my peace of mind, it's not." Oh, Molly would never understand. She and Marcus were *in love*. With each other. Frustrated, Sarah picked up her cinnamon buns again. "But this time, I have a new plan. A plan of my own devising."

Molly bit her lip. "Perhaps you should sit down. You look a bit feverish."

"No! I've too much to do. Beginning with these cinnamon buns. And a few other items, now that school is dismissed for the day." Moving quickly, Sarah headed for the bakeshop's exit. "Don't worry. I've got everything well in hand."

Skeptically, Molly shook her head. "I've seen your plans before. They're nearly as...imaginative as mine."

Hah. Her family was chock full of doubters. It was a good thing Sarah had faith enough for all of them.

She waved. "Wish me luck!"

"You don't need luck," Molly called. "You need a dose of common sense!"

But by then, Sarah was already making good her escape. The door shut behind her on a squeak of hinges and a thump. She clattered down the steps to her next destination.

At the apothecary, Sarah consulted confidentially with the pharmacist. She held up two bottles of elaborately labeled patent remedies, then gave him a hopeful look.

"Which of these would be best to give me spots?"

Frowning, he peered through his spectacles. "Spots?"

"Just minor ones. Nothing terribly gruesome." She thought about it. "Something...off-putting would do."

"Most young ladies want to remove their spots."

"That's fine for them. *I'd* like to add some, please."

She waited impatiently.

The pharmacist's expression suggested she was mad. He pointed to the bottle in her left hand. "That one has a quantity of lanolin in it. It might conjure up some blemishes for you, if you put enough on."

Excellent. She vowed to slather on handfuls. Beaming, Sarah placed the remedy on the counter, along with a jar of Miss Olga's Original All-Natural Wart Cure-All and Preventative.

"I'll take these."

At the mercantile, Sarah selected a length of hideous green flannel. She squinted at the grotesque purple flowers printed on it and decided it was perfect. Four yards were enough.

Next she sampled all the ladies' fragrances on display. The first smelled too lovely, similar to the lavender she used. The second smelled too sweet, a keen competitor for Molly's cones of baking sugar. The third smelled like a man's cologne. Frowning, Sarah turned the bottle so the label faced her. It *was* for men.

She considered it, then added it to her goods, as well.

Only a few more purchases remained. Those and a few fresh eggs to be claimed from Mrs. Harrison on her way home, that is. Feeling more hopeful than ever, now that she had nearly everything she needed to execute her plan, Sarah added a pair of thick wool socks to her load. She plucked a handful of garlic bulbs from the corner, then made her way past the store's potbellied stove to the barrel of crackers.

"Three pounds, please," she told the proprietor.

Then she was off to her mother's for a frenzied bout of sewing. If there was one person she could count on to help her with this dilemma, it was her mama. Especially now that her sisters' advice had turned out to be so foolhardy. *Their* counsel had only led to Daniel's pursuing her ever more boldly. Without his love, that was one thing Sarah could not withstand.

Satisfied that her own ingenuity would save the day, she gathered her bundled purchases in her arms. She waddled to the street as burdened as any pack mule. Now that her day of teaching was completed, her most important task lay ahead.

She had a husband to outwit.

Daniel was late coming home that night. He'd lingered apurpose at the smithy. A part of him wanted nothing more than to see Sarah and Eli—to take his wife in his arms and kiss her hello, to hoist his boy on his shoulders and then tickle him till he laughed near to puking. Those were the moments that made his life his own...that made his life a life.

Yet he'd stayed away as long as he could. Because the rest of him knew of a certainty that it was up to *him* to save them all from the dangers of "love." So Daniel had labored over his fire till long past sunset, diligently repairing metalwork and trying not to think of the family he was missing. But eventually he hung up his hammer. He faced the night instead.

This time of night, when Morrow Creek turned snug and all the families joined for their evening meal, was difficult for him. All his years as a bachelor, Daniel hadn't known the pleasures of having someone there waiting for him. Of seeing a lantern lit as he approached and knowing there'd be soft voices and laughter and togetherness inside his cramped household.

Now he did. And he could not claim any of it.

The real devil of it was, every day Daniel felt more drawn to his "convenient" wife. Every day he wanted her more. Every day he edged closer to something he knew could prove disastrous. For Sarah's sake— and Eli's—he had to hold firm. He had to resist. Otherwise, who knew what he'd feel compelled, like Lillian, to do?

At first, after his blurted-out confession of what his sister had done under the damnable influence of "love," Daniel had tried to stay away from Sarah. He had. But that had lasted him no more than half a day. Perhaps less. Thinking on it now, he gave a wry shake of his head.

Without her, he felt empty. 'Twas plain as that.

With that failure behind him, Daniel had reverted to his original plan. The fact of it was, he needed to assert his husbandly dominance over his household.

Otherwise, things would only become more complicated. He could not have his wife in charge! As Marcus and Jack had pointed out, seduction was his likeliest skill *and* his best chance of winning, besides.

Daniel hadn't given up hope of his seduction tactics working, either. Just yesterday, in fact, Sarah had been so preoccupied by an encounter between them near the water pump, she had mistakenly served him a biscuit. *With* honey. And she'd smiled at him, too. Four ticks of his pocket watch had passed before she'd realized the gesture lay at odds with her strike.

That was progress.

Feeling hopeful—and willing, with his gambler's heart, to take his chances on this night—Daniel strode inside his house. Eli ran to greet him, a toy train in hand and a bone-crushing hug in mind. Naturally enough, that turned into a rowdy mock wrestling match on the woven rag rug. Ten minutes later, Daniel found himself pinned by a triumphant little boy with eyes as brown as his own and an arrogance to match.

"I've got you!" Eli said. "You'll never escape now."

"Let me up, you hooligan."

The boy gave him a crafty look. "Say please."

Hellfire. Sarah's influence was everywhere. "Did Miss Crabtree tell you to say that?"

Eli shook his head. "Aunt Sarah did."

At that, all the fight went out of Daniel. He stared at the boy, agape with wonder. All these weeks later, Eli had finally given over to the woman who cared for him, who cooked endless mounds of stinky cabbage for him...who loved him.

"She did, did she?" With a scowl, Daniel pretended to consider it. "Well, then. I guess I'll have to...*tickle you!*"

He rose with a deafening roar that sent the cat fleeing beneath the sofa. Holding Eli in his arms, Daniel lumbered upright like a bear. He swung him to and fro by the armpits, then set him on his feet. The tickling started. They both collapsed again, laughing till their sides ached.

Gruffly, Daniel hugged him close. Eli's answering embrace warmed him in turn. Just for a minute—no more than that—he allowed himself to enjoy it. To lock it in his memory. The boy had a piece of his heart in his grubby fist, that was for certain.

Now on to more practical matters. "I could eat a two-ton buffalo. Hair, hooves and all." Sniffing, he rubbed his belly. "Where's our dinner?"

Eli shrugged. "I already ate mine. Aunt Sarah said to go ahead, since you were working at the smithy so late. But maybe there's something left over for you."

"All right. Go and finish with your trains. Then it's time to clean your teeth afore bed."

The boy gave a grudging nod. Daniel sent him to play. Then, drawing in a deep breath, he tucked in his mussed shirt. He raked his hand through his tousled hair. He rubbed his whiskers and verified them exactly prickly enough. Then he steeled himself.

It was time to confront the hardiest obstacle of all. The greatest challenge to his self-control. His wife.

He found her, befuddlingly enough, seated at the kitchen table with her feet propped on a chair and her father's *Pioneer Press* newspaper in hand. Her skirts billowed to the floor, looking somehow more voluminous than he remembered. A cup of something terrible-smelling sat at her elbow.

Daniel made a face. "What is that stench?"

Perkily, Sarah lowered her newsprint. "Hello, husband!"

He gawked. "What is that on your face? Did some ruffian hold you down and smear chicken droppings on you?"

Blithely, she touched the sticky-looking goo. She seemed uncommonly satisfied with it. "It is a beauty concoction. Made of miller's bran, whole eggs and a quantity of ground herbs."

He sniffed. No, the smell definitely came from her cup, not her face. "What are you doing with it?"

"Making myself more beautiful, of course. I intend to use it regularly from now on. *Extremely* regularly."

Daniel grunted. Drawn by a movement glimpsed from the corner of his eye, he glanced at Sarah's pert feet. Or at least at the place where her pert feet in their ladies' button-up shoes *usually* were found. Not tonight. Tonight, in their place, wiggled two bulky wool-shrouded *things*. Doubtless, given the vagaries of women's fashions, they were designed to make her head seem small by comparison.

He frowned in confusion.

"You don't need to become more beautiful," he managed, as he knew she expected. As, privately, he thought was true. "You look stunning already. Rivaling the ladies' pictures in *Godey's,* in fact. You could model dress patterns and the like."

"Honestly? Looking like this?"

Arching her eyebrows…no, more truly, her *muck pack* brows…Sarah regarded him. Skepticism emanated from her.

He could not lie. That was the first rule of honorably seducing a woman. Straight-faced, he pointed. "You may need to remove those…stockings first."

At that, she laughed. The stuff on her face crackled in reaction. Daniel recoiled. There were some things about living with a woman that, evidently, no one had warned him of.

He would *pound* Marcus Copeland when he had the chance.

"Sit down, sit down. I'll get you some tea."

Busily, Sarah stumped to the stove. Those had to be men's socks on her feet. They made her ankles look as big as an elephant's. Not that Daniel had ever seen an elephant in the flesh, but he had studied drawings of them in Sarah's schoolbooks. He reckoned the creatures could not be any baggier, bulkier or grayer around the ankles than his bride.

Kettle in hand, Sarah glanced coquettishly over her shoulder. Daniel knew what she wanted—what he'd given her for the past week or more. Gamely, he attempted to steal a forbidden glimpse of her ankles...wherever they were. Let no man claim Daniel McCabe was easily deterred from his goal.

Sarah did not appreciate his fortitude at all. In fact, she suddenly looked downright vexed.

She hobbled nearer and slid a cup beneath his nose. A horribly familiar stench wafted upward. It made his eyes water.

Daniel balked. "What the hell is this?"

"Brewed garlic tea. Triple strength. I understand it does wonders for the masculine constitution." Sweetly, Sarah offered him a spoon. "Sugar?"

Masculine constitution? Offended, he glared at her.

He didn't need any assistance with his constitution, damn it. He'd prove it to her, too. Just as soon as he managed to quit gawking at that concoction on her face, he would take her in his arms and kiss her. First he would need a face cloth.

Then something else occurred to him. "You just served me."

With a placid nod, Sarah settled on her chair.

Unbidden, his gaze went to her elephant feet. Strangely, they seemed almost endearing to him now. It was a brave woman who dared appear before a man dressed that way. She was one in a million. At the realization, Daniel put his chin in his hand. He smiled—unable to help it—fondly at her.

"Yes, I did serve you." She gave his smile a displeased glance. "The good news is, I've decided to resume cooking your meals, et cetera. Your dinner is in the oven, and you have a stack of mended shirts just there, on that chair."

She nodded to them.

Daniel could not believe his good fortune. Delighted, he picked up his shirts. They filled his arms in a clean, sweet-smelling mass.

"You are hugging them," Sarah observed.

He felt ridiculously enraptured. They were only laundered shirts, that was true. But still, Sarah had washed them for him. She had… "They're stiff as a board!"

"Are you criticizing my use of laundry starch?"

"No. Never." He petted the items, then wanted to grin like a loon when an unyielding sleeve poked out of the mass. In all his paltry attempts at laundering, he had never achieved this degree of fineness. He felt absurdly cared-for. "What is the bad news?"

Sarah hesitated, her beauty concoction gleaming thickly in the lamplight. Now that he'd become used to it, Daniel reflected, her face didn't look so bad. Beneath all the mess, he could still glimpse Sarah. His Sarah.

Driven by impulse, he put down his laundered shirts and leaned nearer. He swiped her chin.

She stared. "Did you just *taste* my beauty treatment?"

"Mmmm." He sucked his finger clean. "Needs salt." He settled back, folding his hands comfortably over his empty belly. "Now. You were telling me the bad news?"

"Yes." Sarah seemed befuddled. "The bad news."

She set aside her newspaper and accidentally elbowed a jar askew in the process. Daniel caught it just as it headed for the floor. He glanced at the fancy label.

Miss Olga's Original All-Natural Wart Cure-All and Preventative. Hmm. Poor Sarah. For her sake, he smiled and pretended not to have seen it. That, he reasoned, was what a good husband did.

"The bad news," she said, "is that I have a great deal to do at the schoolhouse for the next few weeks. There is the annual spelling bee to prepare for, and the holiday pageant, besides. I may be up late every night for a while. Burning the midnight oil, as they say."

"Fine. I'll keep you company."

"Oh, no." She waved her hand in dismissal, then rose to fetch his meal from the oven. Bearing it in her apron-shrouded grasp, she slid a plate of roasted beef and potatoes in front of him. "That won't be necessary. There's no sense keeping the whole household up at night."

"Not the whole household. Only me."

"It's my work. My responsibility. I'll do it."

"You might just find that your responsibilities are lessened soon." Winking at her, Daniel forked up some beef.

"What does that mean?"

"You'll see. Mmm. This is delicious." He caught her hand across the table and squeezed it. "Thank you."

Sarah looked taken aback. At least, he thought she did. It was hard to tell beneath all the stuff on her face. But, true to her nature, she recovered quickly enough.

"Well, enjoy your dinner. Take your time." Wriggling her hand from beneath his, she gathered her newspaper and a pile of wool with knitting needles poked through it. "I have much to do before bedtime."

He shot an appreciate gaze to her bosom. Blessedly, it featured no muck, nor a dingy gray covering. "Don't tire yourself overmuch. I have plans for you tonight."

Daniel waggled his eyebrows, making his romantic intentions plain. Sarah blanched. She glanced to her feet.

"But I look…"

She faltered. Her meaning was clear, though. She thought she looked unsightly.

Daniel didn't care. She was still Sarah. Warts, muck and elephant ankles could not change that.

"You look like yourself. The woman I plan to have our usual kissing lessons with in—" he consulted his pocket watch "—about forty minutes. Once Eli is asleep."

"You're serious."

He nodded, then returned to his meal.

"Horsefeathers!" she muttered, then stomped away.

A few moments later, Eli's loud chortles came from the far end of the house. Daniel guessed the boy hadn't seen Sarah's getup till now.

Smiling to himself, he went back to his dinner. He didn't know what his wife was playing at, but it was plain she was up to something. The funny thing was, Daniel almost looked forward to finding out what it was.

Filled with anticipation, Daniel carried a lantern to the chamber he shared with Sarah. Light bobbed along the hallway, illuminating the plain wood walls. Keeping his footsteps light, he traversed the short distance quietly. Eli was safely abed, and the house felt still. Daniel wanted it to stay that way.

He relished this time of night. Darkness meant he and Sarah would be together with no pretense between them. Climbing in bed beside her these days, he felt a curious sense of homecoming. It was strange, but there it was. He was not a man to question the truth, especially when it met him between warm sheets and an even warmer woman.

A sliver of light came from beneath their door. Good. That meant Sarah had waited for him. Tilting his head, Daniel lifted the latch. Inside, his wife sat propped on pillows in their bed, her face scrubbed clean. Thank heaven for small favors. He could not glimpse her feet, but he trusted she'd bared them for sleeping.

She bent her head industriously over her knitting, not seeming to notice his arrival. Daniel knew that would soon change. He set down his lantern, arranging it in place beside his washbasin. He cleared his throat.

Sarah did not so much as glance up. Her knitting needles flashed, fashioning what seemed to be a hideously ugly and very lengthy stocking. It occurred to him that she might be making yet another pair of elephant stockings—this time in mold green.

He had to stop her. "I guess I'll get undressed."

It was an announcement that never failed to stir her interest. Tonight, though, Sarah did not seem to hear him.

Frowning, Daniel flipped down his braces. He unbuttoned his shirt and pulled it over his head, being sure to flex his arms as he did. He tossed his shirt on the quilt, inches from Sarah's pile of green wool.

She went on knitting. Disbelieving, Daniel shed his undershirt and boots, then his trousers. He did it slowly, giving Sarah extra time to notice. By the time he'd stripped himself to his drawers alone, his remaining clothes were flung noticeably from the quilt to Sarah's bent knees to the bed post…and she'd progressed a few more rows on her socks.

Something was wrong. Daniel wasn't used to being ignored—at least not by women. And especially not while he stood in the lantern light practically naked. But to his surprise, Sarah seemed capable of it. While he stood there, first subtly posing with his arm on the bedpost and then with his leg propped on a stool, she didn't even stir in recognition of his manliness.

He felt thoroughly disgruntled.

He strode to the bed and yanked back the linens on his side, intending to get in and get on with his plans anyway. He had cuddling to get to, and soon. And after that, his favorite part of the night, kissing practice. But when he looked to Sarah's now-uncovered form...

"What is *that?*" he blurted.

"What do you mean?"

"That...*thing* you're wearing."

"Oh. This?" Sarah stroked her high-necked green flannel nightgown. "This is my new winter nightgown."

The thing bore several deep ruffles and a nausea-inducing print decorated with hundreds of purple flowers on a field of green. It had a prudish neckline that covered every inch of Sarah's enchanting bosom. Worst of all, it appeared to be fastened with at least sixty tiny buttons. Buttons too numerous for even the most patient man's hands.

"What—" He hesitated, feeling absurdly choked up at the loss of the sheer lacy gown he loved seeing her in. "What happened to your other nightgown?"

She shrugged. "I think I may be getting too plump for it."

Meaningfully, she reached for something on the night table. Spicy sweetness drifted toward him. For a moment, Daniel felt heartened, thinking it must be perfume of some kind. But then Sarah bit into it, and he recognized it for what it was.

A cinnamon bun.

She licked her fingers. "Mmm," she said with her mouth full. "I can't seem to get enough of these. This is my third one today! I'm afraid I'm going to get dreadfully fat."

He stared. *He* wanted to be the one to put that rapturous expression on her face. Not a stupid bakery bun.

"It's a good thing I've already snared myself a husband," Sarah went on blithely. "Now I can indulge to my heart's content and not worry about winding up a tubby old maid." Cheerily, she patted the mattress. "You go ahead and go to sleep. You won't disturb me. I've only got a bit more work to finish on my knitting, and my small lamp is fine for that."

He hesitated, baffled by her talk of plumpness. She looked wondrously fine to him. Sarah glanced up. Her gaze whisked over him, as though by accident, then returned to her handiwork. Daniel remembered he still wore nothing but his drawers and felt even more befuddled. Was *this* her only reaction to his near-nudity?

Had he somehow lost his appeal to women?

Heartily appalled at the notion, he got in bed, feeling he had no choice but to do so. For several minutes, Sarah knit vigorously beside him, pausing only to polish off another cinnamon bun. Crumbs scattered on his bare chest. Grumpily, Daniel brushed them off.

"What of our 'practice'?" he asked.

She shrugged. "It will have to wait for another night. As you can see, I am far too busy. And much too full of sweets."

"I'll change your mind." He rolled over. Smiling, he stroked his hand suggestively over her flannel-clad hip.

"Oh, Daniel. Honestly, you shouldn't...."

But gradually, as he caressed her, Sarah slowed her knitting. Her needles clacked at a lethargic rhythm, and she squirmed in the bed beside him. Daniel *hadn't* lost his ability to entice her, after all. Encouraged, he swept his palm to her daunting row of buttons.

If any man could defeat them, it was him.

"Ouch!" Feeling a sharp pain, he scowled at his hand. "Your damn nightgown gave me a splinter."

She blinked. Relief showed plain on her face as Sarah set aside her knitting. "Well, then. I'll just doctor you up! What you need is a good night's sleep to recover."

Grumbling, he watched her scurry for the basket

of remedies she kept on a corner shelf. Damnation. That nightgown of hers was a veritable man repellant. What had possessed her to put it on tonight, of all nights?

Daniel didn't know, but he had a few suspicions. All of them had to do with his success in wooing her.

Thoughtfully, he endured Sarah's fussing and bandaging. Imagining himself burying his wife's knitting needles, burning her new nightgown and buying every last cinnamon bun Molly's bakery produced helped greatly to distract him. Sarah might think she had deterred him, but Daniel knew better. This was only temporary. He would not give up that easily.

Especially not now, when her resistance all but proved the very thing he'd been hoping for.

He was winning.

Chapter Thirteen

When Daniel came to bed several evenings later, Sarah was ready for him. She'd had to nearly sprint through her chores to do so, but she beat him to their chamber. She felt determined to win this tussle between them. She would meet her husband on *her* terms and not be unsettled by his seduction tactics.

And she would make him love her, too.

She heard his footfalls outside their door and hurriedly grabbed a handful of the crackers she'd purchased. She crumbled them all over the quilt. Originally, she'd planned to eat them and produce the crumbs naturally. But after all the cinnamon buns she'd ingested in her attempts to make herself too plump for Daniel's liking, Sarah did not have the appetite to eat anything more.

Surrounded by cracker fragments, she fussed with the rag rollers in her hair. She adjusted the high neck of her new spinster's nightgown, then patted it in place. Given its coarse flannel and many buttons, it felt about as comfortable as a prickly pear corset, but it had been effective in deterring Daniel's too-rousing touch. For the past few nights, he'd only given her a brief kiss, a puzzled look and a strangely dispiriting "good night" before rolling over and falling asleep.

To be truthful, she missed his attentions, seductive and thought-scrambling though they might have been. She missed his touch and his smile, and even his kissing lessons. Without those things, her nights felt oddly…empty.

She prayed she was doing the right thing.

The door creaked open. Hastily, Sarah grabbed her knitting. She'd never excelled at women's handiwork. Unless Daniel sprouted an abnormally huge foot, in fact, he would never be able to wear the sock she'd been making. But he didn't need to know that, she reasoned. So long as she remained busy.

"Hello, husband!" With forced cheer, she held out a snack. "Would you like to join me in some crackers? They're crunchy and delicious."

"No." Daniel shook his head. "I am not hungry."

He began undressing, this time with less fanfare than he'd exhibited on previous evenings. Sarah couldn't help but sneak a peek at him, all the same. This activity of his was a particular favorite of hers—although she never would have admitted it to Daniel. Clothes rustled and flew. In the low lighting of their chamber, his muscles rippled with power. His skin gleamed, sun-browned and darker than her own.

In every way, her husband was a fit specimen of manhood. He was hardy and agile and plainly in his prime. To her eyes, he was also intensely beautiful. Glancing away between his shed articles of clothing—so he wouldn't catch her looking—required Sarah's most determined acts of will.

Silence descended. Daniel did not throw back the linens and shake his head at her prim nightgown, as had become his habit. She sensed him standing there, waiting.

"What's the matter?" Hopefully, she patted her face's coating of lanolin cream. It had turned out to be distressingly slow-acting in its effects. "Do I have spots?"

"I don't care if you do."

Oh, dear. Given the rumbling, purposeful tone in his voice, he meant it. Sarah didn't understand. She'd done all she could to seem unattractive to him—to deter his advances. She wanted Daniel to be forced into dealing with her on a non-physical basis. It was the only way she could retain enough sense to cope with him. But this…

Had he suddenly gone blind?

"You must be looking at my warts, then," she fibbed, staring fixedly at her knitting. It had gone slack in her hands. "I've been trying a new remedy—"

"You've never had warts."

This time, he sounded unnervingly certain. Exactly the way a man who'd known her since childhood, Sarah remembered too late, had a right to. Drat that wart removal remedy. Could it have made Daniel guess what she was up to? Impossible.

"They're...a recent development. Perhaps they were brought on by the strain of preparing for the school spelling bee."

He grunted, sounding surpassingly unconcerned as he turned back the bed linens. "Don't worry. I'll wager you'll have help with that soon."

Again with that promise. What did he mean?

Before she could ask, Daniel got in bed, upsetting her balance in more ways than one. The mattress dipped beneath his weight, and his nearness made her forget what they'd been discussing. It made her heart patter instead.

Stoutly ignoring it, Sarah reached for the bottle beside her nightly cinnamon bun. It contained the last item in her arsenal. Hastily, she dabbed on some of its contents. She thrust her wrist toward Daniel.

"Here. Smell my new perfume. It's delightful."

He inhaled. "It's bay rum hair tonic. For men."

Oh. A glance at the bottle confirmed it. A nervous titter escaped her. If that was true, then why did Daniel smell it again? Why did his lips brush tenderly over her wrist as he did so? Why...*oh, my!*...

did he press a kiss just at the spot where her pulse beat strongest?

Could she possibly have reckoned wrong?

"You seem to like it well enough," she pointed out.

He glanced up at her, glorious in his near-nudity and completely unselfconscious about its effects upon her. He did not release her wrist. Indeed, Daniel inhaled again, and the sensual way he did so was impossible to ignore.

He smiled. "I like the woman beneath it."

"You can't possibly smell...me...beneath that stuff." Forgetting she meant to ignore his appearance, however compelling, Sarah caught an accidental glimpse of his brawny torso and acres of bare skin. Flustered, she looked away. "It's much too strong for that."

"Nothing is strong enough to keep me away from you."

Her heart leaped again. Foolish, *foolish* of her to hope he meant those words. But still, Sarah couldn't help it.

Struggling to retain her composure, she patted her armored nightgown. Its fabric felt so coarse, it probably *had* given him a splinter. She felt sorry for that.

"I never meant to wound you, you know," she blurted. "With my new nightgown, I mean."

Oh, dear. She hadn't meant to admit that at all.

"I know." *Stroke, stroke* went his fingers over her wrist. "It was my own fault. I couldn't keep my hands from you."

At the husky note in his voice, at the caress of his hand, Sarah felt herself tauten with anticipation. Why was Daniel being so nice to her, anyway? Why wasn't he repelled by her bay rum scent, her wool-shrouded ankles, her hair curlers?

Abruptly remembering them, she patted the multiple pieces of muslin she'd twisted in her hair. Without Molly's ever-primping example, she'd never have thought of them. But since she had…

"I hope my hair curlers don't bother you." She looked a fright in them, and she knew it. "The rags simply can't be helped. I wasn't terribly adept with the hot tongs, and curls are all the fashion right now, you know."

Daniel threaded his fingers between hers. Absently, he stroked his thumb up and down hers, making her shiver.

"I wouldn't think a woman so eager for spots and warts would care about fashion," he remarked. Tellingly.

"I don't," she prevaricated. Desperately. She was so close to weakening. To losing her resolve altogether. "It's only… I want to look nice for you."

"Mmm. You always look nice to me."

It was true, Sarah realized as she stared at his absorbed expression. It was as though Daniel saw her clunky "beauty" implements and treatments, saw her ugly nightgown and her curling rags and her cracker crumbs…and cared not a whit. He *knew* her, she understood just then, in a way no one else ever had. And he accepted her, too.

A tiny shimmer of hope came to life inside her.

"You look good to me, too," she confessed.

Drat it! She hadn't meant to admit that either.

He arched his brow. Seductively, his gaze met hers. "Then look your fill."

Unabashedly, Daniel shoved aside the bed linens. Without their partial covering, he appeared magnificent and manly. Sarah knew it was dangerous to gaze at him so openly, especially in fulfillment of such an invitation, but she simply couldn't help it. Not when intriguing sprinklings of dark hair embellished his muscular chest and legs. Not when his arms looked as large as tree branches, perfect for holding her. Not when nothing but those well-fitted underdrawers hid the most secret parts of him from her view.

She guessed, trying to regain a measure of composure, that blacksmithing did wonderful things for the masculine form. Either that, or Daniel had simply been unfairly blessed.

He grinned at her gawking, and she decided the latter was definitely the case. The scoundrel knew she liked looking her fill of him. He'd baited her into doing it.

Too late, Sarah whisked her gaze upward. Her mouth felt dry. Curiously, her skin *hummed* all over her body, warm and tingling and somehow needful of touching. She would never have believed merely *looking* could have such an effect on a person.

Daniel's too-knowing gaze met hers, taking in her eyes, her parted lips. "Now you know how I feel," he told her soberly, "when I look at you."

Oh, but that couldn't be true. Especially lately. Feeling even more muddled, she told him as much. "Not when *you* look so… Well, the way you do. And *I* look so…"

"Perfect. So perfect and so…Sarah." He plucked her knitting from her lap. Dropped it to the floor. "You won't be needing this anymore tonight."

Dumbfounded, she stared at her discarded wool. Her knitting needles jabbed outward at mocking angles. "I wasn't done with that. I—" She struggled to recall what she was supposed to be doing. "I have a stocking to finish."

"No doubt you will finish it, with a determination like yours. But not tonight. Tonight, I want your full attention."

"What for?"

He sighed, looking beleaguered. "So much conversation. I should have known I could not just *do* this."

"Do what?"

"*This,* for a start."

Daniel put his hands gently to the sides of her head, right over her rag rollers. Then, *then,* he kissed her.

Caught by surprise, Sarah muttered a protest against his mouth. An instant later, helplessly, she melted against the pillows at her back. Ahhh. It had been so long since he'd done this. Especially this way—so thoroughly, so expertly, so hungrily. She'd forgotten how much she'd yearned for it.

She found herself clutching his shoulders, every inch the wanton, when at last their kiss ended. She made a distressed face, unable to prevent a grumble of disappointment.

"Hmm. You haven't forgotten how to kiss," he observed teasingly. "Only how to keep your food in your mouth."

Demonstrating, he swept a small mountain of crumbled crackers from the sheets. They pinged to the floorboards for later sweeping, and Sarah felt herself flush. Daniel caught her. A smile quirked the corner of his mouth.

"I forgot to ask you." His eyes grew wide with sham-serious consideration. "Can you wait for your cinnamon bun tonight?"

What? Who cared for food at a moment like this? Sarah needed a chance to recover, though, so she grasped at the opportunity he'd offered and did her best with it.

"Mmm. I don't know." She pretended to ponder the question. Thinking proved difficult while her heart still pounded from the last kiss they'd shared. "Those cinnamon buns are awfully tasty. You know I relish my occasional treats."

In truth, although they *were* delicious, she never wanted to see another cinnamon bun in her life. Ever. But now she was caught in a trap of her own making. Stupid, *stupid* plan.

"That's too bad," Daniel mused. "I had a different sort of treat in mind."

His deep voice, so rich with promise, thrilled her.

"What…kind of treat?" She hoped it involved kissing.

He gave a cavalier wave as he settled beside her, his head sharing her pillow. "You're not interested. It's all right. You can carry on knitting."

Knitting. As though she cared to knit one or purl two.

Disappointment assailed her. The flush of victory she'd felt earlier didn't seem to matter one whit now—not while Daniel seemed to have given up the fight altogether. What was wrong with him? How could he kiss her so stirringly, only to abandon the effort moments later?

"I *might* be interested," she allowed.

Not replying, Daniel flung his arm overhead, comfortably settling in. Absently, he played with one of her curlers. She could not believe he wasn't horrified at the thought of touching them. She could not believe he intended to withhold his "treat" from her.

"I'm *definitely* interested," she tried.

That moved him. A little. "Hmm. Well, the treat was going to be a kiss—"

Yes! She had guessed correctly.

"—but you don't seem interested. Go ahead. Knit."

Was he deaf? She looked at his latest offhanded wave and wanted to tackle him to make him stop the gesture. Daft man.

"I told you I was interested. Twice."

A low rumble of assent. "I'll tell you what. You can kiss me," Daniel offered generously. "If you want."

She turned her head. His profile greeted her, obdurately male and typically handsome. His nose jutted at a belligerent angle. His mouth pursed in thought, finely shaped and, she knew, marvelously talented. He appeared both cocksure and curiously… hopeful?…at the same time.

You can kiss me. If you want.

Sarah *did* want. She wanted very much.

"I wouldn't know how," she protested, but it was only an excuse. They both knew it. The knowledge was there in Daniel's face as he went on gazing at the ceiling.

"I need you, Sarah," he said simply. "I need you, and I need to know you want me. The same way I want you." He hesitated, not looking at her. "These past few days—"

"Have been foolish," she said, understanding just then exactly how foolish. She'd set out to prove something to Daniel. She'd only succeeded in teaching something to herself. Something remarkable.

Only a man who loved her—who truly *loved* her— would still want her now, she realized. Only a man who loved her would see the real her, would look beyond her nightgown, her beauty treatments, her socks and her curlers and everything else. She'd tried her best to deter him.

Thrillingly, she'd failed.

That could only mean one thing. Even if Daniel couldn't bring himself to say the words, as Sarah moved to meet him, she knew then that he felt them.

Poised on her forearms, her nightgown billowing behind her, she stared at him in wonder. Although he said nothing more, Daniel had never before seemed so vulnerable to her. So open. For the first time, Sarah felt she held a piece of his heart in her keeping. All she wanted to do was to treasure it.

"I do need you," she whispered, and dared to press

a kiss to his waiting mouth. The motion felt awkward, unfamiliar, until Daniel moaned and cupped the back of her head in his hand, holding her to him. His reciprocity made it right.

"I do want you," she said, and braved a trembling touch to his face. The slant of his cheekbones, the arch of his brow, the bristly texture of his skin all felt different, forbidden, until Daniel smiled and covered her hand with his own, making sure she went on touching him. His assurance made it perfect.

"And no matter what else, I do love you," she said, and risked laying herself half atop him in an untried caress. Her breasts pushed against his chest. Her bent knee touched his thigh. The closeness they shared felt almost overwhelming, nearly too exciting, until Daniel looked into her eyes and kissed her back, quieting her fears. His sharing made it love.

"I do. I do love you," she said, needing him to know it in the same way she needed to arch against him, to touch him, to breathe. "I love you."

"Ahhh. Sarah. Then let me love you back." He brought her forehead gently to his in that familiar, uniquely caring way he had. Their gazes met. "Let me love you. I know I don't have the words, but—"

"Shhh." She kissed him, feeling better at it now. "I know. It's all right."

At that, he seemed relieved. A little of the cockiness

returned to his expression, and Sarah couldn't help but love it. She'd always been drawn to his surety, his strength, his way of taking life lightly.

"Are you sure?" Daniel asked, giving her one final chance to resist. "Because stopping won't be easy, after—"

"If it's not easy, just beg me," Sarah said, striving to sound ever-so-sensible. "And then we'll stop. Someone once told me there is plenty of begging involved with these sorts of romantic moments, although I've yet to experience it myself."

He grinned. Wolfishly. "That sounds like a challenge."

"*That* sounds like you're eager to fulfill it." She smiled, feeling all the more a seductress as she grew accustomed to the press of their bodies, the heat of their togetherness, the role of the pursuer. "But if not, there is always knitting. You might enjoy it. Wool, needles—"

Daniel growled and kissed her. She squealed as he squeezed her middle in his powerful hands, then yelped aloud as he lifted her higher. After a stunned moment, Sarah found herself straddling him, her scratchy nightgown covering most—but not all—of her legs.

His gaze went straight to her bared knees, then roved higher. He swallowed hard. "Do I look like I want to knit?"

"No. You look like you want to kiss me again." Sweet heaven, she hoped he kissed her again. "But looks are often deceiving, you know."

"Hmm. I reckon you'll have to wait to find out which one I'd rather do, then."

Hah. "That's what you think."

Emboldened by his love, Sarah knew she was more than ready for this game. Feeling no shyness at all, no hesitation, she grabbed handfuls of her hem. Daringly, she lifted her nightgown. It flew to the bedpost, then slumped to the floorboards to join Daniel's discarded britches.

He stared. "You vixen! I wondered how you didn't wind up scraped to pieces by that attacking night-gown of yours."

Flirtatiously, she smoothed her lacy white gown in place. "Yes. It felt far more comfortable to wear this beneath it."

Daniel's appreciative gaze was that of a man glimpsing a long-lost friend. He captured a bit of filmy white between his fingers.

"From now on, wear only this," he ordered. "Or wear nothing at all."

"Yes, sir."

His grin widened. "I like the sound of that. All right. You can kiss me again."

Feeling beyond willing, Sarah did. With her hands pressed to Daniel's broad chest for balance, she leaned closer. Her mouth touched his, and she was lost. All banter, all playing, all sense of mastery flew from her head as their kiss went on and on.

This was what it felt like to share a kiss in love, she realized, and wanted to sigh with the wonder of it. Daniel's care, his attention, his *need* were all for her, and in that moment, Sarah savored them all.

"Very good," he managed when they were through. Despite his carelessly said words, his voice sounded throaty and needful. "But I'll need another to be sure."

She gave it gladly, this time splaying herself flat against him as their mouths met. Daniel felt warm and solid and beloved beneath her, and her whole body tingled in the places where they touched. Sarah knew she needed more. In frustration, she wriggled atop her husband, then stopped in shock as another, warmer and harder and more compelling, part of him met her sheer-gowned backside.

He groaned. "Careful. Unless you mean for this to end too quickly between us, you'd best stop that."

"What?" Arching her brow, Sarah swiveled her hips the merest degree. It was all she dared. "This?"

Another groan, louder this time. Hearing it filled her with a surpassing sense of feminine power—and a wonderful sense of longing, too. Daniel wanted her. He wanted *her*.

"Yes, that. Stop wiggling. I can't stand it."

She couldn't let that pass. "Stand…this?"

Fiercely, he grabbed her hips. His hands clamped in an especially sensitive—and until now, un-noticed—spot. Sarah gasped. Having him touch her there aroused all sorts of fluttery feelings in her belly and lower. Heat pooled in the same places her virginal nightgown did. She scarcely knew how to express everything that was happening to her.

Somehow, Daniel knew. "You're blushing."

She couldn't speak.

He lifted his hand, freeing one side of her from those engrossing sensations. Before Sarah could take any relief in that, though, Daniel traced his fingertips over her partly bared bosom. He examined her there, appearing fascinated.

"You're blushing here, too."

"I can't help it. Oh, Daniel. How long will this go on?"

His rakish grin surprised her. "As long as you want."

"Oh." Restlessness seized her, making her impa-tient for…something. Sarah didn't know what. "Then please—"

"I'd say that sounds like pleading. Almost—" his brow lifted "—begging."

"Not fair!" she cried. "You have me at a disad-vantage."

His expression sobered. His gaze met hers as he

lifted his hand from her bosom to her cheek. "Ahh, Sarah. You have no idea."

She couldn't reason what he meant, but the look on his face bespoke love. Devotion. Wanting. Those were all she could have hoped for, so Sarah didn't question him any further.

"Please love me," she whispered.

Everything in her heart agreed. So when Daniel tenderly turned her in his grasp, she let him lay her down on the soft, warm linens. When he kissed her, she opened her arms and held him to her. When he placed his hand beneath her nightgown and slowly, slowly slid it past her calves, her knees, her thighs… she welcomed him.

Finally, after countless kisses, he coaxed her upright to sit. Although Sarah didn't know why, she did so agreeably. Trustingly. She found herself with both legs parted on either side of his torso, meeting him chest to chest. She couldn't move her gaze from Daniel's rugged, handsome face. Never had he seemed more wonderful to her…never had he felt more necessary.

He showed her his intentions. Sarah nodded, wanting this new and magical time between them to go on and on. An instant later, as she'd known it would, her nightgown whisked over her body. The cooling touch of the night air gave her goose bumps—or maybe her husband's touch was responsible for that. Either way, she longed for more.

Her wedding-night gown dropped to the bedside in a flurry of white, as tangible as the fears she'd discarded with it. Bravely, Sarah faced Daniel again. Under his loving gaze, she lay back against the pillows.

"You are beautiful." He touched her with awe, his deft hands skimming her bared curves with something approaching reverence. He shook his head. "Too beautiful for me, by far."

"No!" Fearing Daniel would stop, Sarah reached for his hand. She wove their fingers together, squeezing hard. "I'm just me. Just Sarah. You know me."

His gaze lifted. "You were never 'just Sarah.' To me, you were always more than that. I should have told you sooner. The funny thing is…" His smile quirked. "I only just realized it myself."

Tears stung her eyes, forcing her to blink them away. To know that he *saw* her, that he *loved* her, was more than she'd ever truly dared to wish for. Sarah touched him in amazement. She knew she would never be the same again.

"You know I've always loved you," she said. Her voice quivered with the magnitude of the admission, with the thrill of finally being able to give him the truth, once and for all. "Always, always. It was always you, Daniel."

He looked humbled. Moved. Gratified, all at the same time. Giving a hoarse cry, he buried his face in her neck. He squeezed her tightly, holding her safely to him. For a man so unused to emotion as Daniel, his embrace was a telling thing. It communicated his feelings as strongly as any words would have done—more so, Sarah thought as she wrapped her arms around him.

He kissed her then, a hot press of his lips to her neck. Then another. Another. They came faster and faster, each kiss more passionate, more intense, than the first. She shivered beneath them, losing herself in feverish explorations of his naked back, his muscular arms, his hair-prickly chest. She arched higher, needing to be closer, and Daniel answered with a kiss fully on her mouth.

Skin to skin they pressed together, Sarah writhing with a need she didn't quite understand. All she knew for certain was that Daniel would fulfill it. He ground against her in his turn, seeming unable to stop himself. Every hot press, heady with the hard, exciting feeling of his manhood against her thigh, intrigued her more.

"You should be naked, too," she managed, gasping.

Within seconds, he'd complied. "Yes, ma'am."

His words echoed her earlier bantering with him, making Sarah feel safe. Comfortable. Beyond ready. This was Daniel. *Daniel.* If anyone would be the first one—the only one—to love her, it was him. And now *he* was ready for that, too.

"Don't be shy. Have a look," he urged. "You know you want to, wife." He posed beside the bed, lingering just for an instant, waiting impatiently. When she glanced up, he tilted his head. "Wife," he mused. "I like the sound of that."

"So do I," she declared. Then, bravely, she peeked.

Her glimpse of him was brief. She had a shocked impression of size and heft, of the sheer impossibility of what she knew they were about to attempt, before Daniel ended her view. He joined her in their bed and kissed her. The rascal plied his kisses so thoroughly that Sarah forgot her worries over what they planned altogether.

All she knew was the deep, delightful angle of his mouth, the sinful swirl of his hands on her breasts, the murmured praise he offered as he encountered every unexplored part of her. He took blatant pleasure in kissing every inch, in touching and squeezing and admiring. His talented hands were everywhere, bringing her shudders of yearning. How he aroused such feelings, she'd never know.

"After this, I'll never want to wear clothes again." She panted, holding his shoulders to keep her steady in the whirl of sensation he'd created. "Since you like me so well naked."

Daniel paused with his head near her belly. His

answering smile was for her alone, and all the more precious for it.

"If you're trying to make me disagree..." He kissed her navel, then pronounced it delicious. "You're failing."

She quivered. The fluttery feeling inside her grew stronger, encouraged by his attention. Her whole body felt powerfully drawn to get closer. *Closer.*

"After this," Sarah persisted breathlessly, "I'll—"

"After this," he promised, offering a scandalous wink to make up for his interruption, "you'll know what it is to be loved. And well."

As sure as he'd predicted it, she did. Shockingly, uninhibitedly, Daniel showed her all the ways he could love her. He stroked her till she shook. He kissed her all over. He touched her in places no other man ever had or would, and all the while, Sarah welcomed him. By the time he'd made his way to the most private parts of her, she had no sense left at all.

"Please, please," she begged. "I need—"

"I know," he said, "and soon—"

Whatever else he said was lost to her. All at once, Sarah's body arched in a moment of perfect pleasure, suspending her between everything she knew and everything she needed. She moaned, unable to help herself. This was...this was...

Bliss. Crying out, she clutched at Daniel. She

squeezed her eyes tightly shut and held him, riding out the incredible sensation. When at last it spiraled away from her, leaving her spent and breathless and pulsing, she looked up to see him watching her with raw need.

"Oh, Daniel. That was…"

"Perfect." He stroked her rag-rolled hair from her face, then kissed her again. He sounded breathless, as though he'd run a long way to find her in their bed. "Ahhh, Sarah."

In his voice, she heard everything she needed. Love and wanting and togetherness. She pulled him closer, opening herself to him, and her reward was a union far more remarkable than any they'd shared till now. Preparing her with whispered words and a gentle beginning, Daniel settled himself between her thighs. Finally, *finally,* he made their coupling complete.

An intense fullness gripped her. She gasped in surprise, her eyes widening. She never would have predicted *this*. This felt…unlike anything she'd ever experienced.

Daniel stilled immediately. He watched her with obvious concern. The muscles in his arms corded with the exertion of holding himself unmoving within her, of denying himself—them—something remarkable.

"Is this all right? Sarah? If it's too much, I'll—"

"No. No." She shushed him with a kiss, drawing him closer with her arms around his shoulders. She wanted this. Wanted him. To know that they were one was all she'd ever hoped for. "It's perfect. *You're perfect.*"

His face eased, gladness taking the place of his concern. "Then hold on to me, wife. We're only beginning."

His caring made their loving easy. His skill made it beyond pleasurable. Only a few heartbeats had passed before Sarah realized something truly unbelievable—this lovemaking of theirs could get better and better. With a hoarse moan, Daniel took them both to new heights, to raptures that made her clutch him still harder…that made him cry out and stiffen against her, thrusting again and again.

At long last he slumped against her, his heart thumping wildly. "Ahhh, Sarah. You are wonderful." He offered her a smile, one as wicked and as tantalizing as any she'd ever seen from him. "I don't think I can ever let you go."

She kissed him. "There will never be a need." She meant it with all her heart. "Never, never, never."

With a gusty sigh, Daniel took her in his arms. He rolled them both to their favorite cuddling position. Sarah happily wiggled her backside in place against him, loving the way he made her feel safe and beloved and cozy. Tonight she lay with a changed man. From here on, everything would be different.

Daniel loved her. He *loved* her!

He hadn't said the words, it was true. But in light of everything they'd shared, Sarah could not believe that mattered. Not truly. Daniel loved her. Their lives would be wonderful now. She couldn't wait to get started.

But first...a tremendous yawn overtook her.

"Tired already?" Daniel asked. Humor sounded in his voice—humor, and something else. Something intriguing. He trailed his fingertips over her middle, then lower. "If I can't keep you awake till nearly sunrise, I haven't done my job properly."

Oh, my. Incredibly, another thrill shook her. Sarah turned her head. "Sunrise? We have work to do and Eli to care for. Our chores will be waiting."

"They'll have to wait longer," Daniel said, and kissed her into a willingness to stay awake...forever, if necessary.

Chapter Fourteen

"*You* seem happy this morning," Sarah remarked.

Smiling and lively, she spooned a tremendous quantity of scrambled eggs on Daniel's plate. Her bustle swayed as she worked. He felt his gaze drawn to it—drawn to her—and couldn't help but grin.

"Why shouldn't I be happy?" He rubbed his freshly shaved jawline and regarded her with satisfaction. "I've got the best wife in the territory *and* the drowsiest rooster."

The blessed animal had actually crowed late for once, allowing Daniel a chance to sleep longer. Refreshed, he'd coaxed Sarah into another round of loving at sunrise. She'd proved a natural talent at kissing and caressing, at giving pleasure and—most importantly to him—at receiving it.

It was no wonder their arrangement was turning out so well, he mused now. He'd found a friend, a wife *and* an uncomplicated lover, all in one. To be sure, he felt a lucky man.

With that thought in mind, Daniel relaxed in his chair, watching Sarah. She puttered beside him in a kitchen turned brilliant with sunshine, arranging his toasted bread just so. A knowing grin enlivened her face. It made her seem surpassingly beautiful, as did her simple care for him. She was a woman unlike any he'd ever known.

"I hope you're hungry," she chattered, ladling on still more eggs before returning her skillet to the stovetop. "I seem to have lost track of how many eggs I was cracking this morning. There's a veritable mountain here, and sausage besides. I don't know what's the matter with me."

"I do." He eyed her confidently, pleased with both of them. "'Tis related to your husband's skills in the bedroom."

"Daniel, hush!" Her eyes sparkled prettily. "Eli's just in the next room, practicing for the spelling bee before school. He might come in. He might hear you talking so—"

"Wickedly? Appreciatively?" Daniel felt a devilish smile quirk his mouth, and knew he'd never met a morning with more robust good cheer. "Truthfully?"

Sarah pursed her lips in pretend chagrin.

"You know," he observed thoughtfully, "when you do that with your mouth, it only makes me want to kiss you."

"I'd say *you* have had enough kissing," she told him mischievously. "Your lips will fall plumb off if you persist."

"Come here." He felt giddy with joy. "I'll risk it."

"Eat your eggs."

Saucily, she sashayed to the stove. Doubtless, her knowledge that he savored every move put extra vigor in her steps. That side-to-side swish of her hips entranced him. Sarah returned with coffee in hand and slid the cup before him.

"Eat," she urged. "Your eggs are getting cold."

"I don't care. I've got other things to think about."

Proving it, Daniel reached unerringly to her skirts. A handful of shapely female backside met his grasp. He gave a hearty squeeze, loving the way Sarah felt. Loving...*her,* almost. Or at least loving her as much as he would have dared. If he'd believed in such nonsense.

Today, he felt too lighthearted to worry over it.

She squealed. "Daniel!"

"What? Are you tender? Did I hurt you?"

"No." A blush colored her cheeks. "It's just that I thought...with these wild curls in my hair..."

He perused them, noticing her hairstyle for the

first time. Truthfully, the top of her head was not the first place his attention had gone this morning. Studying her now, Daniel saw that tendrils of corkscrew hair sprang all around her head, barely contained by her chignon.

"You look…vivacious," he said.

"I look crazy!" she fretted. "Absolutely ridiculous. I *knew* I should have taken time to remove those rag curlers last night! Now the curls are set and won't cooperate."

Ineffectually, Sarah shoved a coil in position.

"You were distracted last night." He said it soothingly. Or perhaps wolfishly, with fond memories of those "distractions" she spoke of. Daniel couldn't tell for certain and couldn't be bothered to decide. He felt exactly that carefree. "Leave your hair as it is. I like it."

Suddenly, she looked inspired. "I'm going to dunk my head in the washbasin! That will solve the problem for certain."

"Here, now." Trying to sound stern, Daniel caught her hand in his. He cupped Sarah's chin. "I thought we'd settled all that. You look fine to me, just as you are."

"But I—"

"But nothing. Believe me. I'll show you."

"You're just being nice. Because I gave you extra eggs."

He frowned. Silly woman. Didn't she know when he meant what he said?

"You do enjoy a nicely scrambled egg," she persisted.

"I enjoy *you*," he said deliberately. Before Sarah could get away, Daniel pulled her onto his lap. The press of her body against him made him feel contented...nigh foolish with the aftereffects of last night.

He gave her a resounding kiss, one meant to give proof to his words. He found himself gazing into her lovely eyes and then giving her another kiss...just because he wanted to.

"No more nonsense. Stay and eat breakfast with me."

"Oh, Daniel." She caressed his face, her freckled features softening as she looked at him. "You really *are* a different man today."

He didn't know what that meant. But he didn't care overmuch, either. Everything was fine. Better than fine, now that Sarah had stopped resisting him. Now that he'd succeeded in seducing them both.

"I'm a *sore* man," he teased, wincing as he wriggled in his chair. "I swear, you've done me in, wife."

Sarah gasped and gave him a playful swat. Chuckling, Daniel kissed her again in retribution.

Before he knew it, though, that kiss deepened. It became something more compelling by far, and much more necessary. With abandon, he delved his hands in her crazy woman's hair and moaned his enjoyment.

He should have been incapacitated, Daniel knew. Unable to rise to the occasion or, at the least, unwilling to subject himself to any more romantic shenanigans. But he wasn't. This sensation of needing, of wanting, of *caring* was the most remarkable thing. He enjoyed it immensely.

It was true that parts of him, lately unused, now felt *eagerly* used near to chafing. But somehow, Sarah inspired him. He wanted to see her smile. If the cost of that was a tender and overworked manhood, he would gladly pay it.

"Do me in again," he growled, filling his palms with her soft hips and wads of skirts. "Again and again and ag—"

"You're insatiable!" She wrapped her arms around his neck, not seeming the least bothered by that fact. "A person would think you'd been denied affection for years."

"I have." He said it soberly, only then realizing the truth of it. "Only I didn't know it."

Sarah smiled. "Hah. After all those women who chased you? Who *you* chased back? Pshaw. You've had more than your share of everything."

"I did not have you. Today that's all that matters."

"Oh." Her eyes turned misty. "Daniel, I—"

"That, and these eggs." Grinning, he released her. He eagerly picked up his fork. "I find I'm starving. Did you say there are sausages, too?"

He tried a bite, groaning his delight. Not only was Sarah a perfect wife, a helpmeet, a lover and a friend, she was also a cook beyond compare. Daniel caught her watching him with a wifely interest and patted the chair beside his. He winked.

"You'd better join me soon. Else everything will be gone."

By the time Eli joined them for his walk to school, the plates were scraped clean, the forks were abandoned and Daniel had a lapful of Sarah again. He kissed her soundly, laughingly aware of Eli's little-boy protests.

"Stop those retching sounds, boy," he commanded. "Someday you might not mind so much, when you have a lady of your own."

"I'd rather eat dirt," Eli told him.

They all gathered their hats and coats and headed off to their days, Sarah and Eli tromping toward the schoolhouse and Daniel striding toward the smithy. He'd swear that he whistled a happy tune the whole way.

"I mean it, Grace," Sarah told her sister at lunchtime, where they sat sharing a noontime meal at her schoolhouse desk. "Everything is wonderful now. Even better than I'd imagined."

"Better than *you'd* imagined? Now that's saying something."

"Yes, it is." Blithely, Sarah plucked a bite of ham from her sandwich. It tasted as delicious as anything she'd ever eaten. In fact, everything around her seemed superlatively good. "See? Even your dour moods can't bring me low today. That is how happy I am."

Grace gave her a suspicious look. "Have you been sampling patent remedies again? Tippling from Daniel's whiskey?"

"No." She gazed at her students, making sure they behaved. Outside, the mild sunshine turned the snowy landscape crystalline and left frost melting on the windowpane. "But Daniel has come around, and he is all I ever wanted."

"You want your schoolwork, too! Don't you?"

"Of course. I feel a burst of pride and accomplishment every time I walk in the door here. Every time I greet my students or see one of them succeed." Sarah knew it was true and relished every minute. "But don't you see? Now I have so much more! A husband who loves me, a warm household of my own, even a little boy who feels nearly my own son." Sarah gave Eli a fond look. "It's more than I ever dreamed of."

"Dreams can't be trusted, Sarah." An unaccountably

solemn look crossed her sister's face. Grace ducked her head, brushing bread crumbs from her skirts. "Even you know that."

Astonished—and more than a little concerned—Sarah regarded her sister. "Of course they can. Why would you say such a thing?"

"I only mean that you should watch yourself. Still. A man like Daniel can't be trusted."

"A man like—" Gawking, Sarah broke off. Then the truth of the situation struck her. "You mean a man like Jack Murphy can't be trusted, don't you? Grace…" She nudged her sister with her shoulder, hoping to jolly her out of her bad humor. "Come along. Have out with it! Why don't you simply tell him how you feel? Heaven knows you're forthright enough about everything else."

"Tell him how I feel?" A snort. "I don't know what you mean."

But as Grace repacked the remnants of her boxed lunch, her fingers trembled the tiniest telltale bit. And as she arranged everything just so, her usual composure seemed shaken. For a person as meticulous as Grace ordinarily was—with her tucked-in shirtwaist, her no-nonsense chignon and her laced shoes meant for bicycling—those signs were alarming.

"I don't even approve of Jack Murphy," she insisted. "He is too frivolous by far, and all the more eager to spread that frivolity around, too. Dance-hall ladies, indeed. And an acting troupe is coming through, too! Did you know, he even has a marked fondness for practical jokes?"

"Hmm. Were you a victim of one?"

Grace looked shocked. "He promised he wouldn't—!" She stopped herself. "The man is a menace, plain and simple."

Sarah hid a smile. She wondered mightily which of the saloonkeeper's jests had snared her sister. She would have loved to have been a fly on the wall during *that* occasion.

"It might do you good to take life less seriously."

"Hah! Now you sound like *him*."

"It's true. Besides, you might find that you enjoy frivolity. You never know what you're capable of until you love someone."

"Apparently *you* were capable of going on strike," Grace pointed out. "Or have you forgotten that?"

"That was a mistake." Dreamily, Sarah hugged herself. "Go on, Grace. Try something new, why don't you? You just might surprise yourself."

"I *do* have a new women's suffrage campaign about to begin." Grace seemed as ridiculously cheered by the notion as only she could have been. "Also, my ladies' bicycling club has a jaunt planned for spring, and I'm considering a temperance rally for after New Year's Day. Let Jack Murphy make a joke of *that!*"

Sarah feared he just might. That was simply how contrary men could be. "Well, I wish you luck with all of it. As for my part, now that my home life is settled, I have grand plans for the schoolroom. I wonder...do you think a class play might fare well?"

Grace seemed interested. "What did you have in mind?"

"Oh, I don't know. Hmm." Sarah slapped on a sham-innocent look. "*The Taming of the Shrew*, perhaps?"

Another snort. Her sister stood. "*That's* one piece of work that should be well forgotten about. Hah! As though a man might actually need to *tame* a woman. The very notion is preposterous."

Sarah widened her eyes, nodding complacently.

But as Grace hurried into her cloak and headed out of doors with her head held high—doubtless preparing to do battle with one particularly charming, ne'er-do-well Irish saloonkeeper yet again—Sarah still had her doubts.

There might be more to the state of affairs between her sister and Jack Murphy than met the eye. And still more there...maybe *much* more...than Grace was ready to admit.

For days after that, Sarah was kept busy with her students, her husband, Eli and the rapidly approaching holidays. All of Morrow Creek bustled with anticipation, even through a fresh snowfall and a surprising cold snap. The mountain air fairly tingled with crispness, and the ponderosa pines stood blanketed with white. The mercantile and apothecary were packed with items newly arrived on the train, and more than one set of hands was busy with sewing or knitting or creating something special for loved ones.

In the Crabtree household, Christmas had always been a close-knit time, full of love and surprises. Sarah felt determined to make sure the same was true of her small family's holiday. They might have come together in an untraditional way, but, Sarah reasoned, that only made their closeness now all the more extraordinary…and all the more precious, too.

By lamplight, long after Eli had been tucked safely abed, she held up a toy soldier. Its body was fashioned of tin, forged and polished by Daniel's skilled hands. Sarah's job was to paint on a face and hair and tiny clothing. They'd stayed awake many a late night recently, trying to finish the set in time to surprise Eli with it on Christmas morning.

"This one is too big." She showed it to Daniel. "See? His feet are tremendous and his head is over-size, too."

Her husband glanced up from the rest of the toy regiment. He'd done as much "arranging" of them as she had of painting, Sarah would wager. But his unabashed playfulness only made him seem more appealing to her. She pretended to go along with his claims of "testing" the soldiers and didn't make so much as a peep whenever Daniel accidentally let slip a command in a tellingly wee soldierly voice.

"It's fine." He looked abashed to have been caught with two soldiers in—apparently—midbattle. He peered at the soldier she held, then nodded. "There has to be one soldier who's bigger and stronger than all the rest."

His knowledgeable tone didn't fool her. "They should all be the same," Sarah insisted. "That's what's fair. That's what makes them a matched set."

He regarded her with amused patience, his face aglow in the flickering light. "Every boy imagines himself the biggest and strongest. This way, Eli *can* be the biggest and the strongest."

She smiled. "Ahhh. I see."

"It will save him the trouble of trying to fuse two pieces together," he said seriously. "To make one big one."

"Mmm." She paused, considering the image of a tousle-haired, little-boy Daniel ferociously trying to create a big, strong soldier. Her heart felt full to overflowing with the love she felt for him. "I take it that tactic doesn't work very well?"

"No, it doesn't." He frowned, a lock of hair falling over his forehead as he absentmindedly arranged both soldiers in a fighting pose. "If you heat the metal enough to fuse it, it drips in the fireplace and ruins the grate. Your papa—"

Daniel broke off abruptly. His face colored.

She found him more adorable than ever. "I'll paint this soldier with the best and fanciest uniform, then." Sarah picked up her brush and stroked on a swipe of blue. She tilted her head, pointedly not looking at her husband. "I'll give him gorgeous brown eyes, and a big, stubborn nose, and two stuck-out ears, just like—"

"Enough." Making a fierce face, Daniel tugged his earlobe. "Else you'll find yourself with coal in your stocking on Christmas Day."

"So long as you're there next to it, I don't care."

Sarah leaned closer and kissed him. Daniel resisted at first, but she knew his mulishly pressed-together lips were all for show. Because as soon as she held his face in her hands and whispered to him—

"I love these ears."

—he kissed her back so longingly that she forgot what they were doing altogether. Heartened by this evidence that Daniel could be vulnerable, too, Sarah promised herself she would do all she could to make him feel loved. For long moments afterward, she cheered him with caresses. She kissed him heartily.

She plied him with words of praise and appreciation, and by the time those stuck-out ears of his turned pink around the edges, she knew she'd succeeded.

He cleared his throat. "If we keep this up, these will be Easter presents for Eli."

Sarah laughed. "Then I'd better paint on spring-time uniforms instead, husband. Because I have no intention of stopping with you. Ever."

Those soldiers—even the markedly big, strong one—did not become Easter presents. Sarah and Daniel finished the troop a few evenings later, freeing her that Saturday to spend the day on her own. With Eli left to Daniel's care, Sarah traversed the short distance to the Crabtree household, where she met with her mama and sisters for a spree of shopping and gift wrapping and even—with Molly's tutelage—holiday baking.

Afterward, Sarah bundled up in her coat and scarf and took to the streets of Morrow Creek. She had a special gift in mind, one that would not be easy to procure. It meant a great deal to her that she find it, though, so she persisted until all the arrangements were set.

Pleased with her progress, she headed home just as the shops were beginning to close—and just as business at Jack Murphy's saloon was picking up. Waving to him as she passed, Sarah gave a thought to what the saloonkeeper might like for Christmas. A new love, perhaps? Or was the man truly all jokes and nonsense, as Grace said?

The two of them might need a matchmaker, Sarah vowed—a matchmaker like the one who had brought Molly and Marcus together. She knew just the person for the task, too.

At her front porch, she stopped. A fine fir wreath decorated the door, nailed firmly in place and embellished with a clumsily tied muslin bow. It could only have gotten there through Daniel and Eli. Grinning with happiness, Sarah touched her gloved hand to the lowest twisted bough. The fragrance of freshly cut pine wafted outward, following her all the way inside the warmth of her home.

"Daniel? Eli? You two have been busy today, haven't you?"

Sarah's good cheer lent the words a knowing cadence. She could just picture her husband and Eli laboring over that wreath, bending the branches in place till it looked full and lovely. It had been very thoughtful of them. Shedding her coat to the peg beside the door, she removed her hat and gloves and dropped them to the table.

"Hello? Where is everyone?"

Silence. That was odd. Then Sarah realized what must be afoot. Wearing a renewed smile, she headed for the kitchen.

"There you are!" She rose on tiptoes to kiss Daniel hello, heedless of the snow melting from her boots. "I thought the whole house was deserted! Then I realized there must be some *secrets* happening here, what with it being nearly Christmas and all." She rubbed her hands together to warm them, then pressed her palms to Daniel's clean-shaven cheeks. The chill evaporated. "See? It's getting cold out."

He gave a wan smile. Likely, he was hungry. Well, that would be remedied soon enough, Sarah knew. She bustled to the stove, sidestepping Whiskers to light a fire beneath the kettle. She'd been away longer than she'd expected, so dinner would be late tonight.

With an apology on her lips, she turned, only to see her husband regarding her strangely.

"Daniel? What's the matter?"

"It's... Sarah..." He stopped. He cast her a confusing glance, then swept his hand through his hair. "I don't know how to say it, except to just have out with it. Lillian is back in Morrow Creek. She arrived today."

Chapter Fifteen

Dumbfounded, Sarah stared at him. "Lillian? Your sister?"

Daniel nodded.

"She is in Morrow Creek? Right now?"

He nodded again, seeming distracted.

Surprise filled her. For an instant, Sarah could only stand there, absorbing the news. Then a new and important thought struck her.

"Oh, Daniel! You know what this means, don't you? It means you were wrong about her, all along. Lillian is a good mother. She *does* love Eli. Truly!" She felt so happy for Eli. So glad for Daniel—for them both. "Don't you see what this means? You can—"

"It means she is here to fetch Eli."

"But—" *Lillian is a good mother,* she heard herself say again, and felt wobbly at the implications. She had realized them herself, right away. But now Sarah wanted nothing more than to deny them. "Fetch Eli? What for?"

"To take him back East with her. And Lyman, her new husband." Daniel sighed heavily. He scrubbed his hand over his features, suddenly seeming weary. "They want to be home before Christmas. They leave in three days' time."

"Three days!" Sarah grabbed his hand, trying to make him look at her. She frowned, puzzling over it all. "But that can't be! Before Christmas? Before...oh, Daniel, I...I thought we were to have Eli forever."

"So did I." He shrugged, the movement stilted. "We were wrong. It's not meant to be."

"But you...surely you won't let Lillian take him, just like that? Will you?" Sarah stood rooted to the spot, feeling her heart race. Her mind whirled with the shock of this news. If she could just see Eli for a minute...

She hurried to his room.

When she returned, Daniel slumped in his chair.

"He's gone!" she blurted.

"He's with Lillian. At the Lorndorff Hotel. There wasn't room for her and Lyman to stay here, otherwise I'd have—"

"She *took* him?" Distraught, Sarah stared at him. "Already?"

"Sarah. It's not as though Eli has been kidnapped by strangers. Lillian is his mother."

She crossed her arms, feeling not much comforted.

"I know this must come as a shock to you—" some fierce emotion contorted Daniel's features before he regained control "—but what's done is done. What else would you have me do?"

"Consult with me, for one!" Fraught with disbelief, Sarah faced him. She could not understand how this had happened in the space of a single afternoon. "I have a right to know."

"It was not your decision to make."

"But...Lillian abandoned Eli." Her voice cracked at the remembrance of it. "She has no claim on him now, does she?"

An odd smile crossed Daniel's face. "Well, now there is the funny part. It seems there was a misunderstanding. My sister and her husband were only having a wedding trip."

"A...wedding trip?"

He nodded. "A trip they ended early, in fact, to come fetch Eli from here. Because they missed him so much. And because they want to spend the holidays as a family."

Sarah's breath felt cut short. She was losing Eli?

"But *we* are a family." Her voice sounded small. "You and me and Eli. Aren't we? I thought..."

Daniel captured her hand. "Sarah, we were meant to care for Eli for a few months," he said gently. "Nothing more."

Stupidly, she stood there, feeling gob smacked.

"The joke's on us, isn't it?" Daniel said, reminding her inappropriately of the tricks Jack Murphy had played on Grace. His voice boomed, suddenly stout with humor. "It looks as though we got married for nothing."

Sarah didn't find that funny in the least. "Perhaps you did. But I got married because I love you."

"Love?" This time, Daniel's puzzled gaze did meet hers. "But I did not think you *meant* that." He gaped at her, astonishment writ on his features. "People say things while they're—" He gestured meaningfully, nodding toward their chamber. "They're not themselves! They get carried away...."

His voice trailed to nothing. He stared at her, looking beset with surprise. Looking, almost, like a charming stranger.

"They don't know what they're saying," he finished.

Remarkably, he sounded as if he found that reasoning sensible.

"Oh. I see." Bleakly, Sarah hugged herself. This was an even larger shock. She could not take it all in. "Then when you said how much I meant to you? When you said you couldn't let me go?"

He gave her a frustrated look. "No woman holds a man to the things he says while in her arms."

"No woman *you've* known, perhaps. Until me."

"We were enjoying ourselves." He seemed unable to comprehend why this troubled her. Offering a coaxing smile, he stepped nearer. "Don't tell me you didn't like it. I won't believe it."

"You should believe it."

New insight came into his face. "Stop. I warned you often enough. Plainly enough! You knew 'love' was beyond me."

"Maybe." Sadness washed over her. Sarah wondered at her ability to continue speaking at all. "But I didn't know love was lost on you, as well."

A frown. "You're not making sense."

She stepped back so his nearness would not confuse her...so his familiar appeal would not weaken her resolve.

She drew in a deep breath. "Do you love me, Daniel?"

Silence. Then, "I don't want to talk about this now."

"*Do you?* I have to know. Because if you can't say the words now—if I've only been fooling myself, all this time—then our marriage is as false as our care for Eli was."

He stared at her, his hand fisted. "Leave off, Sarah.

Can't you see how hard this day has been? This is no time for—"

"For what? For you to be stuck with an inconvenient 'convenient' wife? A wife you don't need anymore, now that Eli is—" The realization struck her, heartbreaking and impossible to ignore. "You don't *need* a wife anymore. You don't need *me*."

He turned away. "Stop. No more talking."

No more loving, he meant, more likely. Feeling tears threaten, Sarah pursued him across the kitchen. She would not give up on this, she wouldn't…yet Daniel already looked set against her, his shoulders broad and impossibly strong.

Beside him, she felt powerless. *Unseen.*

"Look at me," she said.

He did not. He only stood there, his whole body tensed as he stared out the kitchen window. His impassiveness hurt her as much as his outright anger would have. Could Daniel not see how much she needed him now? How much she would need him *always?*

"You must wish I would vanish as easily as Eli has." Her voice shook as she said it, some hurting part of her demanding a reaction—any reaction—from him. "You must hope I will simply leave off, as you said, and let you go back to your bachelor life."

A pause. "I never said that."

"It's true, nonetheless! Isn't it?" She grabbed his shoulder. Tried to make him face her. But Daniel remained unmoved, as resistant to her as he always had been before they'd—no—they'd never loved. Not the way she'd thought. "Just tell me. Tell me the truth."

His sober glance—an answer in itself—broke her heart.

"Leave me be." Daniel put out his palm as though to stop her from saying more. His hand trembled with the force of his emotions. "Just leave me be."

She could not believe it. "But I—" *I love you,* her heart supplied. *I love you.*

She could not bring herself to say the words again. Not when Daniel so clearly did not want them.

"Well. I guess it's time this 'joke' of ours came to an end, then. Isn't it?"

Blinking back tears, Sarah strode to the chamber she shared with Daniel. Although she waited just inside the door, hoping to hear his heavy footfalls behind her, he did not follow.

Far sooner than she wished, she'd packed a bag of essentials. She carried it to the kitchen, feeling peculiarly unsurprised to find Daniel exactly where she'd left him. His pose looked the same, as though he'd turned to granite between the cookstove and the old scarred table, and might never move again.

She raised her chin. It was hard to force words past her aching throat, but somehow, Sarah managed.

"Do you mind if I visit Eli at the Lorndorff? I should like to say—" her voice quavered, forcing her to clear it "—say goodbye to him before he leaves."

Silence fell between them. For an instant, she dared to believe Daniel might come to himself again— might turn to her with a smile and a tender touch and tell her it had all been a mistake. Tell her he *did* love her, as she'd believed.

He raised one shoulder. "That is not up to me."

Fresh misery struck her. Daniel did not even care if she saw Eli again, if she even said goodbye. It was as though the past weeks they'd spent as a family had never happened at all.

When she didn't acknowledge his answer, he turned. His gaze fell to her hastily stuffed bag, then to the bit of spare petticoat she'd accidentally gotten stuck in the clasp when she'd fastened it. His brow furrowed.

"What are you doing?"

He hadn't even noticed her packing, she realized then. Hadn't *seen* that she'd left him at all. With a deep and unwelcome familiarity, Sarah recognized the feeling that struck her next. Once again, she was invisible to him. Or, more likely, Daniel had never seen her at all. Not the way she'd wanted him to.

"I can see when I'm not wanted." *Tell me I'm wanted,* a part of her begged silently, but he did not comply. She tightened her grasp on the handle of her bag, lest her stupid soft heart should get the better of her and convince her to stay anyway. To go on hoping. "I'm leaving."

"Leaving? Where are you going?"

How could he look so perplexed? "Probably to my parents', I suppose. I'll return for the rest of my things later."

She couldn't bear to sort them all now. To go through her belongings, to pack them beneath Daniel's uncaring eyes, to pretend she didn't want to stay…

She could not endure it.

A fresh onslaught of tears stung her eyes. Stifling a sob, Sarah hurried to the front door. Her only thought was to leave before she crumpled, before she lost her pride completely. She dropped her bag, wriggled her arms blindly into her coat sleeves, concentrated fiercely on wrapping her scarf with fumbling fingers.

"Stop," Daniel demanded.

Helplessly, Sarah did. Her heart hitched in her chest as he came nearer, a scowling look of bafflement on his face.

"Just…*wait,*" he said, his tone gruff. It looked

as though he'd raked his hair clean upright with frustration. "Wait. This is not right."

Once more, she dared to hope. She gazed into his eyes—eyes that had looked at her with kindness and friendship for as long as she could remember—and knew it was only right to give them another chance to succeed at this.

"Do you love me?" she asked.

Daniel's frown deepened. A long moment swept past, while she waited pointlessly for him to give her the one thing that should have come easily—that had always come easily, in her feelings for him.

Sorrowfully, Sarah put her hand to his face. She released a pent-up breath, searching his gaze with her own. This was the last time she would have the right to touch him this way...to pretend, with his unwitting help, that they might truly be one.

"Never mind. You were right. It's not right between us," she agreed quietly. She could not blame him. Not justly. The risk in this had been hers. "The trouble is, for a little while there...I truly believed it was."

She lowered her hand, ignoring a foolish yearning to hold on to the warmth of him for just a little longer. Then she picked up her bag and left him behind, closing the door on all the hopes she'd ever had—and all the future she'd ever dreamed of.

* * *

The door snicked shut with a sense of finality that Daniel could not deny, as hard as he tried.

Deeply confused, he stared at the barrier of wood and wrought iron separating him from Sarah. She was the only woman he would have listened to for this long—the only woman who would have dared to speak to him the way she had. But still, despite all her words, he had no idea what had just happened.

Damnation. Swearing ferociously, he slammed his palm against the door. Pain vibrated up his arm. Making a wry face, Daniel cradled his hand to his chest. This pain proved he wasn't dreaming, at least. He really *was* having the most godforsaken day of any he'd ever spent.

First Eli. Now Sarah. Both gone.

Alone, he stared at the door. Even as he puzzled out this day, the hand-wrought wood creaked open, admitting a sliver of wintery air.

She was back. Hopefulness thumped in his chest. He should have known Sarah could not stay angry with him for long, Daniel told himself. What woman ever did? His knack for pleasing females was, after all, nigh unshakable.

Feeling a fool—but a desperate one—he wrenched the door wide. All that greeted him was the dusk-darkened snowy landscape…and the sight of Sarah striding purposefully away.

She looked small and distant—disconcertingly so. Her scarf trailed, bedraggled, down her back. In her hand she gripped her overstuffed bag, nearly dragging its contents through the snow. Her footprints marched from his front porch to the street, headed in the one direction he'd never thought she would take.

Away from him.

Clutching the door frame, Daniel frowned. What was wrong with her? He could not reason out why Sarah had left, nor where her haste for doing so came from. He'd needed her today. He'd needed her to understand how wrenching it had been to let Eli go...how hard it had been to give Lillian his blessing, when doing so meant losing the boy who had become like a son to him.

Instead of helping him, instead of understanding, Sarah had given him those tearfully accusing looks. She'd insisted on having *words* from him—coherent words when he could least muster them. She'd demanded and pushed, just as any other woman would have, and then she'd gazed at him with those eyes, brimful of damnable tears.

Worst of all, she'd left.

Daniel didn't know how long he stood there. Long enough, he realized belatedly, to freeze his nose and cheeks. His breath gasped in frigid puffs. His fingers felt numb with cold. If he hadn't known better, he would have sworn his heart had iced over, as well.

He refused to consider so daft a notion.

Feeling woefully bereft all the same, he closed the door. By rote, he strode to the woodstove and added a log. The fire crackled, illuminating his empty hands. The silence pressed down on him, forcing his awareness of his empty household. No little-boy laughter greeted him; no soft welcoming murmurs came from Sarah as she cooked an evening meal.

This was how it would be from now on.

Shaking off the thought, Daniel went to the kitchen. More silence waited there. In Eli's room, everything had been packed and hauled away, down to the last puzzle piece. He searched in vain for some sign of the boy he'd cared so much for, but it looked as though he'd never been there at all.

I've got you! You'll never escape now, echoed Eli's voice, and Daniel felt a fresh pang of regret. He wished there had been another way…wished, almost, that he'd never had the boy with him. 'Twas funny—all this time, he had imagined Eli to be the abandoned one, when now it was Daniel who felt forsaken.

A few steps carried him across the hall. He found himself staring at the bed he and Sarah had shared, its quilt rumpled with the imprint of the bag she'd packed. Signs of her were everywhere. A lone glove flopped forgotten on the floor, and a silver-backed mirror lay on the bureau.

Daniel strode to the far wall and caught hold of the thing hung from its peg. Sarah's fancy white nightgown met his grasp, as cool and pristine as if it had never been worn.

I got married because I love you, he heard anew, and the ache inside him gnawed even more intensely. He would not have guessed. Sarah loved him. *Sarah* loved him.

He could not take it in. Daniel rehung the night-gown, then caught himself smoothing a crease from its soft folds. He swore aloud, feeling a fool. Anyone would have thought him a softhearted woman, the way he mooned over his empty household.

He was a man. A brawny man, with strength he'd always been proud of. And yet…now his eyes burned with something suspiciously close to tears, and his throat felt raspy enough to hurt. Daniel swallowed hard, fighting an odd impulse to just lie down and have done with this day. All he wanted was to turn back the clock. To set things the way they had been. Before.

Mustering a pained resolve, he glanced around the room once more. He could not stay here. That much was certain.

By the front door, Daniel snatched his hat from its peg, intending to go…anywhere else. The motion accidentally knocked Sarah's warm winter bonnet to the floor. Stupidly, he stared at it. Then he reached for it. Sarah would need it in this weather. She would be cold without—

He stopped. His life was changed now, whether he wanted it to be or not. But Daniel McCabe was not a man to sit around brooding over the differences. He was a man of action. With a fierce frown, he jammed on his own hat, then headed outside.

The chill winter wind fit his insides exactly. It only took a determined step in a new direction before he'd blotted out the sight of Sarah's trailing footsteps. If he were lucky, time would blot the memories of what they'd found together—and lost—with self-same efficiency. Until then, he refused to think on it anymore.

Chapter Sixteen

Sarah entered the ornate lobby of the Lorndorff Hotel, Morrow Creek's fanciest meeting place, and found herself in another world. Although the ordinary commotion of town waited just outside, here it was calm and quiet. Velvet-upholstered furniture occupied a rug near the fireplace, and a marble-topped reception desk stood nearby. A few travelers milled here and there, their accents sounding decidedly unterritorial.

A uniformed hotel employee hurried past, carrying a railroad schedule and an air of importance. Wiping her damp palms on her skirts, Sarah made herself progress past a stand of potted palms, through a plastered archway, to the dining room. She was to meet Eli and his mother there, and could not be late.

At this hour—just past schoolhouse dismissal time—few guests occupied the cloth-covered tables. Their silver place settings and fine crystal sparkled in readiness, though, and a pair of employees worked nearby to position the centerpieces. Another cluster of workers labored to arrange the heavy-hung draperies at the windows, their voices muted.

The whole place bespoke finery and elegance, another world from the practical one Sarah usually occupied. She had come to the Lorndorff dining room only once before, on the occasion of Molly's wedding breakfast. Then, the Crabtrees had all giddily put on their nicest clothes and trooped to the hotel. They'd all felt quite fancy and in good cheer, especially Sarah—who'd felt like a princess in such surroundings—and her papa, who had declared himself "a fine dandy!" and smoked a cheroot.

The memory conjured a smile, however short-lived. Sarah's own wedding had been too hasty to allow for a lavish breakfast beforehand, and the truth was that on today's visit to the Lorndorff, she felt anything but cheerful. She'd passed two mostly sleepless nights in her old Crabtree bedroom now, tossing and turning with memories of Daniel.

She hadn't known a person could shed so many tears, and her puffy, red-rimmed eyes doubtless told as much to anyone who cared to see it. A hurried glance to one of the mirrors lining the wallpapered wall confirmed her fears. She appeared wan and pale, her hair haphazardly twisted in a knot at her nape.

Perhaps Lillian would view her paleness as fashionable, Sarah told herself, striving for optimism. Perhaps Daniel's sister, not knowing Sarah's usual robustness, would simply assume she always looked a fright, with dark circles beneath her eyes and a rat's nest of hair.

The notion proved not quite as encouraging as she'd hoped.

Nonetheless, Sarah lifted her head and surveyed the hushed dining room. The least Eli deserved from her was a proper goodbye. She didn't feel she could give him that from a train depot platform, especially not with Daniel—more than likely—lingering nearby, too.

She spied a woman in a blue dress and fancy hat, seated with her back to the dining room doorway. Her movements were languid, her manner refined… her hair, what Sarah could glimpse of it, a dark brown exactly as rich as Daniel and Eli's. This had to be Lillian, the woman who'd left Morrow Creek to marry not one but two wealthy men, and to travel the world along with them. Heart hammering, Sarah proceeded toward her.

"Aunt Sarah!" came Eli's voice, of a sudden.

It came from another direction—from the doorway leading to the hotel's Sonoran-style courtyard, now knee-deep in snow. Confused, Sarah turned to the sound. Footsteps scuffled, and a woolen scarf flew to a nearby chair. Eli had not been to school today, and she yearned to see him again.

She saw him an instant later, clattering across the polished floorboards at full tilt. His small face shone with glee. His hair stuck up at odd angles—owing its style, she reckoned, to his wool hat having been cast aside, as well. She couldn't help but smile. Some things, at least, did not change.

"Aunt Sarah!" An instant later, he clamped both arms around her middle and squeezed with all his might. "You came!"

"Of course I came." His embrace brought tears to her eyes. He felt perfectly right, fitting precisely beneath her chin in a wriggling mass of boyish vigor. She sniffled, then found herself laughing, too. "I wanted to see you. Besides, did you honestly think you could play hooky from school and not have a talking-to from me in the end?"

Her avowed sternness did not fool him. "My mama said I could do it. That makes it all right." Eli released her, grinning. Never one to be still for long, he glanced over his shoulder as he shucked his coat to another chair. "Look, here she is. Mama!" he yelled. "Come and meet Aunt Sarah. Hurry!"

The fancily bonneted woman turned, her nose wrinkled in disapproval. She peered at them, her low opinion plain.

Any minute now, she would rise, Sarah knew. She

would rise, and she would deepen that disapproving look, and she would cut this visit short before it began. With one hand on Eli's shoulder, Sarah steeled herself. No matter how unpleasant Lillian turned out to be, she was still Eli's mother. Daniel's sister. She deserved respect.

Oh, but *please* don't let her be that prune-faced snob!

"Eli, stop," came a voice from behind her. "You're giving the wrong impression entirely, and I'll never recover!"

At that happy-go-lucky tone, Sarah turned, befuddled. Those words hadn't come from the snobbish woman, as she'd expected.

They had come instead from the woman hurrying toward them just now, her crooked arm draped with Eli's familiar cast-off hat and scarf and gloves. She dumped the lot to the same chair that now held Eli's coat, then faced Sarah.

"Eli will be back with his tutor once we reach Philadelphia again," she explained in confiding tones, as though she and Sarah were long-lost friends. "But until then…" She winked. "Well, after being apart for so long, I was just greedy enough to keep him all to myself. I hope you understand."

She smiled, pausing in what looked—almost—like uncertainty.

Sarah gawked, momentarily taken aback. She felt

speechless. She didn't know what she had expected from Daniel's grown-up sister, but the woman before her was decidedly *not* it.

Lillian had laughing eyes and messy, partly tumbled hair, and a haphazard way of wearing her clothes that said she did not care a fig for fashion or its vagaries. She was hatless and out of breath, pink-cheeked and as full of life as Daniel was. She possessed nearly—unbelievably—the same quantity of his charm.

"I'm *so* happy to see you again," she said, and engulfed Sarah in a hug whether she felt prepared for it or not.

Evidently, that had *not* been uncertainty Sarah had detected in her. Muffled, muddled, she embraced her sister-in-law with no small amount of awkward surprise. Lillian smelled of fresh air and damp wool. She felt, beneath her layers of overcoat and skirts, almost as hearty as Sarah fancied she herself did.

Lillian squeezed mightily, gave a pat, then stepped backward, beaming.

Disbelieving, Sarah recognized the maneuver. It was Eli's hug, fashioned in feminine form. It contained the same squeeze, the same pat, the same enthusiasm. Eli had, it struck her, learned to offer hugs so generously from his mother. The realization made her heart twist strangely.

Looking carefree, Lillian turned to Eli.

"That last snowball was a trick shot, you rascal." She ruffled his hair, then tickled him into gales of laughter. "I'll get you later, just wait and see."

Eli laughed, his face shining as he regarded his mama.

"Not if I have anything to say about it, you won't." A man entered the dining room from the same direction they'd come. He was graying at the temples, but looked strikingly hale, all the same. He shook a telling coating of snow from his coat, then strode nearer, grinning. "I may be old, but I still have a few good snowballs in me. I'll be the victor yet."

"Oh, you aren't so very old," Lillian teased. "Although I do know you do have a strong arm and an *exceedingly* clever way of making a snowball. I'll consider myself forewarned."

They exchanged a loving, intimate look. This must be Lyman, Lillian's second husband, Sarah realized. He did seem wealthy, but not inordinately so. His air of exuberance exactly matched his wife's. So did his level of merry dishevelment.

"See that you do," Lyman said, lightheartedly.

To Sarah's astonishment, the two of them kissed. Right there in the Lorndorff dining room, with the other patrons and the staff and Eli and she, herself, looking on. Embarrassed, Sarah turned hastily away. When she dared to peek again, Lillian and Lyman regarded Eli with identical affectionate glances.

The picture the three of them made was of a happy family, indeed. Confused by the realization—one she had heartily *not* expected—Sarah heard herself stutter a greeting.

"Oh, but we're leaving poor Sarah by the wayside!" Lillian exclaimed. She took her by the elbow and, looping her arm companionably within hers, guided them both to a waiting table. "Come, let's have some tea. I ordered some refreshments, so I hope everyone's hungry for something tasty. Like chocolate!"

Eli cheered. "Chocolate! Chocolate!"

Towed along in her sister-in-law's wake, Sarah could not find the heart to resist. There was something happy about Lillian. Something generous and witty and irresistible.

"Come along, everyone. It's time for treats!"

Lillian cast a secure glance behind her, probably not truly needing to do so. The men in her life trailed her with absolute adoration. Lyman kept his gaze fixed dotingly on his wife's face as he pulled out a chair for her, and Eli patted her arm whenever he was within reach, as though assuring himself his mama was still there with him.

"You must be terribly angry with me. Are you? Tell me you aren't," Lillian encouraged, facing Sarah after they were all seated. "I could not *live* with myself if I thought you were."

She offered another smile, equally charming as

the first. Feeling unaccountably affected by it, Sarah realized that this, too, felt familiar. Lillian possessed the sense of engagement she'd always found so appealing in Daniel.

"Why would I be angry?" she managed.

"Because I missed your wedding, of course!" Lillian glanced at a waiter, who instantly snapped to attention. She folded her hands beneath her chin, propping her elbows unconcernedly on the tabletop. "I had *no* idea Daniel was ready to be married. You must tell me all about it, and your courtship, too. I'm simply dying to know everything."

Feeling nigh swept away beneath this unexpected turn of events, Sarah hesitated. In that moment, a cadre of servers rushed to their table. One bore a teapot wrapped in a fine embroidered towel and delicate matching cups. Another brought sugar and cream, another coffee and another a platter of pastries and other treats.

Delicious-looking comestibles were passed all round. The conversation was momentarily lost beneath the heated swirl of tea, the sugary crunch of sweets and the happy chatter of a troupe of snowball-throwers recently in from the cold.

Looking at her companions, Sarah knew she should have felt excluded. She should have felt resentful, or angry, or worried for Eli's future. But as she gazed upon Lillian's openhearted smile and Lyman's jovial face, as she heard Eli's contented sigh, she simply could not be. She felt weary, that was true. Also, saddened near beyond bearing to be losing the boy she loved. But she also felt heartened, and that was one thing she hadn't reckoned on.

Lillian caught her staring, doubtless appearing overwhelmed at the hubbub surrounding their table. She patted her hand with clear commiseration.

"Money is useful for doing exactly as a person wishes to," she told her with a wink, "but beyond that I haven't a care for it. Please, enjoy yourself. This bit of fuss is the least I could do, to thank you for all you've done—" she caressed Eli's unruly hair, casting him a warmhearted look "—and for all you *will* do, in making Daniel happy. I wouldn't entrust my brother to just anyone, you know."

Daniel. Talk of him only made Sarah ache. Their parting was too recent...their mistakes too fresh. She should have tried harder not to love him. Or to keep her feelings hidden. Or, failing that, to stop herself from marrying him and entering into this mess at all. But what was done was done. All she could do now was to see through this goodbye with Eli.

She drew in a bolstering breath. She could not fall to weeping again and ruin this for everyone. "Thank you. That's...very kind."

Lillian's brows puckered with concern. "Did I say something wrong? I only meant that I remember you, Sarah. I remember you and Daniel, together, when we were all just children." She rolled her eyes at Lyman. "Sarah and Daniel were wild, but positively inseparable," she told him. "We all should have known they were meant to be together."

Meant to be together. Hearing it said hurt even more.

"What of you two?" Sarah asked, forcing herself to lighten her manner. She angled her head to indicate Lyman. "How did you meet?"

They told her a delightful tale of a springtime in Philadelphia, a millinery shop, a mixed-up order for hats that had gone to the wrong people at first...and brought the right people together in the end. Holding hands, Lillian and Lyman described how they met and how they married; how they decided to travel to the continent for their wedding trip, how they thought of no one to care for Eli in their absence save Daniel.

"It was so important to me that Eli know his uncle," Lillian said seriously. "With Daniel here in the territory and me all the way in the States...well, it's been very difficult."

Lyman gave her a consoling look.

"My mother and father are in Philadelphia, as well, of course," Lillian continued. "But with Mama so caught up in the social whirl, and Papa so involved with his various business ventures, I fear it's just not the same. But I'm being silly. Here *you* are, Sarah, with a whole new family to begin! Tell me. Are you and Daniel hoping for a great many children? Because I can tell you, there is nothing more—" She broke off, looking to Sarah with concern. "Oh, no. I've done it again, haven't I? I can tell I've said something wrong."

To her horror, Sarah felt tears well in her eyes. Children, with Daniel, were something she'd long dreamed of…but hardly dared to hope for. Now, the entire notion felt impossible.

"I'm fine." It felt the biggest falsehood she'd ever uttered. "It's only that I'll miss Eli something terrible, after he leaves. It won't be the same without him here."

She gave him a fond look, smiling though her tears as he chomped happily through an elaborately iced pastry. Eli swallowed. He swiped his fist across his mouth, scattering crumbs.

"I'll miss you, too, Aunt Sarah."

Lillian and Lyman looked on, beaming.

"But I won't miss the 'rithmatic you taught me."

They all laughed. Sarah sniffled, hoping her watery eyes would clear before the too-perceptive Lillian noticed. For a woman who should have been self-absorbed and standoffish, she seemed to discern a remarkable amount.

"Tell us about your schoolteaching," Lyman invited.

So Sarah complied. She described her students and her schoolhouse, the challenges she'd faced in her teacher's exams and in being appointed Morrow Creek's schoolteacher. She laughed over funny stories of recitals and of the memorable time Grace had visited to speak on women's suffrage.

"The girls did not *truly* have a march down Main Street afterward," Lillian insisted, her eyes sparkling. "Did they?"

"Indeed, they did. My sister has a very persuasive personality. Daniel says—"

Jolted from her happy mood by her remembrance of him, Sarah lapsed into silence. Tellingly, Lillian and Lyman exchanged a glance.

"Says what?" Eli asked, a smear of chocolate on his chin.

Sarah mustered a smile for him. "He says that Grace could talk the sky into turning green, if she set her mind to it."

And that I could make gold from a gadfly, just by wishing as hard as I do.

Unfortunately, no amount of wishing, she'd learned too late, would make Daniel love her.

She lifted her gaze to find Lillian watching her

with sympathetic eyes. Another squeeze of her hand followed. Sarah had the unmistakable impression that Lillian knew something of the hurt she'd been through…that she'd guessed, somehow, at the troubles between her and Daniel.

But all she said was, "More tea, everyone?"

Stuffed and sated, they spent a long afternoon at the table, sharing stories. Sarah stored up memories of Eli, finding occasions to hug him and reasons to give him a smile. He, in his turn, reacted as any boy would have—with intense interest in the treats and a whooping joy over the renewed snowball fight they all engaged in in the courtyard together.

Breathing heavily, packing another snowball, Sarah could scarce believe she was here, enjoying a diversion with Eli's family. She would miss him, it was true. But by the time she had been thoroughly trounced by another of Eli and Lyman's sneak attacks, she realized one thing for certain.

Eli would be fine—he would be *more* than fine— with his mother and his new father. Sarah only wished, as she trudged home to the Crabtrees' after she'd left him, that she could hold out the same hope for herself.

Frowning, stripped to his shirtsleeves despite the brisk December weather, Daniel swung his hammer. Its steady, clanging contact felt the only secure thing in his world. Nearby, his fire burned hot and golden, casting the walls of his smithy into shadows.

'Twas devilishly hard to work past dark. That was why he did not usually do it. But these days, two lanterns and a fierce determination made all manner of things possible for Daniel. Tonight, he intended to labor as long as he had for the past few evenings. No damnable sunset would stop him.

"I'll stay, if you want."

Sweating, scarcely hearing the words, Daniel glanced up. His apprentice, Toby, stood beside the bellows. His concerned expression wasn't lost on Daniel—it was the same face the irksome boy had worn for days. The same one he'd spied on the faces of his friends, late of night, when he trudged into Murphy's saloon for a pint that might help him sleep.

"I'll stay. To help you. That plowshare over there—"

"Go." Irritably, Daniel gestured toward the huge sliding doors at the smithy's entrance. The gap they created loomed large enough to allow a wagon and team to pass through, but tonight it showed only the hushed, snowy street beyond. "I don't need help."

Toby hesitated, his youthful features surpassingly sober.

"Be gone now or don't bother to come back to-morrow." Daniel's hammer struck steel, splattering sparks. "Go."

"Fine." Shoving his hat on his head, Toby shouldered past.

Daniel didn't bother to look up. He concentrated on the sleigh runner he was fashioning, all his attention for the work at hand. Tempering and bending metal required skill and strength. Of those qualities in him, at least, Daniel felt justifiably proud. He clung to them fiercely, needing nothing else.

"Ha. Maybe *you* can talk sense into him," he heard Toby say, nonsensically. "Afore he works himself to death."

Irritating bastard. The boy needed a lesson in not mouthing off to his elders. Right now, Daniel wouldn't mind an excuse to give someone a good pounding, either. Clenching his hammer in a fist roughened by more work than usual, he turned to confront his apprentice. Instead, he stared at his sister.

Lillian tilted her chin, standing bundled in the place where about-to-be-shod horses usually did. Her stubborn posture was one thing he hadn't missed while she'd been in the East.

Knowingly, she regarded him. "Well, I guess you've gone and done it again, haven't you?"

He refused to consider what she meant. "I'm busy."

"Ahhh." Unbothered by his harsh tone, she stepped nearer. With an interested expression, she examined his darkened smithy. "I might have known you would bury yourself in work. Men are like that, aren't they? Dead set on ignoring the truth. And you are nothing if not a big, tough man."

Her taunting tone goaded him. He *was* a man. A strong man, Daniel knew. A man to be feared and, preferably, left the hell alone. Why couldn't Lillian see that?

Instead, she looked at him as though he'd stomped on a field of wildflowers. Kicked a puppy. Dipped her pigtails in ink...again.

He glared. "I don't want company."

"When has that ever stopped me?" She smiled, as audacious as he remembered and twice as annoying. "You need help, you idiot. I'm here to give it."

Daniel grunted. He adjusted his grip on his hammer, then studied his working piece. "This has cooled too much."

He tromped through the darkness to his fire. Lillian watched, arms crossed, as he held the clamped metal to the flames. He felt undesirably aware of her scrutiny.

All he wanted was to be left alone. In time, he would crush the sadness that kept him turning in his lonesome bed each night. He would forget the sound of Sarah's voice and the delight of her touch, and he would go on to pleasure many other women. He would be the same man he had been. He would.

Determinedly, he carried his half-formed sleigh runner to his anvil. He scowled at the metal's glowing surface, strangely unable to recall his plans for shaping it.

Lillian stood nearby, arms crossed. "I've seen you break hearts before, you know. I had to see for myself if this time you've had yours broken, as well."

Despite her gentle tone, Daniel refused to meet her gaze. "I never broke anyone's heart," he said, his tone gruff. "Every woman I dallied with knew the right of it. I warned them all. They were fine."

He needed to believe it was so. *Did* believe it.

Lillian shook her head. "You broke many hearts, Daniel. Only you were too busy, too carefree, to see it. Who do you think those women came to for commiseration? For answers?"

Stubbornly, he refused to guess.

"Yes. Me." A faint smile. All at once, Lillian seemed uncommonly wise. Tenderhearted, too. "They all came to me, afterward. At least when I lived in Morrow Creek, they did. So I know the signs of a woman who's been left brokenhearted by my scoundrel of a brother."

He glanced at her, stricken.

"Oh, don't look at me that way." Lillian touched him with affection—and no small measure of exasperation. "You know how you affect women. Likely, it's the same way *I* affect men."

At that, an impish look crossed her face, making her look the way she had as a girl. Suddenly, Daniel realized he'd missed her mightily while she'd been gone.

"We simply can't help it." Lillian offered a matter-of-fact shrug. Her gaze was warm, though, and so was her voice. "But that doesn't mean *we* aren't affected, too."

It did. It always had. Daniel needed it to be true.

"I have *never* been 'affected.'"

His sister seemed unconvinced. "You cannot avoid it. Love finds you eventually. It did me."

He scoffed. "Yes. And look what it did to you."

The puzzlement in her gaze confused him. "What did it do?"

"It made you send Eli away. Made you—"

"—come back for him?" Lillian shook her head. "Because that's what I did, in the end, you know. We've been over this before. It was a simple misunderstanding! I was head over feet for Lyman, about to leave on my wedding trip, and my message to you was unclear. I'm sorry for that, but it's settled now."

Yes...settled, because she'd come to reclaim Eli.

Daniel stared at his sister, a heated, indignant reply instantly on his lips. Yet there was something about the way Lillian stood patiently by, secure in what she'd done. Secure in her belief that he would understand it eventually.

Something that stopped him.

If Lillian did not forsake Eli under the influence of love, Daniel thought suddenly, *then that meant love was—*

"I know the signs of a woman who's lost you." Her voice interrupted his thoughts, scrambling them half formed to the darkness. "Until now, they've all moved on."

"Until—" He clamped his mouth shut on the question.

"Until Sarah," Lillian answered, nonetheless.

Daniel couldn't bear to hear it.

"I can't believe she would come to you to tell you that." He let his hammer fall slack, its head resting on his cooled metalwork. "Sarah is not like other women."

It hurt even to say her name. He didn't know how he managed it. Scowling, Daniel gazed to the snowdrifts outside his smithy door. Soon it would be Christmastime. He'd never looked less forward to making merry.

"She didn't tell me. She didn't have to. I knew when I looked at her, and I knew doubly when I looked at you."

Daniel glanced to his fire. He would need to tend it, else lose its heat.

"You're wasting your breath. Sarah left me. She left me when I—" *Needed her,* he thought, but would not say the words. Not now. "When I would have let her stay."

It was true, he realized then. Whether Eli was with him or not, whether Daniel himself required a wife, he would have wanted Sarah nonetheless. Not that it mattered now.

He turned to Lillian. "It's late. You have a train to catch in the morning."

His sister bit her lip. "Daniel, I—"

She hesitated, then crossed the smithy in one swift movement. Before Daniel could guess what she was about, he found himself engulfed in her familiar, caring embrace.

"I'm sorry," Lillian murmured against his shirtfront. She squeezed harder, as though her very grasp could melt the iciness around his heart. "I only want you to be happy, that's all."

Then you are wasting your time, Daniel thought, but for some reason he could not say so. Not now, not in the midst of Lillian's comforting hold. He relaxed for a moment, patting her hair with his hand. He hugged her in his turn.

When he released her, he even managed a smile.

It was the least Lillian deserved. For caring. For being there. For trying, in her obstinate, sisterly way, to help him. The only trouble was, Daniel knew happiness was beyond him. Without Sarah, he could not see how it would ever touch him again.

"I'll walk you to your hotel," he said, and finally abandoned his work for the night, at long last.

Chapter Seventeen

Three ales and one whiskey later, Daniel had the answer he needed. Of course, he felt nearly too bleary-eyed to concentrate long enough to receive it, but receive it, he did.

"Women." Jack Murphy raised his glass, his brogue as thick as the boggy, unidentifiable stuff he'd poured into it. "Who needs them?"

"Exactly!" Daniel quaffed his drink, then pounded the bar. He wobbled unsteadily on his stool. "Another!"

Obligingly, Murphy poured. Although it was past closing time, and the saloon deserted save for Daniel and his friends, the barkeep showed no signs of being ready to quit drinking.

"To bachelorhood!" he declared. "Long may it hold."

"You two are drunk. Or delusional. Or both." Marcus Copeland strode to the bar, crossing the saw-dust-covered floor with the hearty steps of a sober man. He pried the bottle from Murphy's hand, then shook his head at Daniel. "Leave this. Go home."

"Hah. Easy for you to say." Daniel frowned into his empty glass. "You have Molly to go home to."

"I don't need *anyone* to go home to." Murphy thumped the bar. "I'm well off on my own."

Daniel brightened. "Hear, hear!"

They saluted, clinking their glasses. Almost. 'Twas a mite hard to do, when the damnable things blurred and multiplied.

"If you think you don't need women," Marcus said doggedly, addressing Murphy, "then you haven't seen yourself mooning over Grace Crabtree."

Jack sobered, frowning. Daniel slapped his knee. "Ha!"

"And if you don't think you have someone to go home to," Marcus added, centering his smug, know-it-all gaze on Daniel, "then you haven't looked at your wife lately."

Daniel glowered. "How can I?" he groused. "She's locked up at the Crabtrees'."

"That's right! Locked up!" Jack bellowed. His gaze narrowed. "Wait, damn it. She is? Your wife is living with her family again?"

Morosely, Daniel nodded. "Why do you think I've been here every night? It's not to see your two ugly faces looking back at me."

Jack waved away the insult. Marcus only shook his head.

"You shouldn't have let her go," he said. "It will only make bringing her back all the more difficult."

Screwing up his face in exaggerated astonishment, Daniel crooked his thumb at his brother-in-law. "Look. Married for a few months and he knows everything about women. Tell me, Copeland. Where was all this know-how when you were working yourself to the ground at your lumber mill, and I was here with four—*four!*—lovely women for company?"

Marcus frowned, but Daniel wasn't done. He waved again.

"Besides, who says I'm bringing her back?"

"Who says he's bringing her back?" the saloonkeeper echoed.

"It's obvious, to a thinking man like me." Dragging a bottle of whiskey closer, Marcus enjoyed a slug. He wiped his mouth. "It's only a matter of time before Murphy, here, gives in to Grace Crabtree—"

"What? The hell I will."

"—which means the saloon might not be open for long, owing to Grace's radical, freethinking ways—"

"That's crazy talk, you rotter. Give me that whiskey."

"—which means you—" Marcus jabbed Daniel in the chest "—won't have any place to wallow in misery about your marriage."

"Get out." Jack cradled the whiskey bottle to his fine suit jacket, his pale Irishman's skin flushed with indignation. "Don't come back, either. Not till you regain some sense." He jerked a thumb toward Marcus, raising his brows at Daniel. "See? Getting yourself hitched only causes trouble."

"He might have the right of it," Daniel allowed reluctantly. He viewed Marcus with clearer eyes. "He's right about you, Murphy."

The saloonkeeper shook his head. But his gaze shot evocatively to the upstairs rooms where Grace Crabtree held her ladies' meetings in her portion of their shared building. His features softened, just for a minute.

"Nonsense," he said, more quietly.

"Maybe I *do* need to bring Sarah back home," Daniel said.

"Do it," Marcus urged. "She might make you pay at first—"

"Pshaw." Daniel puffed out his chest, dismissing the notion without another thought. He grinned, feeling lighter than he had in days. "She's a woman. What could she possibly do to make me pay?"

The first high-heeled ladies' lace-up shoe hit Daniel squarely in the shoulder. The second sailed past his head with less-than-deadly accuracy.

"Now leave, you drunken lout!" Sarah yelled,

silhouetted in the window of her parents' house. "I have a candlestick in here, and I'm not afraid to use it next."

Shutters banged open. "Please, don't use it!"

Fiona Crabtree eyed her daughter from a nearby opened window. Her shawl looked bedraggled, her eyes wild.

Apparently, the tendency toward rag curlers among Crabtree women was not limited to the younger generation. Cheerfully, Daniel waved.

"Hello, Mrs. Crabtree! Sorry to wake you. I'm here to fetch Sarah and bring her home."

"Home? With you? Hah!" Sarah hurled another shoe.

It flew toward his manly regions. Drunkenly, Daniel stepped sideways. Then he opened his arms in pleading fashion. "Come home, Sarah. Else I'll have nowhere to get ales from."

She scoffed. Daniel paused, wondering at her reaction. The reasoning seemed sound to him—as true as it had when Marcus had explained it an hour or so ago at Murphy's saloon.

There was more to this than that—such as his need for her, of course—but a self-respecting man did not grovel. Begging Sarah to come smile at him or touch him or force-feed him vegetables would not do. He had a reputation to uphold.

"Get out of here!" His runaway wife hefted a chamber pot.

Daniel wasn't worried. Because what had occurred to him, what he'd realized after doggedly pondering over his talk with Lillian, was that love was *not* dangerous. It did not make a man do rash, horrible things. Lillian's return for Eli was proof enough of that. Her arrival had changed everything 'round.

Love only made a man lonely when it was withheld, Daniel knew now. He was done with being lonely. He wanted warmth and laughter. He wanted Sarah.

He began a song to that effect, a bawdy ditty with her name substituted for all the ribald ladies' names in the original. Pouring his feelings out in the lyrics, Daniel swayed and sang, his hand over his heart. This would touch her for certain.

Someone else leaned irritably from the window. "Dear God, McCabe!" Adam Crabtree said. "Stop that caterwauling."

"It's almost sweet," Fiona judged mistily. "Only off-key."

"It's ridiculous and misogynistic." Grace opened her shutter, gazing down at him with weary impatience. "If I agree to speak with Sarah for you, will you stop it?"

Abashed, Daniel shut his mouth. A searching glance at Sarah told him she hadn't been properly moved by his tribute. He frowned. He'd felt so certain, when setting out from Murphy's tonight, that coming for her was the right thing to do.

He nodded to accept Grace's starchily spoken offer.

"No!" Sarah cried. "All of you, just quit it. I *won't* come back to you, you whiskey-soaked oaf, and that's my final word. Because of *you,*" she informed Daniel, "the school board is reviewing my teaching position. They think I don't have the 'necessary dedication' to go on as schoolmarm."

Foggily, he recalled his attempts to ease her workload.

"I never meant—" Daniel broke off. He was forgetting his usual charming tactics. He needed them, tonight of all nights. He gave Sarah a lopsided-feeling grin, certain, of a sudden, that his teeth might actually be whirling around with the rest of his head. "Come out with me, Sarah. Come back."

Her look of disdain wounded him. Especially with nearly the whole of her family looking on. Daniel staggered beneath it, his hand over his heart again. It ached, exactly as it had for all the past days. That had nothing to do with whiskey.

"I need you," he said.

Sarah paused. She stilled her grasp on the hairbrush she'd doubtless meant to hurl next and regarded him with a look he murkily recognized. Dread gripped him. 'Twas the look she had worn before asking him, twice, if he loved her.

Something else crossed her face. She tightened her lips. Daniel felt her slipping away from him, slipping as surely as had his grasp of standing upright, or of speaking sensibly tonight.

Perhaps he *had* imbibed too much, he decided in afterthought. Especially while celebrating, upon Marcus's advice and Jack's grudging agreement, his impending reunion with his wife.

"I want an annulment," Sarah said quietly. "I'll be by to collect my things later this week."

Then she closed her shutters and darkness fell, leaving Daniel to stand there alone in the street… bereft of hope in a way he never had been before. Because now he *knew* he needed Sarah—and he knew, equally surely, that she was well and truly lost to him.

Sarah sat in her family's parlor the next evening, her lap full of knitting and her mind full of thoughts of Daniel. She hadn't slept at all after closing the shutters on him last night. Now, after a day's teaching, she felt scarcely like herself. Tiredness bore down on her, along with a sadness deeper than she'd felt before.

What had Daniel been about, coming to her past midnight the way he had? He'd hardly looked the same man, with his whiskered face all miserable and beseeching, his speech broken and his steps lumbering. That he'd been drinking had been plain. Whether doing so had loosened his resistance to her *or* kindled his desire to have a handy washerwoman in his home seemed less clear. Either way, Sarah could not risk trusting him.

Tightening her resolve, she knit a few rows. Soon she would go back to the small house she'd shared with Daniel and take away her things, once and for all. But today she hadn't been able to face the prospect—not with Eli leaving on the eastbound train, and not with her many sleepless nights weighing on her. Tomorrow would be soon enough.

"Sarah, did you hear me? You look far away."

At the sound of Grace's voice, Sarah glanced up. "I'm sorry. I find myself woolgathering a lot these days."

She cringed inwardly, regretting the words instantly. Her family was bound to leap on them and chide her for being too dreamy, too prone to fanciful imaginings. If only they'd known how such wishing had come crashing down around her.

After a thoughtful perusal, all Grace said was, "I was merely mentioning how solidly Lillian has won me over. I know you believe Daniel has all the charm in that family, but I think Lillian wound up with her share of it, as well."

Mama nodded. "She's a lovely woman. It was very kind of her to visit all of us yesterday. We *are* family now, you know."

Sarah decided it would not be diplomatic to remind Mama of her impending annulment. She sighed, remembering it herself.

"Lillian shows a fine appreciation for a good newspaper." Papa turned the pages of his periodical. "That's an excellent quality in any woman."

"Also, she has several very interesting ideas about housekeeping." Mama leaned forward with enthusiasm. "Lillian is quite clever with a box of borax and a horsehair brush."

"She may have a position for me with a charity organization in Philadelphia," Grace confided nonchalantly. "Lillian may well change my life."

Sarah gawked. She hadn't been the only one who'd been affected by Daniel's sister. Her whole family adored the woman.

"I'll admit, it's enough to make me wish Lillian and Eli and Lyman hadn't had to leave today," she found herself saying wistfully. "But it's a long way to Philadelphia. If they're to arrive there before Christmas—"

"Leave?" Her papa looked surprised. He lowered his periodical, peering at her over its pages. "*You,* my girl, have obviously not read your father's newspaper today."

He tsk-tsked, then went back to it, leaving Sarah baffled. She gazed to Grace, then her mother.

"It seems the eastbound train has been delayed," Fiona explained. "Due to bad weather farther down the tracks. It will be past Christmas before it's cleared."

"Yes, I understand the Lorndorff Hotel is completely full, and so are all the boarding houses in town," Grace added. "Jack Murphy has delayed travelers sleeping on his saloon floor for a nickel apiece."

"Hmm. Very enterprising of him," Papa approved.

"*I've* charged four cents apiece for a place upstairs and booked twice as many travelers." Grace's mouth quirked with suppressed amusement, even as she placidly examined the political pamphlet she'd been reading. "Jack was fit to be tied at being undersold."

Papa hooted with laughter. "That's my girl."

Mama only shook her head. "Grace, have pity on the man."

But Sarah couldn't listen any longer. Somehow, being among her close-knit family only made her feel more alone. She stood, trailing yarn from her cupped hands.

"Good night, everyone."

Her mama blinked with surprise. "Going to sleep already?" Her gaze meandered to Sarah's handfuls of wool, then lifted. "Why, if you stop knitting now, you'll never finish that innovative pair of woolen britches you've been making."

"It's a sock, Mama. A sock." Sarah didn't want to say so, but knitting the green monstrosity somehow made her feel closer to Daniel. By now, he could have fit one whole leg in the thing—up to his hip. "Good night."

She headed upstairs, her mama's voice following her in puzzlement. "My goodness. Daniel must have *very* large feet, mustn't he?"

"I think you should stay here." Daniel studied Lillian and Lyman seriously, feeling as though the snowstorm in Nebraska had granted him a rare reprieve. "Eli took to the territory right away. There are business opportunities aplenty here for Lyman. And Lillian, you—"

His sister eyed him interestedly from across her hotel room. She'd always been eager to leave Morrow Creek.

"Eli hasn't even been fishing yet," Daniel finished heartily. It was better, he reckoned, to bypass any problems. "He *has* to go fishing with his uncle."

"I'll send him for another visit. Maybe next summer?"

The boy perked up. "We can fish in the summertime!"

Damn it. That would be fine, but it wasn't the point.

"It's wholesome here. The city is filled with soot and grime and criminals. It's no place for a child."

Lillian rose, looking amused. "It's filled with museums and parks and wonderful shops, too. Besides, a little dirt didn't hurt *you* as a boy. I recall your coming home grubby-faced on a daily basis, with snakes in your pockets."

Daniel and Eli shared a befuddled glance.

"What's wrong with snakes?" they asked.

His sister smiled. She gave Daniel's shoulder a gentle squeeze as she passed by on her way to retrieve something.

"Perhaps if you would take care of your own life," she suggested with care, "you wouldn't be so interested in mine."

Daniel frowned. He should have taken exception at that, but there was something about the way Lillian said things that made staying annoyed with her difficult. Besides, he *had* tried to take care of his life with Sarah, had tried to make her come back and love him again. It hadn't worked.

He watched absently as Lillian selected a cut-glass jar from the bureau. She dipped out some of its contents, spreading cream on her hands.

"Isn't Sarah coming to see you today?" she asked.

Jolted from his reverie, Daniel nodded. "Tonight. She's coming tonight to collect her things."

Lillian knew all of the story. He'd confided as

much to her. She offered him a sympathetic look. "Be nice to her."

Nice to her? Sarah was coming to force an annulment from him. An annulment *he* did not want! On the verge of reminding his sister of that appalling fact, Daniel stopped.

There was something familiar about that jar of hand cream, he mused. Something that, with to-night's unwelcome encounter looming, gave him a desperate, last-ditch idea....

Feeling shaky, yet blessedly dry-eyed, Sarah stood on her former front porch. The holiday wreath Daniel and Eli had made stared her in the face. It felt eons since she'd first seen it. Now it hung there, inno-cently festive and woefully crooked, reminding her of everything she'd lost.

With a gloved hand, she straightened it. There. That was better. Now the wreath looked a merry harbinger of the coming holidays. Sarah drew in a deep breath and prepared to knock.

Doing so felt beyond peculiar. She'd grown accus-tomed to coming inside at will, to thinking of the household as hers as well as Daniel's. She wondered if he'd ever felt the same.

I need you, she recalled, and felt her resolve to be firm—to behave with decorum and dignity—waver, just the merest bit. If he truly needed her...

The door opened. It was a shock to find herself face-to-face with her husband. It was a larger shock to find him sporting a face full of polka-dotted splotches.

She peered closer. "Is that…Miss Olga's Original All-Natural Wart Cure-All and Preventative?"

Looking mortified, Daniel touched his cheeks.

"We can't do this today," he blurted, then shut the door.

Sarah found herself staring at the wreath again. Perplexed, she knocked once more.

"Go away," came his muffled voice from within. "You'll have to get your things another day."

Was he fooling with her? Frowning, she marched to the window. She could just make out Daniel standing in the front room, his shaggy-haired head cocked toward the closed door. He had on a pair of britches and a misbuttoned shirt, and aside from his wart cream application, looked very manly.

Although he also *did* seem as if he could use some caring for. His shoulders still were broad, but there was a…*hungry* sort of look about him, too. Sarah bit her lip, worrying.

She rapped on the window.

He jerked, startled.

"Please cooperate, Daniel." Her breath made a frosty pattern on the window glass. She gestured to the door, turning her hand to indicate maneuvering the knob. "Let me in."

She would just as soon have this finished. It was painful enough without dragging it out unnecessarily.

"Come back tomorrow," he yelled.

Then he bolted for the kitchen and disappeared from sight.

The next day, Sarah felt more prepared. Outfitted in an old dress topped with the dark blue cape Daniel had always liked, she marched to his house with deliberate steps. Today she would reclaim all her belongings and demand his cooperation with their annulment. She would have this finished.

Just *see* if she didn't.

Her mind filled with bolstering images of herself regally carrying away a box of her belongings, she ascended the front steps. She would hold her head high, and not let Daniel know how he'd hurt her. She would smile, and not let him know how he still occupied her thoughts. She would calm her frantically beating heart, and not give away the fact that she still felt madly, stupidly in love with the husband she was about to sever relations with.

Preoccupied with trying to achieve such miracles, Sarah stumbled into something. She nearly slipped. Crying out, she braced herself with one arm against the house's siding, then glanced down at the snowy porch floorboards.

A pile of lumber had tripped her. Its pungent pine smell should have been a warning, since it looked freshly planed.

Daniel came round the corner, another board tucked beneath his burly arm. Around his coat-covered waist he'd buckled a tool belt of some kind. A pencil showed, workmanlike, behind his ear. He moved with purpose, frowning slightly as he approached the front door.

He saw her, and his whole face brightened.

She saw that happiness in him and wanted desperately to respond in kind. But she was here for a purpose, Sarah reminded herself staunchly. She could not be swayed. Not even by Daniel's beloved, warmhearted…oh, sweet heaven…knee-weakening smile.

Not even if that smile seemed meant for her alone.

"Sarah." His voice rumbled with pleasure.

"Daniel." Hers trembled with uncertainty. She cleared it, endeavoring to muster some discipline. She had missed him so! "I trust you'll let me in today? I don't have a great many things to take with me, but in light of our impending annul—"

"Can't do it today." Cheerfully, Daniel slung his board around and planted it on the porch. He stood behind it with his legs spread and his arms gripping the wood, looking like a brawny, jolly lumberman. "I've taken up woodworking. I have a great deal to do. All this lumber to whittle."

He nodded to the pile.

"Whittle?" Dumbly, she stared at the wood.

"Yep." He nodded. He breathed hard, as though he'd been busy at "whittling" all morning. "I'm making toothpicks."

"Toothpicks!" The notion was outlandish. Disbelieving, she examined the boards. "Are you mad? That will take weeks!"

"If I'm lucky," he agreed amiably.

His gaze traveled from her boot tips to her wrapped cape, then seemed to get stuck, lingeringly, on her face. His perusal made Sarah feel hot all over. It was a most unwelcome feeling. She'd come here for an annulment. For a gathering of her things. *Not* for a scandalous flirtation with her almost-former husband.

"You're looking well," he said.

Aggravatingly, his words only made that heated feeling increase. Sarah unwound her woolen scarf, its knitted texture soft against her neck. Uncommonly soft, in fact. Almost as soft as the way her skin had felt beneath Daniel's rugged hands when he'd—

"You're looking well yourself," she forced out. "I trust your wart problem is solved?"

Her arched brows did not seem to fool him. Daniel

chuckled, not nearly cowed enough by her practiced schoolmarmish demeanor.

"As solved as it ever will be." With outrageous calm, he selected a knife from his belt. Examined his wood. Scraped away a sliver of it. "I'd better get back to work. As you so ably pointed out, this will take some time."

He pursed his lips and blew away sawdust.

Irresistibly, her gaze centered on his still-puckered mouth. She could not believe he would remind her—so blatantly!—of all its talents. Of all the ways she'd enjoyed feeling that mouth of his against hers.

It would serve him right if she just turned heel and marched away, Sarah told herself. But somehow, she simply went on watching him instead. He blew once more, very gently, and she knew she wanted to kiss him. Wanted…

Daniel's mouth quirked in a grin, startling her from her reverie. He leaned nearer and tipped her mouth closed, the motion so quick she might have imagined it. Sarah frowned in the wake of it, not pleased to have been caught out.

Although Daniel did not seem, she noticed, *entirely* unaffected by her presence, either. His gaze strayed to her face often as he whittled. His expression looked contemplative…almost hopeful. He gave a gusty sigh.

"You'd better be on your way," he announced.

"What? No. I came to collect my things." That was the heart of the matter. She had to remember that. "Also, we still must discuss our annulment. I know you made some... arrangements when we married."

His frown told her she'd recalled their conversation about that correctly. As part of their unconventional union, Daniel had arranged to have their marriage license remain unofficial for a time. If they both requested it, she knew an annulment would be granted.

"You must be eager for your freedom," she said.

His piercing gaze struck her. "As eager as you are for yours."

Well. Since *she* was not eager at all...

Sarah cleared her throat. "There's no reason to delay this. Just let me in and we'll have this done. I don't have much to take with me."

"I'll help you." He went on carving, not looking at her. "Just as soon as my whittling is done. Until then..."

Daniel spread his arms in helpless fashion, one hand holding his hunk of lumber and the other grasping his knife. He indicated the tremendous woodpile with a nod, then shrugged.

With a narrowing of her eyes, Sarah examined his guileless face. She knew him well enough to know that an overriding interest in wood carving was *not* one of Daniel's passions. There was only one reason he'd begun this now, and that was to delay her. What she could *not* reason out was why.

Sarah drew her cape closer around her, staring him down. The man she loved looked back at her, utterly unperturbed.

"Have you been eating your rutabagas?" she demanded.

Drat it. Where had that come from?

His expression grew even cockier. Daniel thought he had her licked, she could tell. *But why?* a part of her wondered. Why would he bother to delay their inevitable parting?

"I mean, fine. Have it your way." The battle lines, as they said, were drawn. "I'll be back later to get my things. Next time, be ready."

His grin flashed again. "Ahh, Sarah." The way he said her name seemed a seductive promise. "I'm always ready for you."

Oh, my. How did Daniel look so wonderful? So tempting? He was a man dead set on whittling millions of toothpicks. That alone should have made him utterly ignorable.

"Hmmph," she managed, despite her wildly pattering heart. "See that you do a better job of it next time, then."

Then she tilted her chin and swept down the porch steps, determined to fashion a better strategy for her return.

Chapter Eighteen

For the third time in as many days, Sarah walked to Daniel's house to reclaim her belongings. She wore a lace-bedecked gown borrowed from Molly, her warm cape and a pair of especially fashionable lace-up shoes. She thought they might have been the pair she'd hurled at Daniel during his drunken serenading. If so, she hoped he would not recognize them, for they were simply too attractive to pass up.

Because of their heels, they lent her much-needed height. Wearing them, she felt a sense of gravitas she would need to deal with her wily almost-former husband. Also, she and Molly—and even, reluctantly, Grace—had agreed they were nearly the most fetching shoes they'd ever seen.

Daniel was bound to find her irresistible in them.

Not that she cared a whit for that. She was serious.

Still, Sarah *had* wrangled with the hot hair tongs yet again, simply to give herself a much-needed boost. Similarly, she'd applied a bit of lavender water and splurged on a pair of fine winter gloves for this occasion. Not because she wanted to look nice for Daniel, she told herself as she hurried through the snow. But merely because she'd…welcomed the practice. Yes, that was most certainly it.

Thus equipped, she reasoned that *she* would have her way with Daniel—rather than allowing *him* to unduly affect her. He absolutely did not need to know that she still thought of him, still dreamed of him… still wished for him.

Still loved him.

Snow crunched beneath her shoes as she trod the final steps to his house. A gentle wind stirred the loosened tendrils of her hair. The distant sounds of Morrow Creek going about its business served as background to her thumping heart. If she did not gain entry today, Sarah didn't know what to try next.

Daniel surprised her by being there waiting.

"Well." He surveyed her from a seated position on the porch steps, his winter coat opened to admit the sunshine. In the gap of its unfastened buttons, his broad chest showed, clad only in a knitted shirt. "You're looking very fine today."

His leisurely perusal gave proof to his words. So did the sinfully appealing grin that followed. It made her want to blush, to giggle, to melt on the spot.

Instead, Sarah mustered her will. "I'm *feeling*

industrious." She nodded to the front door. "Shall we go inside?"

"Not right now." Daniel tucked his chin, indicating the tabby cat sprawled on his lap. He petted him, his fingers moving in a slow, hypnotic rhythm. "Whiskers is napping. I don't want to wake him."

She must be hearing things. Daniel had never deigned to use the name she and Eli had given the tabby. He'd groused that it had been too silly.

"Did you just call that cat 'Whiskers'?"

A nod. "'Course. Whiskers has had a rough time of it, though. Neither of us has been sleeping very well lately."

"Neither have I," Sarah admitted before she considered it. "I've been—"

At the interest in Daniel's face, she abruptly shut her mouth. Drat it! The confiding habits of half a lifetime were hard to break. Since she and Daniel had been such long-standing friends, she'd always told him nearly everything...except her feelings for him, of course.

"I've been up late worrying about my work at the schoolhouse," she prevaricated. It wasn't *too* far from the truth. "Trying to dream up ways to convince the school board I'm still capable of doing my job."

Daniel's clear-eyed gaze met hers. "I'll talk to them."

"No. If you'll just—"

"I was trying to help. I didn't mean to stir up trouble for you."

His kindness only stirred up more. More trouble, more feelings, more regrets. "Daniel, open the door. Please, let's don't drag this out any longer."

"I'm sorry."

"Daniel."

"Forgive me."

His serious look encouraged exactly that. Sarah knew she had to be strong. He did not love her, and that was what mattered most.

"If you'd kindly cooperate," she told him, "I could go on with the rest of my life."

He shook his head. "No. Can't do that."

He seemed peculiarly blithe about the admission. He went on stroking Whiskers, his cuddling attitude impossible to ignore. If Daniel could learn to love and appreciate that old tomcat, Sarah thought, then surely he could...

No, she told herself. *Be firm.*

Still, she fancied she heard the cat purring beneath his attention. It was a reaction she heartily understood.

"*Why* can't you?" she asked, fighting for strength.

At this rate, it would take them months to settle this.

Again Daniel's gaze roved over her, uncommonly

bold and undeniably affecting. "Well, it seems I'm on strike."

Sarah could not believe it. "On strike?"

"Yes." *Pet, pet,* went his fingers over Whisker's fur. "Until you give me a proper demonstration of wifely affection, I won't be opening that door. Which means you won't be taking your things from here."

She gawked. "'Wifely affection'?"

That term sounded *awfully* familiar. It bore more than a passing resemblance to "husbandly duties."

"You know." He lifted one powerful shoulder in a shrug. "Small tokens of wifely fondness. Like…a kiss."

His eyes gleamed at her, richly brown and filled with an *I dare you* aspect Sarah recognized only too well. That bravado had always been present in Daniel. Only she had never found it directed solely at her.

Now that it was…

She heaved a sigh. "Very well."

Before she could lose whatever courage she'd mustered, she marched to him. She noted with abstracted dismay that Daniel's gaze did not so much as dip to her adorable shoes.

So much for that tactic. This was the last time she'd let her sisters advise her on *anything*.

Daniel smelled of soap and man, lounged with a

casual disregard of the cold that told of his strength and fortitude. He looked as wondrous as always, clean-shaven and tousle-haired.

Determined not to care, not to be pulled in by his charm, she put both hands on his shoulders. Leaned over.

Their kiss was done within moments. A brief pucker, a barely registered contact…a flood of heart-twisting memories. Sarah straightened, regarding him with impatience. Why did he have to make this so difficult between them?

"There. *Now* will you let me in?"

Daniel shook his head. "I meant a proper kiss."

"That *was* a proper kiss."

He smiled. "You only think so because you're still a beginner."

She took offense at that. "Is that so? Perhaps if I'd had a proper teacher—"

His laughter confused her. Still smiling, Daniel gave the cat one last, long stroke, then released it. Whiskers jumped gracefully to the porch rail. He stalked to its end and then headed to the trees beyond, doubtless to pester the squirrels.

"Your teacher was fine, and your lessons even better." He rose. "They ended too soon, is all."

Oh, they had, her heart agreed. Foolishly.

"They ended in time for our annulment," she

pointed out. Her throat rasped in protest. "That is soon enough."

Seeming unconcerned with that, Daniel came nearer.

At his approach, she became aware of her heart pattering unevenly in her chest. Her mouth felt dry, her palms damp beneath her gloves. She felt unable to move at all.

There was something about this new, cat-petting Daniel. Something Sarah certainly hadn't reckoned for and did not know quite how to deal with.

He stopped, looking at her with a glance that held much more familiarity, and more compassion, than she'd expected. He leaned his shoulder against the porch post, as easygoing as she'd ever seen him. Yet there was something purposeful in the way he looked at her, too. Something determined.

With a jolt, she recognized that look. It was the one he'd worn on the occasions when he'd kissed her. It was bold, sensual, compelling. *Tempting.*

"I like you in that dress," he said.

He made no move closer. Not even to hold her hand.

Unaccountably, Sarah felt her spirits sag. If her baited comment could not induce Daniel to prove her wrong with a kiss, if her fancy dress and shoes and curly hair could not lure him, then…well, the snow might as well sprout flowers. Both notions seemed equally unlikely. Daniel, giving up?

She refused to feel disappointed.

She did not succeed.

"I can't come back tomorrow," she warned. "I'll be with my students for the spelling bee. Half the town is coming—"

"Then I guess you'd better try kissing me again now."

"I'm not going to kiss you!"

"That," Daniel said, "is what you think."

He caught her in his arms, making their bodies press together. Sarah felt the muscles of his shoulders bunch beneath her gloved hands, felt warmth penetrate her skirts where his thighs met hers. Her mind whirled with protests, but the rest of her…oh, the rest of her merely wanted to enjoy this. It felt good. It felt right.

"Kiss me," Daniel urged. "I need you to—"

"Stop talking. You'll ruin it."

Sarah pressed her mouth to his. Instantly, he opened his lips beneath hers, taking all of her in his kiss. His arms tightened around her, squeezing as though he'd never let her go.

Daniel groaned. She thought she heard an answering sound of pleasure come from her, but she couldn't be sure. She felt too swept away to reason it out. All she knew was the union of their mouths, the glide of his tongue, the sensation of homecoming that came bundled with Daniel's kiss.

This was bliss. This was...*wrong.*

She broke off. "You're trying to confuse me!"

He blinked. Disappointment crossed his face, then resignation. "Hmm. Is it working?"

Of course it is. "Of course it's not."

Daniel did not believe her. She could tell.

"Fine." Sarah stepped backward, pretending to be occupied with shaking out her skirts. She cleared her throat, trying to ignore the fluttery feeling in her middle. Then she nodded to the house. "You know what I need from there. If you won't let me get it myself, then kindly pack it up and have it delivered to my parents' house, please. I won't be back here again for more of your shenanigans."

He seemed even more puzzled. "But...you *love* my shenanigans!"

She always had. Now, sadly, Sarah shook her head. "Not when they cost me this much."

Then she picked up her skirts and turned back the way she'd come, leaving a befuddled-looking Daniel to stare after her.

"Something is wrong." Daniel flexed his arm, examining the muscle bulging beneath his shirtsleeve. He practiced a smile, aiming it to the mirror behind Jack Murphy's bar. He ran a hand through his hair, testing it for thickness. "Am I losing my hair again? Maybe that's it. Have a look."

He bent his head toward Marcus.

The irritating man only guffawed. "Your hair is fine, McCabe. It's the brain beneath it that needs work."

Jack chuckled. "To be sure. Look. You haven't even touched your whiskey."

Daniel grunted. The truth was, he had no appetite for spirits. He only wanted Sarah—wanted her to come back to him. How he'd failed in that pursuit, he didn't know.

"Every time I'm with Sarah, something happens," he explained, needing to reason it out. "It feels as though my heart gets lodged—" he gestured to his throat "—right here and won't budge. I can barely speak!"

"That's what the whiskey is for," Jack said, reasonably.

"No. That didn't work at all." Daniel winced, recalling a particular ladies' shoe headed for his groin. "It's not just that, either. I've tried to hide it from Sarah—and I've done a damn good job of it, too. But aside from the throat problem, my belly flip-flops like a trout every time I'm with her."

"Dyspepsia," Jack pronounced.

"Love," Marcus countered.

Daniel stared at them both. "This cannot be love.

It feels terrible! Yesterday, when Sarah visited me, my palms got sweaty at the sight of her. At the sight of her! Thank God I had Whiskers to hide the—"

"Whiskers?" His friends shared a glance.

"The cat. It's going with Eli back to the States soon, but until then..." Distractedly, Daniel turned his whiskey glass. "Hell. I just like having the cat around. It's not a crime."

The truth was, cuddling Whiskers on his lap made him feel a little less lonesome. He would have worn a dance-hall girl's feathered headpiece before admitting as much.

He scowled at Jack and Marcus, to be sure they understood. He wasn't getting soft. "He's a good cat."

"Oh, we're sure of that." Grinning, Marcus held up both hands in apparent surrender. "But about this 'love' thing—"

"It's not love, damn it! It's sweaty palms and a churning stomach and a thumping heart. It's that irritating feeling of having my necktie strung too tight." Daniel sighed. He examined his reflection again, feeling doubly confused when he appeared as ordinary as ever. "I should see a doctor."

Jack squinted. "I think Copeland has the right of it. You're bad off." He shuddered. "God help us all."

Daniel ignored him. "The worst part is, now I've lost my only link to Sarah. She won't come back now, not even to get her things." He stared morosely at the crate of feminine fripperies packed at his feet. "I overplayed my hand. Pushed her away. After all this time of us being friends—"

"'Twas more than friendship," Marcus insisted.

"—to see it all ruined this way—"

"*You're* ruined for other women now. Admit it."

"Damn it, Copeland!" In frustration, Daniel slapped his hand on the bar. "Shut up. You sound like a moony old spinster. If I'd wanted addle-headed advice, I'd have—"

"Come here," Jack said, nodding.

Marcus agreed.

Daniel frowned at them both.

"It's what you've been doing all along," Jack added.

This was too much. "I may be *dying*." Daniel held his hands to his throat in demonstration of the symptoms he'd described earlier. "But you two—" He shook his head. "The hell with it. Just let me meet my maker in peace."

They had the audacity to laugh. They'd probably dance on his grave someday soon, too. The sons of bitches.

Too bad they were all he had.

"How can I have failed? With a woman?" Daniel stared at them, feeling forlorn and confused. "I thought I could persuade Sarah to come back to me. Something is wrong, plain as that."

Maybe his charm had broken somehow. He'd never thought he'd see the day, but there was no denying the evidence.

"Fine." Marcus stifled his amusement. "Tell me this. Why do you want Sarah to come back?"

Daniel was wise to that trick, though. He knew Marcus wanted to hear something mush-hearted and sappy, something that would prove his point. Something like *she should come back because I love her.* But Daniel knew better.

"I'm not talking about this anymore," he said.

He dropped a coin on the bar, then hefted the box of Sarah's belongings. It felt heavier than it had a right to.

"I'll take that." Marcus held out his arms.

"The hell you will." Daniel cradled it. "I'll carry it myself."

"You've been hauling that box around," Jack reminded him with a pointed look, "ever since last night."

That was true. Daniel had packed it shortly after Sarah had left him on his front porch. Then, he'd been fired up with indignation…and the aftereffects of that churning gut, those sweaty palms, that choking, heart-in-the-throat sensation. He'd hardly known what he'd been doing.

"So?" he demanded.

"So I'll save you the trouble of delivering it."

Marcus offered him a damnably sympathetic look, along with a second hand-it-over gesture. "I'll see Sarah at the schoolhouse later for the spelling bee. I can give it to her then."

"No. I'm supposed to take it to the Crabtrees'."

Not that he had moved so much as a step in that direction over the past day and a half.

"Be reasonable," Marcus said. "In the state you're in, you're liable to confront Sarah and demand to know if she finds your muscles too puny—"

"Or your hair too thin," Jack contributed.

"Or your smile too wide. Just save everyone the trouble," Marcus urged, "and give me the box."

Daniel didn't want to. It was his only link to Sarah.

Mulishly, he held on to it. "I'm not giving her up."

Jack and Marcus gawked at each other, then at him.

"What's the matter with you two?" Daniel demanded irritably. "You're grinning like loons."

From Marcus: "You said, 'I'm not giving her up.'"

Daniel stopped. He could scarcely breathe. "You're hearing things. Not giving *it* up, I said."

"'Her up,'" Jack insisted. He elbowed Marcus. "*Her.* Sarah. Daniel's not giving *her* up."

They gave him a jointly expectant look. They seemed fit to wait on him all day, with the patience of two men who would leave him to go toes-up over love—or deny its very existence to the last. Exactly as he had done till now.

That was when it finally struck Daniel.

He loved Sarah. *Loved her!* Only his love had seemed so near to friendship, had masqueraded so well beneath comfort and laughter, that he hadn't recognized it.

Amazed at his own daftness, he turned over the notion in his mind. Yes. It fit. Remarkably, it fit exactly.

"You don't kiss your friends," Daniel marveled.

"Hell, no!" Jack held up his hands to ward him off.

Marcus did, too. "Sorry, McCabe. Molly's prettier."

Unbelievably, Daniel laughed. "Not *that* way," he continued, remembering all the times he'd fallen, head over boots, near swooning while kissing Sarah. He should have been warning himself of that danger— arming himself with smelling salts instead of worrying over her supposed delicacy. "You don't kiss your friends *that* often. Nor do you enjoy it that much."

"I wouldn't enjoy it at all," Jack warned. "Back away."

"Keep your 'often' to yourself," Marcus ordered.

But Daniel only looked at their appalled faces and grinned. Miraculously, relief spread all through him. He was not dying. Marcus had the right of it.

He loved Sarah. And he was on the verge of losing her forever.

"This stays here." With sudden decisiveness, Daniel shoved the box over the bar to Jack. "I'll be back for it."

Then he left his whiskey and his gawking friends behind, and hied himself off to the schoolhouse. He had a wife to reclaim, and not a moment to waste.

Chapter Nineteen

With trembling fingers, Sarah reached for little Emily's dress collar. She straightened the calico, offering a smile for reassurance.

"Don't worry, Emily. You'll do fine."

The girl gave a wobbly grin. She ducked her head to continue studying the list of spelling words Sarah had issued over the current term. All around them, the schoolhouse teemed with gussied-up children and interested parents.

As they traditionally did, much of Morrow Creek had turned out for the spelling bee. The event was a source of entertainment—and sometimes enlightenment—to the children and their families alike.

Ordinarily, the attention didn't bother Sarah. This year, though, she felt extraordinarily nervous—mostly owing to the presence of several school board members in the front row. They sat on the collected and borrowed benches Sarah had assembled, all waiting in judgment of her.

The hubbub rose. Determinedly, Sarah blocked it out. She concentrated on each of her students in turn, giving reminders here and encouragement there. There would be a few recitations to open the event, mostly given by older students. Then, the spelling bee. At the last, a holiday song.

All of it was designed to demonstrate, to the waiting parents and the students themselves, how much the students had learned so far during the year. It was a standard practice—one Sarah typically enjoyed. She was terribly proud of her students. She never minded an opportunity to let them demonstrate their learning.

It was nearly time to begin. Hastily, Sarah darted a glance to the school board members. Every one of the officials looked impatient—probably to replace her with a newer, unmarried teacher. To a man, the board members had insinuated that the "distractions" of being married had adversely affected her ability to teach. Doubtless, they all expected her students' learning—or lack thereof—to reflect the "overly difficult workload" Daniel had complained to them about.

She knew he'd meant well. Daniel was a man, after all. It was his way to solve problems. But this one…it was a regular fix, indeed. It was true that most schoolteachers were unmarried. And that often schoolteachers retired their duties once they wed.

But Sarah was different, and tonight she intended to show everyone assembled exactly that.

The schoolhouse felt jammed with people. They milled about, talking while they removed their coats. Every time a newcomer entered, the scents of tobacco, bay rum and dress starch swirled in the air, carried on a chilly December draft. Sarah sent one of the older boys to stoke the woodstove again, then called for attention.

"Thank you all very much for coming tonight," she began. "I know the students are delighted you're here, and so am I."

She centered her attention on the assembled families as she went on talking. She explained the program and did her best not to let her voice quiver as she felt the intent gazes of the school board members upon her. It felt as though they measured her—as though they saw through her practiced preamble to the spelling bee—and judged her lacking.

Well. If she was about to fail—to lose her schoolteaching as abruptly and unwelcomely as she'd lost Daniel—she would not go down without a fight. Mustering a smile, Sarah introduced the first set of children. She announced their recitations, then started the applause for them herself. If nothing else, she was heartily proud of these students. They deserved a chance to shine.

The coughing and rustling in the room settled as

the first child began. Holding his hands behind his back, he recited a poem in a determined voice. By the time the proceedings moved on to the spelling bee portion of the evening, Sarah felt looser. Her hands didn't even tremble as she gripped the list of spelling bee words and took her place at the podium.

From the front row, one of the school board members looked on approvingly. He gave her a subtle nod. Jubilation shot through her. She was succeeding! Her students were performing wonderfully, right down to the smallest.

There was a general murmuring as they lined up in the front of the room. A late arrival entered, making the schoolhouse door creak. Determined not to be distracted, Sarah examined her list. She swept her gaze over the crowd, making sure she had their attention, then began.

"Supposedly," nine-year-old Emily said a short while later. "S-u-p-p-o-s-e-d-l-y. Supposedly."

Applause shook the rafters, exactly as it had following the last few successful spellings. The girl grinned, showing a gap in her teeth. The next round began with Eli, who'd been allowed to participate because of his delayed trip.

"Change." He caught his lip between his teeth, pondering the word. "C-h-a-n-g-e. Change."

"Very good." Sarah offered him a smile.

From a few rows distant, Lillian and Lyman cheered raucously. The Crabtrees shouted encouragement.

Grinning over their enthusiasm, Sarah turned to the next student. "All right, William. Your word is 'love.'"

The boy hesitated. Spelling was not his strong suit.

"I know that one."

The hearty male voice came from the back of the schoolhouse. Shielding her eyes with her hand, Sarah peered in that direction. It wasn't uncommon, in their small community, for those watching the spelling bee to become caught up in the excitement. Even grown men were liable to shout out a word.

Ready with a gentle admonishment, Sarah searched the crowd. Her reminder would be more effective if she delivered it directly to the man who'd spoken.

"Love," he said again. "S-a-r-a-h. Love."

Sarah stilled. That voice…

The crowd turned in obvious puzzlement. In their midst in the last row, a man stood, hat in hand. He had serious brown eyes, dark hair and resoundingly stuck-out ears. *Daniel.*

Her heart pounded. "I'm sorry, sir. I'm afraid that's not the correct spelling. If you'll just—"

"Give me another try," he said.

Another try. Did he mean another word? Or something entirely more meaningful? Flustered, Sarah glanced to the assembled friends, neighbors and students. She gripped the sides of her lectern with suddenly damp palms.

Her muddled mind registered that she'd never seen Daniel look so serious, so resolute...so wonderful.

"William?" she croaked. "Your word is 'love.'"

The boy stared at Daniel, doubtless recognizing the schoolmarm's husband from his visits. A girl nearby elbowed her neighbor and pointed. Giggles erupted.

"Love?" Sarah tried again.

A murmur rose. "Give him another try!" someone yelled.

General shouts of approval were heard. A woman in the second row nodded, as did one of the school board members. The Crabtrees looked on avidly from their seats. Little Eli watched from his place among the spelling bee participants, wearing a wide grin. There probably wasn't a soul in Morrow Creek, Sarah realized belatedly, who did not know of the troubles between her and her husband.

"Yes," Daniel urged. "Give me another try."

His deep voice shook her to the core. Drawn to look at him again, Sarah could scarcely believe he was here. Here, in her spelling bee! What was he about? He didn't look drunk. Yet to him, the spelling of *love*...translated to *Sarah?*

"You, Mr. McCabe, are a disruptive influence."

But there was a smile in her voice as she said it. There was not enough schoolmarm starchiness in the world to squelch it.

"Love," Daniel announced again in a booming, sure voice. "S-a-r-a-h. Love. I know that one for certain."

For certain. That could only mean…

Resolutely, Sarah managed to stay her course—albeit with a silly-feeling grin. She did her best to smother it beneath a pretend frown. Her pulse quickened still further.

"But since you seem determined to participate in the spelling bee…very well. I'll give you one word, then we will go back to the *real* students."

The crowd approved. All rustling stopped, although several more smiles could be seen. Obviously, people in town loved good gossip much more than they did a responsible spelling bee. Even the clearly tolerant and now bemused school board members.

Daniel waited, his gaze fixed on her. There was something changed about him, something solid and sure that she could not identify but liked, all the same. He straightened his spine, muscles rippling along his shoulders. He looked as ready as a man could be.

Sarah breathed in. "Your word is…'reunion.'"

A broad grin split his face. "Reunion," he said solemnly. "Y-e-s. Reunion."

Tears blurred her vision. Hastily blinking them back, Sarah cleared her throat. "You're correct, Mr. McCabe. Absolutely correct, I think. However—" here her voice wavered, tugged by emotions too powerful to contain "—you will definitely need to see the teacher after the spelling bee is finished."

Seriously, Daniel nodded. He clenched his hat harder in his fingers, still watching her with that curious expression of his. Sarah fancied she glimpsed yearning in his face. Love, too. She didn't doubt the same was reflected in hers.

The spelling bee finished to a rousing success. Somehow, Sarah managed to announce a few more words, then to applaud the winner. In a haze, she introduced the song finale. The students took their places, the lot of them giggling and sneaking glances toward the crowd and her.

Never had Sarah heard a song performed so rapidly. Her students sang in double-time, finishing the tune almost before she'd cued them to begin. Astonished, she gawked at them.

As a unit, they beamed mischievously back at her.

"Go, Mrs. McCabe!" One of her students stage-whispered, shooing her to the back of the schoolhouse. "Fetch your husband, afore he starts spelling badly again!"

Miraculously, when Sarah stepped forward, the

crowd parted. Her friends and neighbors made way for her, leaving a trail clear to...Daniel. She saw him waiting there, looking as fine and as beloved as he ever had, and knew that these were the most important steps she would ever take.

"He's a mighty poor speller," O'Neill, the butcher, said as she passed. "I'm purty sure that ain't how you spell 'love.'"

But Sarah—S-a-r-a-h—felt heartily glad that, for Daniel at least, it was. She clenched her skirts in quivering hands and approached him, finally stopping to gaze into his face.

He seemed surpassingly pleased with himself. "I reckon I'm in a heap of trouble, if the schoolmarm wants a word with me."

"This is a *familiar* sensation for you, then, is it?"

"Ahhh, Sarah." He caught her hand, oblivious to the eagerly watching families nearby. "Nothing could be newer or better. Only it nearly took me too long to realize it."

She hardly dared to ask. To hope. "Realize it?"

Daniel gave her a solemn look. "I love you, Sarah. I love you with all my heart and all my soul. Every time I looked at you, every time I held you in my arms, every time I said your name...what I really meant was, *I love you.* I love you, Sarah, and I want never to be without you."

"You...love me?"

"I'm pretty sure I just said so." His smile flashed, endearing and wicked. "About half a dozen times. But just in case you didn't hear me properly…"

Daniel flung both arms outward and bellowed in a happy voice. "I love you, Sarah!"

Laughter erupted. Her friends and neighbors nudged one another, the women whispering and smiling. A few dabbed their eyes. Nearby, Marcus offered Molly a handkerchief.

"There." Daniel drew Sarah against him, then tilted her chin up. With ridiculous fondness, he regarded her. "I know it took me a while to realize it. I'm sorry for that. If it takes me till the end of my days," he promised, "I swear I'll make it up to you. You'll have more happiness than any one woman has a right to, more flowers and more sweet words and more babies than any woman has ever—"

"Babies?" Sarah gawked. Her heart already felt overflowing with love, but the notion of having children with Daniel was more than she'd hoped for. "Babies?"

"A whole passel of them," Daniel confirmed, his dark rascal's eyes twinkling. "As many as you want. So long as you stay with me, Sarah, so long as you let me love you forever, I could not ask for more."

"Oh, Daniel." Sniffling, she swabbed tears from her eyes. No ladylike tears from Sarah, she noticed with considerable chagrin. She might have known she'd bawl like a slobbering idiot, with no pretense of delicacy. "I hope you know what you're getting into."

He thumbed a tear from her cheek. Kissed it. "I know. 'Tis what I want, for all the rest of my life. I want *you*, Sarah. I love you." A cocky look crossed his face. "L-o-v-e."

"Silly man. I always knew you could spell it."

He shook his head. "Only with you to show me."

"See? You're not the only one who can teach things." Sarah smiled, nearly overcome with the joy she felt. "Although I'm fairly certain there are still a few lessons in store for us. We should probably start studying now."

Daniel gave her a perplexed look. "Studying?"

"Like this."

She lifted on tiptoes and pressed her mouth to his. Their kiss felt warm and wonderful and exactly right. Sarah could not imagine how she'd survived the past days without it.

"Ahh. Now I remember." Daniel winked. "That is how I finally knew—sometimes love looks like friendship. Till the kissing starts."

She laughed. "I do love you. So much." She touched his jaw, ran her thumb over his cheek, savored the rugged features she'd missed so much. "Let's never be apart again. With no one to kiss me, to befuddle me, to challenge my authority over vegetables, I scarcely knew what to do with myself."

Daniel grinned. "Let me love you. That's all you need to remember."

He kissed her again, stirringly. The crowd cheered.

Horsefeathers! Sarah had forgotten their presence altogether. Feeling herself blush, she pulled away.

Deliberately, Daniel caught hold of her hand and kept her beside him. His gaze flicked to the milling, interested crowd.

"Do you have to stay here?" he asked in a quiet voice. "I'd just as soon take you home and 'study' a little harder."

There was nothing she wanted more than a private reunion. Taking in his merry eyes and devilish grin, Sarah felt hard-pressed to admit the truth.

"I should stay until I learn if I've kept my school-teaching position or not. Until the school board members come speak with me—"

"There'll be no need for that," the nearest official announced. He turned, obviously having overheard part of their conversation. "After examining your students, and your obvious dedication to them, we could only come to one conclusion. We would be foolish to lose so fine a teacher in Morrow Creek."

"Then you won't replace me?" Sarah asked.

"We might even consider that assistant school-marm your husband suggested," the board member replied, sporting an uncharacteristic grin. "Provided, of course, that he promises never to attempt public spelling again."

Dutifully, Daniel nodded. "O-K."

"That's my brother for you." Lillian approached with Lyman at her heels and Eli close behind. She shook her head in mock disapproval, but could not hide her smile completely. "A scoundrelly example to the very end."

"No," Daniel declared. "I have been tamed."

The women snorted with laughter, Sarah the loudest.

"Tamed by love," he amended firmly, and Sarah felt moved to kiss him once more.

"That's good." Lillian shared a coconspirator's glance with her husband, then with Eli. "Because we've decided to move to Morrow Creek. Lyman, Eli and I. I'd hate for your scandalous example to—"

She broke off, muffled by an enormous hug from her brother. Daniel seemed cheered mightily by the news—so much so that he hugged Eli and even Lyman in turn. Sarah followed his example, while the spelling bee participants and their families talked and laughed all around them.

"Did we hear correctly?" Fiona Crabtree asked from behind Sarah. She bustled nearer, along with the other Crabtrees and the Copelands. "You're staying in the territory?"

Lillian nodded, seeming exceedingly pleased. "It was an easy decision. After all, the city is filled with soot and grime and criminals. Or so I hear. Here there is plenty of…what was it? Fishing and snakes. Isn't that right, Daniel?"

He nodded. Fiona looked confused.

"Just accept it, my dear," Adam advised with his usual paternal head shake. "It's easier that way."

"Hmmph. Try telling that to Grace." Molly pointed.

The eldest Crabtree daughter stood nearby, decidedly *not* gazing at Jack Murphy. Mostly.

"Or to a certain saloonkeeper," Marcus added.

The Irishman lounged near the schoolhouse globe, decidedly *not* mooning over Grace Crabtree. Nearly.

Daniel heaved a sigh. "Crabtree women are never good at giving in." He gave Sarah's hand a squeeze. "Fortunately for some of us, that's exactly what we need."

"Well, *that*…" Sarah replied primly, "and a few good rutabagas."

And although it took them hours to greet their curious neighbors, and still more time after that to walk home hand in hand, they knew in their hearts that all anyone *truly* needed was love. Without it, life felt as nonsensical as…well, as nonsensical as a single three-foot-long, green knitted stocking.

On Christmas Eve, Sarah held up that stocking.

She puzzled over it, reminded of all the silly notions that had made her knit it. Somehow, it didn't seem right to discard it.

As though sharing her thoughts, Daniel took the enormous yarn clump from her hand. He pinned it to the mantel, then regarded its droopy, lumpy shape with evident satisfaction.

"There." He nodded. "That ought to be big enough to hold *all* your wishes."

"Nonsense." Sarah snuggled closer, happily examining the effect. It was a fitting place, she decided. And Daniel was a wonderful man, to know her so well. "All my wishes have already come true."

"Hmm." He gave her a long, loving grin. "I'll wager you can dredge up a few more wishes, given enough time."

She smiled. He knew her almost *too* well.

"Hmm. I suppose I could come up with one or two more." Sarah offered him a sham-innocent look. "If you insist."

"I insist," Daniel said.

And although *he* didn't look the least bit innocent, nor behave the least bit like a reformed scoundrel, Sarah truly didn't mind. Because Daniel *did* proceed to make her wishes come true just then…and for all the rest of their lives, as well.

* * * * *